Keepers

In the Forgotten Valley

by K. J.& A. Bryant

National library of Australia Cataloguing-in-production data:
Bryant, Kevin J.
Keepers- In the Forgotten Valley
1st.edition Pre-Teen Fiction
ISBN: 978-0-646-48877-6

Published by K. J. Bryant
Email: kevinbryant5@bigpond.com

Cover Art by, Fran Haine
franhaine@harboursat.com.au

Design and layout by; K.J. Bryant

First edition 2010

This edition of **Keepers** is offered to the **kids of the valley** .

They will know most of the following geography and hopefully forgive me if it seems that some of the places and even the rivers appear to have moved around a little.

If you are not from the valley then come and see it, you will understand how real the connection can be when you take the time to feel it for yourself.

The **Forgotten Valley** is a real place to the northwest of Sydney. The settlements of Wisemans Ferry, Spencer, St. Albans, Peats ridge, the city of Hornsby and the town of Galston are also real, as are the Hawkesbury and Macdonald rivers. The Ancient Spirits and the Rainbow Snake are real and respected by all who know and feel '**The Place'**. The names of Steve Irwin and Jacques Cousteau are mentioned with the greatest respect and within the context of their contributions to the planet. Reference made to Harry Potter is intended to indicate that he is now part of popular culture and rightly so.

Now it is time for you to decide which part of The Place you are willing to be. Enjoy the **Keepers.**

K.J. Bryant

To our nephew Steve, he was born a Keeper

His spirit was called to return in 2006

Too soon for us, but now he is one with The Place

The pain in my head is killing me.

I bet Dad is burned about the house...they didn't have to wreck the whole place!

I know I'm bleeding but I can't see anything.

These guys may not be too bright but they sure are dangerous.
I thought we got away. They should have got us after the plane crashed or when we came down that cliff or running for the boat.

I thought we were safe...I wonder if they got the others?
I can't hear them, can they hear me?
I think I am passing out...maybe I am dying. Mum will kill me if I die out here.

Where is Jack? It's his fault...catch the truck, save the world, hug a tree. Him and his dreams!

That was the start of this whole thing, yeah, I remember...him and his birthday dream.

Doesn't matter now.
I'm cold, really cold.
I'm going to sleep now.

How did it go again, was it a Lobster and a Magpie...where are you Jack? Why am I here...

Keepers

In the Forgotten Valley

Chapter One

Dream Time

The claw of a huge mangrove crab sifts the sandy bed, I pass him by. A school of mullet swoop, then as though in a mirror, dive up toward the sky, they breach. I am not in the river, I am the river. No time to notice the change but the sounds are clear and sharp, the perfect feathers of a giant sea eagle flutter then stiffen as she plummets toward the surface seeking food, I am the sky as well. Now the camp fire is calling, the Elders and the others are waiting there for me. It is time to meet them, time to hear of the past and of the future.

In a language I have never learnt I begin to understand that I can just be Jack Kipley, and still be a real part of The Place. There is so much to hear and see, even more to learn, but only I can decide which part is waiting for me to be.

———————

Kate and Alex watched their son all through the night. They did not know if there would be any sign.

Jack slept peacefully. He knew that when he woke he would be thirteen years old but he did not know that his parents were so concerned about the exact time as it drew closer.

Next door, in her bedroom, his sister Emma also slept peacefully but she knew what was coming.

She had turned ten two months ago and the first dream was on the night of her birthday. At four thirty five in the morning, the exact time of her birth. She had woken in fright to find her parents by her bedside, waiting and wondering.

Inside the place of his dream, where the parents could not see, Jack sat with Emma at the meeting fire of the Ancient spirits. They sat quietly while the Elders explained to Jack that there was danger coming to the Valley. He would be needed to help his sister and the other Keepers. The old man waved to the other side of the fire, one by one he saw Penny, Jamie and Gazza appear. Each of them looked like they were just waking up. Gazza rubbed his eyes and said, "Can't you guys work sort of nine to five or something?"

The wrinkled speaker took no notice "Our people come from a place called The Dreamtime. In your dream time we will plan to keep this place safe from those who do not see the beauty and feel the life that is here."

Jack looked at each of his friends. They all smiled back waiting for him to make the decision that each of them had made at their own birthtimes.

Dream Time

The only distraction for the parents was the wind. On what had been a calm moonlit night, it had sprung from nowhere and was battering the house, bending trees and howling as it cut across the nearby cliffs. It brought clouds that tried to cover the moon and make the valley dark, but the moon would not be hidden. It shone even more brightly and veered from place to place around the scudding clouds; showing like a beacon should to a ship in raging seas, giving a place to measure from, a place that meant safety from the storm.

At three am Jack began to murmur in his sleep. He seemed to be talking with someone. He rolled from one side to the other as though he was unsure about something.

The surface of the river now was leaping and tossing as the wind pulled at it to follow and parts of it did, but most of it remained and waited. She would not be blown off course after all this time.

His parents waited those last few minutes to see Jack accept his destiny.
They could tell that the clock had ticked over to three fifteen. It was the exact time thirteen years ago, that one more spirit was borrowed from The Place. This one was to be known as Jack Kipley. As with all life forces, when the time was right, it would return to The Place but until then, it had work to do.

Jack relaxed, became calm and peaceful.
The wind died down, the trees stood up, and the river settled back to its smooth glimmering self.

Alex and Kate knew that their son had agreed to be the next Keeper in the Forgotten Valley.

Keepers

Even though they had discussed it, Alex was still not sure of exactly what it would mean to Jack and the rest of the family. He was bothered, he had been almost positive that nothing would happen tonight. That thing with Emma was just some sort of coincidence, now he was not so sure.

The parents of the newest Keeper sat on the jetty sipping steaming tea and talking, while the shining black river lay resting, waiting for the light of day so that it could continue its journey to the sea. They spoke about the history of Kate's family in the valley, or the whole country, if you believed what her father had to say.
Now that both of their children had been called, Alex had to think more about the legend.
He was from a river family and he had heard the stories of the old days, when every now and then, according to the legend, if there was going to be trouble in the valley, the Ancient Spirits would call one or more of the Kerry's descendants to become the Keeper and protect the Valley.

Until he married Kate he did not know that the legend was about her family and particularly about her Ancestors. The family tree showed Kate as one of the descendants of the first European family in the Valley. There are others spread around the country and they keep in touch from time to time. They were most often in touch when one of them had a child approaching 'the age'.
There was no set formula. Sometimes a girl from one family could have the dreams, and a boy from another branch might be called. There were stories about all sorts of combinations and about how some Keepers had saved the town, the valley, even the planet. Then sometimes a whole generation went by and no one had the dreams. Even without the dreams there were those who shared their love of the country. Not just the flag and the name and that

sort of thing, the real meaning of country, the old name for everything, 'The Place'.

The Place is the whole thing. Land, water, air and every thing that belongs in it or on it, animals, birds, trees, snakes, sharks, crocs and people as well, if they behave. These days the people forget that we are all connected to each other; if you make a change to one thing, it will always affect something else.
The ones that are called Keepers know about the connection, some don't have the dreams, they just know. Anyone can be a Keeper, they only have to care.
A long time ago people understood that they belonged to the land the land did not belong to them, then, everyone was a Keeper.

As time went on people began to think they were so clever. They could control The Place. They could cut and tear, kill and clear, just to make money and never have to count the real cost. The number of Keepers became smaller but the need for them became greater.
Now there was one more to join the battle.

The sun was rising behind the mountains in the east, the first rays of a new day filtered through the trees up on the ridges and the ancient valley began to stir to life. The Cockatoo, the Currawong, the Kookaburra, Magpies, Finches and the rest all started to call to the river to wake and move on to the sea as she had since before time was measured by man.
The river heard them call and as dawn climbed lightly down the mighty cliffs and over jumbled hills to light the way, she began the winding twisting trip. Like the Rainbow snake that had made her and the mountains, she followed the ancient trail because, for the river, that was 'The way'.

Keepers

There was no breeze as the sun came up. The river was like glass, or more like a mirror. The reflection was so perfect that Alex could not tell where the time worn sandstone cliffs that faced their house ended, and where the reflection began. As he gazed at the raw beauty in front of him, he realized that thousands of years ago the Ancients could have been in this very spot, looking at this exact reflection.

In so many other places this sort of beauty was lost. Gone to careless development where there was no thought about fitting in with The Place only what could be taken from it.

He turned to Kate and he could tell from her eyes, full of tears but not crying, that the legend was real to her, her heart was with the Ancients and with The Place.

If her children were called for the good of the Valley then she would help them if she could.

Alex spoke quietly, "To be honest, I thought this legend thing was just something that your family wanted to keep alive when the other kids were 'called'. So I thought I should play the game but after Emma and now Jack, I think you'd better tell me the whole story."

Kate smiled, enjoying the warmth that came with sunrise. "Believe me my dear, very soon my Dad, his sister and the rest of the bunch will be arriving and as this day goes on you will hear everything that you ever wanted to know about the legend of the Kerry clan in the Forgotten Valley."

Chapter Two

Wake To Fright

Jack did not feel any different when he woke on the morning of his birthday. He washed and dressed and made his way downstairs without seeing any of the family. Maybe it was too early for them. As he approached the kitchen, the door was closed but there was heaps of noise coming through. The voices were familiar, he stopped to listen. It sounded like everyone he ever knew, or at least all of the family.

He opened the door slowly, they all looked around and were suddenly silent. There was Grand dad (Mum's father Reg Kerry), his long grey hair tied at the back, ever present overalls, stretched across broad shoulders. Great aunt Pearl (Grand Dad's sister), smiling pink face under sort of blue grey hair. Mums sister, Aunty Anne and her husband Barry, Dad, Mum and Emma. His mates were there too, Jamie and his folks, Penny with hers and Gazza with his as well.

No one said a word so Jack cleared his throat and said with a smile, "Good morning every one, Ah, isn't it a bit early for a birthday party?"

He almost panicked at their reaction. Every adult in the room charged at him. Great Aunt Pearl was not the quickest but she was the nearest. As he half turned to run she got him in a bear hug and when she was sure that all of his ribs had cracked, she passed him on to Grand dad. He did that hand shake back pat (like belting a rug) thing. Now that he was squashed and battered he might as well be embarrassed to death by aunty Anne who never seemed to be fully dressed sort of, at the top, anyway. When her hug was over his face was red and luckily his Dad was there to shake his hand and give him time to breath.

Mum stood on one side with her arm around him and they all sang happy birthday in that noisy way that families do.

Thinking the worst was over while everyone got stuck into toast, cereal, tea and coffee, Jack pulled his father aside. "Come on Dad, what's really going on, this mob are never together at this time, even if they are awake?" There was an expression on his father's face that he could not read.

"Relax son, just have your breakfast, there's a family meeting on after, don't worry". He smiled and went back to his coffee.

"Alright, Quiet now, let's begin". Jacks Grand dad was calling for attention.

They had all moved out to the Old Stone House, the one that had been built by Grand dad's Grand dad. Huge stone blocks had been cut from the floor of the valley and put hard up against the sheer rock wall so that it almost looked like it was part of the cliff, after all this time it looked like part of the valley itself.

The house was in good condition and even the old furniture was still there.

For some reason, a long time ago Grand dads father had built another house nearby. That's where Jack lived now with his sister and parents, grand dad lived up at his rock quarry high above the river. The old stone house was hardly used for anything anymore. Jack's Dad did use the big boat house which was built into the main part of the structure, to keep his cruiser in, but that was all. He had asked about the stone house more than once but never really got an answer.

The place was never locked so Jack and Emma had looked in a couple of times but it was sort of spooky, not scary, it just felt like they should not be there. It always looked like someone still lived there, this time was still weird but with the whole family together, it felt right.

Granddad looked at Jack, "Do you know why we are here?"

Jack was about to say he had no idea and maybe they were all insane but he thought he should wait and see.

So he shook his head and watched as his Grandfather unwrapped the large parcel that had been on the table in front of him. The wrapping was a soft oiled chamois material and inside, was a large leather bound book with a brass clasp on the front and big brass hinges on the back. It was hard to say how old it was, the leather was a rich dark reddish brown and the brass shone in the light from the window. It was obvious that it had been well cared for. Jack looked around the table. Everyone had gone quiet again; they were all either staring at the book or at him.

Grandfather spoke, "You have all heard the family legend in some form or other, but this book has never been part of the story. While there is no guarantee that a Keeper will be called from every generation, there has always been a Guardian. It is the Guardian who cares for the book and passes it on to the Guardian in the next generation. That way the legend will not be lost or changed, I am the Guardian now and soon I will pass it on to the next,"------

Emma called out, " What's in the book Grand dad?"
Reg looked startled, he cleared his throat, "Yes, the book, quite right young Emma, what's in the book."

The family members were all relieved that Emma had caught Reg just as he had started to ramble. It was often difficult to keep him on track once he started a story. Now as he continued he seemed a little more focused.
"This book was started by Clancy Kerry in the year 1789. Clancy was the first Guardian and wrote the story of the family from the time of their beginning in this country. Since then each Keeper or Guardian has added the story of their own generation. Because there are five Keepers called for this generation, it will be the Guardian who will keep the book and record the events as they occur. The next Guardian will ------- ,"
Pearl interrupted, "Hang on Reg." then to the rest,
"This may take a while, why don't you all get a fresh cuppa while I try to move things along a little."
The group was grateful and did not need further encouragement to escape while Pearl turned to her brother.

This was the first that the kids had heard about Keepers being real. Jack was stunned, "So all of you have had the dream?" he asked as soon as the crowd separated into two groups.
The adults had headed for the kitchen. The five kids were in a huddle in one corner of the room. The other four looked at each other.
Jamie spoke first "I had a dream on the night of my birthday when I was thirteen but it was just a dream about the Ancients, no body made a fuss."

"Yeah" said Gazza, "Same here, no one told me that it meant anything," he looked ay the others, "So what does it mean?"
Penny quickly answered his question, "It means the Ancients are not fussy if they called you to be a Keeper."
Gazza made a face.
Emma spoke to Penny, "How come no one has said anything to the boys when we have been told so much?"
Jack was surprised again, "What sort of things?"
Penny cut in, "Well we knew that you would be called next and we are always at the meeting fire, like last night. The boys looked blank, she felt nervous," That's all really, but it's different for the boys. I don't know exactly how but it just does not work the same way as it does for girls."

Just as the boys were going to ask what she was talking about, Grandpa Kerry called them all back to the table.
"Come on, everyone take a seat, there's more to do."

The parents had been drifting back in with hot cups of fresh tea and coffee, now they seemed ready for another session with Reg.
As the last of them sat and turned to face the end of the table, he began, "My sister informs me that she will take over from this point and since she is the last called Keeper of the Valley and I am only a Guardian," Reg could be quiet a sook, "I will hand over to her."
There was a murmur around the table.
Reg made an old style bow to his sister and stalked off in a huff toward the kitchen.
More murmuring at the table.
There was no murmuring when Great Aunt Pearl stood to speak.
She was not a big lady but she could be scary sometimes.
The kids always thought it was funny when their parents sat quietly or did exactly as she said, without argument. It looked like they

were all back in kindy. They would not say they were scared exactly, maybe like Jamie's Dad would say, "There is always someone somewhere who is tougher or smarter," it seemed like Great Aunt Pearl might be both.

She began, "All right, so, this book was left in the care of my brother who was not called as a Keeper but as a Guardian. I was the last Keeper called here, there has been no more in this district for two generations. Lord knows I could have used some help, however. Now that we know there are five in this generation we must help them prepare for what ever may be ahead."
That brought a murmur but it didn't last long.
"The book contains the story of each Keeper in the past and will record the events of the new ones as well. There is also a tale that says the blank pages contain information from the Elders which can only be read by one of the Keepers, only one."
There were some skeptical glances shared around the room.
She went on, "The book will only reveal its secrets when it is in the proper place and when the time is right. That place and time will be revealed to the Keeper with the most vision. I myself, have never seen any secret writing so I don't think it is a true story, but there you have it." Pearl seemed to think some one might argue as she looked around but no body did.
Gazza whispered to Jack but the others heard, "Hey man, that's me. I see stuff that no body would believe, oh yeah, I've got the vision."
The other four just stared at him.
"What?" He pleaded.
Penny said softly, "I believe you Gazz, I really do."
The others started to laugh then realized that Pearl was watching.
"What?" he whispered then looked up directly into the eyes of Great Aunt Pearl. He swallowed hard.

She looked at each of them in turn, then continued slowly and deliberately, "The reason that I will read the legend now is that the book may not be passed around, and if you all hear the same story in the same place at the same time, there should be no confusion," again she looked around the group, "Is that clear?" she asked everyone as she stared at Gazza.

Most of them nodded vigorously, some said, "Yeah, sure, OK," then went quiet.
Gazza gulped again.

"The business of the Keepers is serious. This is not the only family to be called to help by the Ancients but we believe it was the first, so please pay attention," she looked once more around the room.

There was no movement.

"All right then", announced Pearl, "I will begin,"

Chapter Three
Legend has it

In the year 1763, the privateer ship, "Free Spirit" had sailed along the east coast of an unnamed and unknown land in the Great Southern ocean. She was a twin mast brigantine displacing one hundred and twelve tons.
There is no other record of a man named Hamish Kerry and his wife Else but they were the only survivors when the 'Free Spirit' foundered on a shoal at the entrance to what was later called 'Kalklyn Bay'.

The northerly breeze that had been so kind to them as they made their way down the coast swung suddenly just as the Captain committed his vessel to the entrance of the Bay.

Keepers

At low tide the channel is narrow and the change in the wind was enough to drive the ship hard on to the ragged edges of rock before the crew could take any action. There are no details about what happened to the Captain and crew, only that Hamish and Else were left with plenty of provisions, some livestock salvaged from the ship and one of the lifeboats which was rigged with a single square sail as well as oars.

They set up their home on a small island not far off the mainland in the bay. It was just as well that the natives were friendly, Hamish was about to be very busy, Else was pregnant. They had eight months to arrange shelter and safety for the start of their family. The two of them were used to hard work. Hamish was a shipwright and Else worked as hard as he did. Over the time it took to build their first log cabin it became clear that there was no threat from the local tribe of aborigines and when their son "Clancy" was born, (That was me) the local women were on hand to help and the men celebrated with my Pa. My Ma had two more children on the Island, "Mary" was born the following year and "Robert" was two years after her.

Legend has It

Life on the Island was fine. The men of the tribe taught us boys many of their ways and Ma had a small school were Mary, Rab, myself and several of the local children learnt reading and writing and speaking English. In return, the wise men of the tribe taught us the local dialect and some of their history.

Over the years Ma and Pa wondered if they should try to return to what was called, 'civilization' where they would have no house, no friends, no freedom to make their own future and no more contact with their new friends. They decided, no way.

They were happy living and learning with the people that had a way of being with the land not just on the land.

My family wandered the district with the locals, we learnt about tribal boundaries. We met with other tribes and because they thought that we strangers were interesting, the tribes learnt about us and about each other as well. Often this led to understanding and even friendship. Further and further up the river the Kerry clan became known as tough but good people and by the time that the next European ship sailed into the bay more than twenty years later, the local folk and us, had high expectations of the people on board.

Keepers

We would all be very disappointed.

That ship was the Barque HMS "Condor" out of Dover.

The trouble started almost as soon as the Europeans found that the Kerrys had tamed the "blacks" as they referred to us and the local people. They did not show any respect for the tribal customs or for the people and it did not take long for us to disagree with the way the locals were being treated.

The Captain of the 'Condor' was a Navy man named Frances Kalklyn, he had spent some time at a convict settlement down the coast called Sydney Town and the whole district was to be named New South Wales. He said that it was all the property of England and under the rule of a Governor, this worried my folks but the words did not have much meaning for the Tribes people.

Over the next few months the newcomers established a settlement in a cove on the mainland. They spread out in an untidy manner all along the shore line of what they called 'Kalklyn Bay'. In a short time their part of the place was dirty and ugly on the land.

Legend has it

Because of the attitude of the newcomers, the locals
stayed away. The new settlers found that life can be very
difficult when you do not know The Place.
They became resentful of the comfort that we enjoyed in
our life on the island.
Captain Kalklyn stopped asking for help and instead,
began to demand it. As the representative of the
Governor, who represented the Queen, who now,
somehow, owned everything that our family had worked to
build for more than twenty years and everything that the
Locals and their Ancestors had ever known.

The life that Hamish and Else had chosen to stay away
from had caught up with them. They did not like it nor did
we their children, or the Local people.
Because the natives were nomads they did not have too
much trouble keeping out of the way of Captain Kalklyn
and his soldiers who were the worst of the new folk.
We Kerrys however, found it very difficult to avoid the
lazy and belligerent crew from the 'Condor". Ma and Pa
still remembered enough of life in England to know that
the Government of that time had no interest in people or
their rights. They knew that if we fought with the army we

would lose, even if we were in the right. Pa went to see the Elders of the local tribe. He told them what he knew about the Government and the army. The Elders believed him.

They could clearly see that all European people were not the same. With my father they began to make a plan. Their plan was not to fight the intruders, but to use their knowledge of the bush and the river to keep their families safe and leave these invaders to fend for themselves.

There was a small inlet in the island, on the side opposite the settlement. We kept our boats there, they were safe from high seas and rushing tides. Over the years as Rab (everyone called Robert Rab) and I had learnt the trade of 'Shipwright' from our father, we had built several boats from local timber. The boats were light but strong, broad enough to be stable but did not draw much water when loaded and they handled well either under sail or by oar Five of the boats were built like small barges, no sail, no tiller and flat in the hull so that they could carry a great deal of weight while being towed by another vessel. The first two to be built were loaded with special cargo salvaged from the wreck of the 'Free Spirit'.

Legend has it

We children had always been told not to ask what was in the sealed casks stored in the cave at the inlet. Now as each one was loaded it was covered with sail cloth and tar to seal it from the weather. The contents were still not spoken of. Father only said, "If the cargo was ever discovered by Europeans it would bring nothing but trouble". Now it had to be moved to some other hiding place before it was discovered by the crew of the Condor.

It was decided that Father and myself would go on an expedition up river with two guides. These were senior members of the tribe, (Ngalpil and Tabui) to find a new site to build on.

Ma, Mary and Rab would continue to load the other three barges with useful equipment from our island. But they must not arouse suspicion in the Condor camp, they must take care. We would all leave this place in seven days when the tide was at its highest and the moon at it's brightest. Sailing the river at night could be dangerous but we would chance it to be free again.

In the small native canoes and with the tide in our favour the four of us travelled up stream, coming to beautiful parts of the district that I had not noticed before.

Keepers

Two days of paddle and sail brought us to a bend in the river. The guides brought the canoes together and agreed that they had arrived. Pa and I were confused, we studied both sides of the river. It was a long wide reach, now with the tide out, there was a mud flat on the Northern side that ran up to thick mangroves. The mangrove trees were too thick to penetrate and ran each way on that bank as far as the eye could see.

The southern bank had much less mangrove and behind that was some good open land running back to the sheer rock cliff reaching up twenty feet in some places and one hundred or more in others. The cliff continued in each direction also, the flat land was cut by a small creek which emptied to the river at a steady rate. There was nowhere to hide a house. These boys must be lost.

Pa spoke in the local language, reminding them that we needed somewhere where we could build again but be out of sight of anyone on the river. That meant we would need somewhere to tie our boats and barges while we unloaded, then move inland to build. He thought they understood.

Ngalpil and Tabui smiled at each other and paddled to

the creek. It was lined with mangrove and river gums and although the water was wide enough, it was heading straight toward the sandstone cliff. Within one hundred yards the end of the creek was in sight. It seemed to come out at the base of the sheer stone wall. The guides paddled directly at the cliff where two river gums and a clump of smaller trees had sprouted on a shelf in the rock face above the stream.

Father was in the lead canoe and as it approached the cliff without slowing down, he braced himself for the collision. The nose of the canoe slid into the overhanging foliage. Ngalpil bent his head but paddled even harder against the current. Pa lent forward and held tightly to the sides of the canoe as the branches brushed over him. Then the sunlight disappeared, it was suddenly cold, he could feel the canoe was still moving. He looked up but could see nothing in the darkness. Suddenly, he was hit in the face and hurled flat on his back in the canoe. He was looking straight up as the tree branch that hit him, then several others, passed overhead. In a few seconds he was looking at the bright blue sky again. He lay there confused as the smiling Ngalpil turned to him, "Hamish, you are home now."

Keepers

Pa and myself lay in the canoes side by side with the same bruise on our foreheads. Laughing with our friends and making jokes about paddling through the rock in magic canoes. When we finally sat up and looked around, we found ourselves on a small sandy beach inside a huge circular cavern which was open at the top. On the other side was a similar sandy bank. The walls of the circle reached to the sky far above. All around the top of the walls were trees and scrub. We could see the opening that we had come in through, it was much bigger on this side than the other, shaped a bit like a triangle cut into the cliff by the flowing water over thousands of years. Opposite that opening was a giant archway like a church except there was water coming out. It was coming out of the mountain like a small river.

On the sides near the beaches the water was calm but in the centre between the two tunnels the current was strong. There was a good piece of high dry land above each of the beaches with trees and even some grass growing. It was a perfect hide away.

As we discussed the place, Ngalpil and Tabui explained that it will be even better than it looked. The reason that these two from the tribe had been chosen to make this

Legend has it

journey was because they were both "Koradji",(we
understood that to mean medicine man or magic man).
For what was planned by the elders at least two "Koradji"
were required.
While Pa and I unloaded the canoes and set up camp for
the night, Ngalpil and his mate were on the other beach
making different preparations.

Because of the high walls it was dark in the cavern well
before sunset. Father and myself sat near the small camp
fire watching the two "Koradji" building a much bigger fire.
They had painted themselves in the traditional way for a
Corroboree and were still busy painting the walls of the
cavern around the entrance. Ngalpil had even climbed the
wall to make a drawing above the entrance. All the
paintings and drawings were from the Dreamtime. They
were mostly of the Rainbow snake, the one that made the
river and the valley, the animals and the birds, all before
any white man arrived and all before time was counted on
clocks.
The drawings were complete. They sat each side of the
fire and chanted to the Spirits of Ancient Elders,
waiting for the moon and the tide.

Keepers

We had built our fire well above the high tide mark on the beach and we wondered why the Koradji had built theirs below the tidal mark. As the water rose in the cavern the two magic men built the fire even bigger but it would soon be extinguished by the rising water.

The cavern began to glow. I nudged my father and pointed to the edge of the wall above us. The moon was just coming into view and the rays were reflecting off the walls of our stone cylinder. The chanting of the Koradji grew louder as the light increased. The tide pushed the water up to the edge of their fire.

Now the water was all around the fire and the Koradji but they were not wet. The water seemed to be surrounding but not touching them.

The moon moved across the sky above and as it reached the exact centre of the circular cavern, it seemed to stop. It got even brighter. The Koradji stood and walked through the surrounding water to the high tide mark.

They made one last call to the Spirit of the Snake, then sat and closed their eyes.

The tide was at its peak, soon it would ebb and turn. My father and I had never seen the like of this. I felt fear and I think he did too, it was fear of things that we did not

understand. We watched and waited. The Koradji sat
quietly. The moon was still not moving.

From the opening in the mountain wall a breeze began to
blow. It became stronger until it was blowing the embers
of our camp fire along the shore line. On the other side,
the fire was undisturbed and continued to burn even
though no more wood had been added.

Now our camp fire was blown out entirely. We stood
nervous in the bright moonlight. The wind became a
gentle breeze again. Just as the tide turned, the water
around the Koradji fire closed in but instead of being
soaked, the fire floated and drifted out to the centre of
the stream.

It floated toward the river with the turning tide. As the
fire reached the entrance it stopped and began to smoke.
The smoke did not blow with the breeze, instead it divided
into streams, one for each of us in the cavern and another
that went straight up and began to cover the wall above
the entrance. As the smoke reached each of us it
wrapped around like a blanket of fog and on the wall
above Ngalpil's drawing, like a painted picture but moving,
we could see into a time that had long gone by. We had
been told the stories of the tribal ancestors being in this

land for many thousands of years, now we could feel that it was true. We began to feel the connection to the land and the water, the sky and the wind. We began to understand the power that could come from that connection.

In an ancient dialect the elders in the pictures on the wall were speaking to the Koradji but somehow, we could understand. "Your request is granted, through all time to come, these people and their offspring will be one with the Valley and its secrets. Outside the Valley they will join with other tribes across the land and the across the water as our people have always done. They will share the power with all who are one in spirit. In this place you see the past, in this place we see the future. A time is coming when the land, the water, animals, birds, fish and the people of the Spirit will need protection. Times will change in ways that you can not imagine. Many will try to trade our world for money. The people of your clan will battle on the sea, on the land and even in the air. You have much to learn but you have time to learn The Way."

The smoke began to drift away although the breeze was gone. The fire, still floating, stopped smoking and moved with the tide into the entrance passage. The moon resumed its journey across the sky.

The fire in the tunnel began to hiss and splutter. There was a last flash of light and the fire was gone, but in the fading moonlight something was floating against the current, back into the cavern. It was dark now and we could not quite see what it was so I set about rebuilding the camp fire.

In the flickering light Father watched as the remnants of the Koradji fire drifted toward him. It looked like the wood of the fire had melted into the shape of a large bowl. Ngalpil was beside him now. He nudged Pa and pointed at the bowl. Father lifted the bowl from the water and looked inside, there was a shimmering silver liquid almost filling the bowl. Tabui wrapped the bowl in a wombat skin and as he stowed it in the canoe he repeated, "You have much to learn but there is time to learn the way."

The first problem was solved, we had somewhere to begin again. Now we had to make it out of the bay and up the river without being caught by Kalklyn and his crew.

By the time Pa and I returned to our island there were only two days left before the full moon. Two more of the barges had been loaded and were ready. The third would be for the livestock, cows, sheep and pigs. The chickens and ducks would fit in somewhere.

Father expected the wind to be in our favour so that we could tie a barge behind each of the boats sailed by Myself, Mary and Rab and two behind his own. He always fancied himself the better seaman.

The day arrived and as soon as the sun went down, we loaded the last of the animals and prepared to set off on our new adventure.

The plan was working well until the moon came up and the rooster, confused by all the activity, started to crow. Our boats were all in line about one hundred yards off shore sailing for the mouth of the river when one of the guards saw us. He raised the alarm.

Captain Kalklyn quickly realized what was happening and ordered his men to their boats in pursuit.

Father was concerned, the Condor boats were bigger than ours. They carried more sail so they would make more speed in the stiff breeze. The crew of the Condor had only been waiting for an excuse to use force against us. This looked like their chance.

Legend has it

The family fleet had a good lead by the time the Condor crew had rigged their boats and set sail from the beach. Father called to the rest of us, "If they get within rifle range cut the barges loose and run for it".
Rab answered, "Father, don't worry, they won't catch us."
I joined in as well, "Yes we will be fine Pa, just hold your course."
Pa did not share our confidence. Already he could see the larger boats heeling and accelerating as they trimmed their rigs and reached across the breeze.

In our time, myself and Rab had sounded and charted most of the bay. We knew where the deeper water was and where the tide ran the fastest so even with the heavy barges in tow we were making good speed.
The Condor crews were tacking their boats on the breeze. They wanted to overtake our fleet before we made it to the river mouth in case the wind failed inside the valley walls.
All the Kerry boats trimmed their sails and ran true on the breeze and close with the tide but still the enemy was gaining. I was in the lead followed by Mary then Father and Rab was in the rear.

Keepers

The two front boats were drawing away from Pa and he called for Rab to overtake and go with us. Rab was laughing at our father and yelling abuse at the soldiers. Pa called to me, " Clancy, what's wrong with your brother, is he mad? !"

At that moment I was afraid to answer.

The mouth of the river was in sight. The first of the Kerry boats would enter the river valley in a few minutes. The first of the Condor boats had tacked across the breeze and gained ground on us. Now as it came hard to port it was sure to cross in front of my boat and cut off our escape. Rab had stopped yelling at the soldiers.

I called to him, he was now a long way behind and about to be caught by the second of the Condor boats, "What say yee little brother?"

Rab's reply came back on the breeze. "Hold your course and hold your nerve Clancy. It must work soon, then this one will tack, then we are safe."

No sooner had Rab replied than I heard a commotion on the Condor boat coming from my starboard side. There was cursing and yelling and the trim of the boat looked wrong. They had eased the sail and slowed the boat.

Legend has it

She came off the heel and settled square on the hull but looking low in the water.
They were about fifty yards from my boat and praise the lord, they were sinking!!

The second boat was within thirty feet of Rab's and for a minute it continued on. Then it peeled away to starboard making a course for their comrades who were now all in the water as their boat and their guns were going down.

Father watched in amazement as the second boat eased its sail and then repeated exactly what the first boat had done. Two of the soldiers fired wild shots as their boat slid deeper into the deep dark water of the bay and began to capsize. Rab was yelling and laughing again, I must say that I was whooping, and Mary and Ma were singing "Rule Britannia" as our small fleet sailed peacefully on, past the panic stricken crew of the Condor, the pride of Her Majesty the Queen. It was not until Father looked back at Rab and saw that he was waving a shipwrights auger that he began to understand.

Keepers

The night before, myself and Rab had swum across to the settlement and bored holes in all the Condor boats on the beach. We drilled just above the waterline so that they would not take water until the boat lent over on a turn. The plan had worked perfectly, almost too perfectly. If the second boat had not heeled over on the tack, leaning on its side and putting the holes deeper in the water, it would have caught Rab before it sunk. However, 'it did and it didn't', and Rab was still cheering loudly as we sailed away.

The two best boats in the Condor camp were gone and it would take time for Kalklyn to rig the remaining smaller boats. We Kerrys would have two days head start, maybe more. That was plenty of time to simply disappear and become just a legend of the valley.

Yes, we heard over the years that followed, that our family had become a story for folks to tell their children on dark and windy nights.

The story goes that the whole family of us had sailed into the 'Dreamtime' with the local folk and when the children see a bright moon and shining stars, it shows that we are happy there. In the years that followed others joined us and the legend included them as well.

41

Legend has it

Maybe we have gone to the 'Dreamtime', for surely
here we have friends to live with in peace, the stars are
always bright and the moon shines on our new home.
Over time the invaders stopped searching for us. They
had other problems to deal with. Captain Kalklyn was
replaced by a man called Brooklyn and our adventure was
forgotten by the settlement.
If we are lucky we will live with the Valley and the locals
who saved us forever and the rest of the world might
forget about our valley for good.

Great Aunt Pearl closed the leather bound book carefully and sat
quietly for a moment with her hand on the Dark red cover.
Then she said to the silent group, "As we know now, the legend is
still spoken of after more than two hundred years and the valley is
almost forgotten sometimes."
That looked like the end of G.P. doing her thing.
Every one assumed that was that and started to head back to the
main house.
All the parents were moving in a huddle as they discussed the
outcome of the meeting. They looked like a rugby scrum that had
lost the football field.

Chapter Four
Takers and Users

Just as the kids got to the doorway, they each heard the voice of Great aunt Pearl. "Keepers will remain please."

They all turned to see Granddad and his sister still sitting at the table. The book lay closed in front of them. Then they heard her say, "Come back and sit down children."

That's when they were sure. She was not speaking. That is, her lips were not moving.

Gazza had time to splutter, "What the----

She cut into their thoughts again, "Don't worry, as Keepers you will find that you can communicate this way, or more to the point. You will all be able to receive thoughts that are properly sent but some of you will not be able to send as well as others."

They took their seats and started to learn what it meant to be a Keeper.

Great Aunt Pearl had been a very active Keeper in her time. She had campaigned against sand mining in the national parks at

Yango and Dharug and other places in the district. She even made a trip to Tasmania when the Franklin River Dam was being protested and Keepers came from everywhere to show the government how much damage the project would do to The Place over there. That was a big win for the Keepers but there had been lots of smaller ones along the way.

She told them how Keepers were ordinary people but they had an extra-ordinary interest in The Place "The sort of interest and understanding that you five had even before you were called," she explained.

"Tell us more about the book G.P." Jack was pushing his luck. No one had ever used the abbreviation to her face before.

Great Aunt Pearl looked at him for a moment, then she smiled and said, "I like that, G.P. eh, sounds like a doctor, maybe that's right, then G.P. it is. That 'Great Aunt Pearl' thing makes me feel old. I might fall asleep before you get to say anything else," they all laughed and G.P. explained more about the book.
"The book tells of how the Keepers were not always in the right place at the right time.
The first of the Keepers had plenty of time to learn the ways of The Place but the ways of people were always a problem."
The kids looked alert so she went on, "There were Keepers when the first rabbits were brought into the country but by the time they realized the danger it was too late. Once the rabbits were released into the wild, the nature of a lot of the country was bound to be changed forever. Then there were foxes, water buffalo, pigs, camels and others but the cane toad could top them all.

The same thing applies to a whole lot of plant life that was brought here by people who either did not know or did not care about what damage it would do. Things like privet, blackberry, patterson's curse and all the others. The point is that the Keepers are called because in their life time there will be an event that will threaten The Place. It might be the whole place say, the world, like nuclear weapons or nuclear waste or global warming. That's when you hope there are Keepers in our governments. Lord knows they have got plenty to deal with. Or it might be just our part of The Place, the Valley, the river, one of the national parks, any of it."

"The legend says to the Keepers, 'You have time to learn the way'. They need to learn the way, then, with each generation the Keepers have to hope they are in the right place at the right time and can see the danger in time to do something."

The five of them found out lots of things about being Keepers from G.P. and G.R, as Grand dad Reg now wanted to be called, when it was Keeper business, but there was a bit of a problem. The two girls seemed to get a lot more information than the boys.
Reg said, "Since G.P. is a Keeper it's just natural that she and the 'women folk' would talk more."
G.P. glared at him. The only thing that they did agree on was that the affect of being a Keeper was somehow not the same for boys and girls.

G.P. was a little unsure of what to do. It was G.R. who came up with the idea, "Let's get one of the male Keepers from another branch of the family to contact the boys, that should help sort things out."
G.P. agreed, "Yes we can call the Mannerings or the Magraths,

they are not far away." Then she corrected herself, "Actually they are both far away at the moment. I just remembered that they are off at the conference about the water desalination plant in Sydney." G.R. cut in, "That's alright I will speak with them when they get back.
I want to know what they think about having five Keepers called in the same generation anyway."

Gazza had been listening like the others, now he asked,
"How come there is such a big deal now that Jack has had the dream. When Jamie and I had it no one seemed to get excited and I didn't even hear about Penny and Emma?"
G.P. and G.R. looked at each other. G.R. shrugged to give G.P. the go ahead and she said, "Well, it has been a long time since there has been a new Keeper in the Valley. To be honest, most of your parents were thinking it was all just an old family story that Reg and I were trying to keep going."
G.R. joined in, "As each of you were called they became more convinced and when Jack's birthday made him the last one for this generation they had to admit something was going on."
G.P. continued, "With five Keepers in the one area we are thinking it might mean something big will happen in your life time. Of course it might mean that because you five have learnt so much from your parents and you work so well together that making all of you official Keepers will just help you do the things you want to do to Keep The Place safe. The legend says "You have Time to learn," so I guess we will all find out eventually."
Then she added, "By the way, don't ever forget, Keepers can come from anywhere. You don't need to be an ancestor of the Kerry's. That does help we think but you all know about Jacques Cousteau for instance or Steve Irwin. Those men were just people who felt the need to work for the planet. I would be proud to have

them as relatives but it is enough to know that they were there."

Penny put her question slowly, not sure of exactly how to ask, "If we were not 'Keepers' what would we be?"
G.R. took a turn at the answer, "Look kids, names are just names, we use them to identify everything and some times they don't fit very well," Reg could see that he was not helping. The kids were confused, he looked at his sister and shrugged.
Pearl took a breath, "Putting labels on everyone can seem ugly but try it this way," she began,
"The world is made up of three main types of people.
'Takers', they are the ones that grab everything that they can and don't care what the cost is to anyone or, anything. Most big businesses are lumped in together there, like oil companies, car makers, mining and others, not all of them are bad but they make a good example because they are big, although it is not always right to attack something just because it's big.
'Users', are the ones who just go along using what the 'Takers' offer and pretend that it's not their fault when resources grow scarce or pollution is out of control. They are the majority, or the consumers, all of us are users to some degree. Mostly, when we are shown a better way to do things, like how to avoid waste, or use less water, the damage from littering and the other simple stuff, a lot of us will try to do the right thing. Then there are
'Keepers', you lot are 'Keepers' because you can feel the pain of pollution in our river. You can see that development in fragile areas is a waste of beauty that has been with us for thousands of years. Others are 'Keepers' if they are the ones to show the way, maybe about, litter, fuel efficiency, better methods of living with The Place instead of on the place.
You and the ones that follow need to learn about both sides, mankind will continue to change the world that is just what we do.

The way we do it is what it's all about. It's just like that movie where the old man says to the kid, "Balance grasshopper" it is all about balance. We need to develop but we need to keep The Place alive as well."

Pearl looked from face to face, "Just relax, it's alright if you don't understand everything at the moment. You will learn as you go along and there are many other Keepers in the world. With luck, one day there will be more Keepers than Users again, then the balance will as it should be."

She sat back in her chair and said, "I think you have all had enough for today. Off you go now and have some fun, get some air and we can talk again some other time."

They did not need to be told twice. Gazza led the charge for the door. Once they were safely out of ear shot, he said "Wow man, that is heavy stuff but I reckon I've got it beat."

Jamie shook his head. He winked at Emma and spoke to Gazza, "Go ahead Einstein, what's your plan?"

"Right, just picture this, we get all the takers to lock up all the users and not let them go,"

Even for Gazza this was sounding 'out there'.

Jack had to ask, "What are you blathering about?"

Gazza feigned exasperation, "Oh you young ones, you just don't think. If they don't let the users go that means they keep them. That means they are keepers, that means they can't be takers and there would be no more users because the takers got them. So everyone would be either kept or a keeper. No more users because they got taken and no more takers because they kept the users they took, simple."

Penny bent down to pick up a fallen branch shaped a bit like a club, she took a test swing to get the feel. Gazza was a bit concerned at the look in her eye as she turned to him and said, "I wonder if they know how long it might take some of us to learn the way."

The parents were not concerned as the kids all tore past in a burst of noise and energy. Gazza's mum was pleased to see that he was in the lead this time. Usually he was lagging behind with young Emma. Just so she would not feel left out, he would say.

No body noticed which of them was yelling, "Save me, save me !!"

Keepers
In the Forgotten Valley

Chapter Five
What's in a Name

The kids knew that they were related somehow. None of them had bothered to think much about it but when they did, it seemed a bit odd. There was Jamie Walker the oldest at fourteen this year. Penny Wilson not far behind at thirteen and three quarters. Gareth(Gazza) Corndiff and Jack Kipley both thirteen this year and of course Jacks sister Emma, ten going on forty as the folks said. Most of them had brothers and sisters but they were not part of the 'click'.

They had spoken about it once or twice, they got as far as, "If we are all related then how come, first, we all have different sir names. We all have different grand parents and we don't even look the same," that was Gazza. Only his mother called him 'Gareth'.
"Yeah" put in Penny, "Like my folks are Chinese somewhere way back. Jamie comes from an Aboriginal Elder. Gazza says he is Hungarian royalty or something (Gazza gives a royal wave) and the Kipleys of course are the direct descendants of 'Long John Kerry' or some other ancient criminal."

Then they would try to rev each other up , like "Hail Gazza, King of the hungry". or "Hey Jamie, you got any Kellogs Witchetties in that back pack". Or "Penny, where did they put your made in China sticker." and of course, " Every body knows that the Kipleys got here before the rest because the pommies sent the worst first!" Emma was the only one who still got upset when they started on that stuff so they gave it up pretty quickly, like it was no big deal, just the rubbish everyone says.

The part that was not rubbish is that their parents got on well. That's why they had grown up with each other like real cousins. Because they were close in ages they found themselves at school together, sports together and of course, adventures together. There was some strange stuff as though. They all sort of knew what the others would do and some times it was a little weird. Like no one would call anyone but they would all turn up at the same swimming hole at the same time. Or they would meet on the school bus and one would say something like, "I just found out--- and one of the others would finish the sentence, they would all look at each other, sort of shrug, and talk about something else.

So it was pretty natural that they would become a gang. They all wanted to do things with the environment when they grew up and from when they were little they all reckoned that Steve Irwin was awesome in the way that he showed how much just one person could achieve. There was no doubt in their minds that if the stories about their Ancestors were true, then 'The croc hunter' had to be a 'Keeper' of the highest order.

So it was Gazza who actually started the name thing, he thought it was brilliant. On the primary school bus one morning he proclaimed, "We will be The WWW."

What's in a name

All the others said as one, "WHAT !!"
He was ready for their jibes. Because he was a computer nerd and the rest of them wanted to be either Tarzan or Jane, he copped a bit sometimes. But they were never too shy to call him when there was a project due or a web search or a virus to kill. That was his sort of hunting, yeah, hunt and kill from the comfort of home and close to the fridge as well.
"Derrr !!!." he said, "Check it out, it is fully adjustable." Wiseman Wild (life)Warriors, or World Wide Warriors, or"—
Penny jumped in "Wild and Weird Whackers".

For the rest of the trip they argued about the name. At first it had to be about the environment so they tried all sorts of strange names. Eventually they woke up to the fact that it is about what you do, not what your name is. Somebody came up with 'XXX' from a movie or something and since it didn't matter that much and when you said 'TripleX' it sounded like action. Just before the bus got to school they settled on 'TripleX' so the five of them would be 'TripleX' members. As soon as Jamie said it that way, Jack said, "Did you hear that, how can five be triple, that's three, in Latin or something, Quin is five, we have to be the 'QuintX' gang."
Gazza was still mumbling that 'Triple W' sounded just as good as they left the bus.
That was a long time ago and the 'QuintX' had just stuck, it didn't really mean anything but every one (except Gazza) thought it sounded cool.

When they were young everything was pretty cool in the Valley too, 'QuintX' looked for adventure and as they got bigger their adventures got bigger. If any of them had seen a documentary on wildlife or conservation or even 'Tomb raiders', when they got together they each picked their favorite character and set off to save the world. That was while they were small and it was usually done on a Sunday when all the folks would get together for a barby. It was good that they all lived pretty near each other on the river. If they needed to throw someone in the mangrove mud so that they could do a 'quicksand' rescue, well, there was always Gazza, at least until his mum cracked up about his clothes.

As they got a bit older they were allowed to start camping out on weekends and holidays. It started in the back yard of Jamie's house. By the time Jack and Gazza were eleven there was four of them up in the national parks that surrounded the valley and they could be even be out over night.

The parents used to say how it wouldn't happen in their day but now with mobile phone reception in a lot of the valley, staying in touch was so easy. If there was a problem there would be a way to communicate but there never were any problems, not really. They were part of the bush and the river. There was no risk for this crew, they were always prepared and alert, that's how you live with The Place.

Of course you can't help bad luck. There had been lots of scrapes and scratches and each of them had learned how quickly a cut can become infected if it is not cleaned and dressed properly.

It wasn't until they got older that they had a sort of serious problem.

Penny was leading the way up through a crevice toward one of their favorite camp sites. They had used this track several times before but today, just as she stepped on the ledge almost at the top of the climb, the sandstone gave way. With no warning and nothing to grab, she tumbled down the sheer face of the wall for about eight or nine metres. She was able to keep her cool, look at what was happening and react, all in an instant.

As she landed on the next ledge she had her knees bent and was in a crouch to absorb as much impact as possible so that she would not simply bounce off the ledge and continue to fall. It worked well but the ledge was not level and as she landed on all fours like a cat, her left hand found a raised section of rock. The load was uneven and her forearm broke.

There are two bones in the forearm she only broke one, that's enough, the pain is intense and the arm is not much use for about six weeks.

'QuintX' swung into action, one of the gang was down !.

Penny tested the arm as the others scampered over the crumbling ledge on to solid ground above. "I think my arm is broken", she called between gasps of pain as Jamie secured a rope to the base of a sturdy gum and prepared to lower himself down to her. It was not a really dangerous crevice. That is, there were plenty of hand and foot holds and from were Penny had landed you would sort of slide more than fall to the bottom but you would not have much skin left when you got there. So the point for Jamie was, preparation. If you are going to help someone in trouble, make sure you prepare so that you don't end up in trouble with them.

While Jamie set his gear, the others hunted around to find something to use as a splint. When a bone is broken it needs to be immobilized, for that, you need something to tie it to, that stops it moving around until the bone gets to a doctor or hospital to have a cast put on. They found a couple of straight saplings, cut them down with Jacks machete and got back to Jamie just as he was ready to go. The whole event took about six minutes from the time that Penny fell, to when Jamie was with her getting ready to splint the arm.

Both Penny and Jamie had done first aid courses about snake and spider bites, broken limbs and lacerations, so they knew how to be careful with the splint. If it is not fitted well or if it is not tied correctly you can cut off the blood flow and kill the arm.

While the splint was being fitted Jack sent Gazza and Emma back down to the bottom of the crevice with Jamie's back pack. He would stay up top and release the rope once Penny and Jamie were down. Jamie fitted Penny with a climbing harness and they worked their way down the wall together.

With the splint on, the pain was a little better but Penny was mostly cranky that it was her that fell. It should have been someone else. Not to hurt them, it's just that she was the one who could climb and jump and run better than them all. That's why you have to stay alert. When you are the best and can't go wrong, nature likes to play games. No body was going to explain that part to Penny just at the moment.

It only took them half an hour longer than usual to get back down the mountain. Penny was too tough to slow them down very much, even with her arm in a sling.

When they got her home her mother reacted a bit different to how they had expected. She didn't go off, like Gazza expected. She didn't cry, like Emma thought she might. She listened to their story, checked the splint and the sling and complimented the kids on their performance in looking after her daughter, 'QuintX' had done the job.

While Penny was going off about how she could have got down by herself and how her arm should not have broke anyway and all sorts of other things. Her mother bundled her into the car saying things like, "Yes dear, that's right dear, oh I know dear."

At least the timing was good, it was the Doctors day on in Wisemans.

They could still hear Penny at it as the car moved off down the drive.

Chapter Six

Lucky Break

It is funny how the world works. If it had not been for Penny's broken arm, the folks would not have had their meeting the next week. If that hadn't happened maybe QuintX would not have found their headquarters a lot of things would be different.

At the meeting they decided that, perhaps the kids had been a little out of control and maybe there should be some new rules. It was not just Penny's folks either, you would expect that.

Emma's mum and Dad were concerned too, mostly about Emma but Jack as well. The result was that they were each going to bar their kids from heading off into the bush any time they liked, so they came up with some rules. Things like, they had to set up a regular camp site near one of the houses, the parents had to inspect the site to make sure it was safe, had water nearby and it had to be easy to get to. That meant no more big rock climbs, abseiling, canyoning, in general, all the good stuff. This was partly because of Emma, as someone said at the time, "she is only nine." The one that nobody said out loud was that it was about Penny as well, in case she had lost her confidence after the fall and maybe it was not what a girl should be doing anyway.

The new deal was announced to the kids at a Sunday barbie about two weeks after the fall. Due to QuintX intelligence methods, there were no surprises, at least not for the kids. Jack's father and Gazza's mother were about the quickest in the bunch. They both got a bit twitchy when the first reaction from the kids was "Oh, gee, golly, that's tough, Okay." It didn't take long for the other parents to catch on that the kids were giving in too easily.

Gazza almost saved the day. He saw the glint in his mother's eye (the one she had when he or his Dad started to explain why something had broken and how it was not their fault. But she wasn't buying it, yeah, that one), and realized that they had outsmarted themselves. Luckily it was only Jamie and Penny who had practiced the 'Okay' part. He was able to kick Jack under the table and point at his mother with his eyes while starting to whinge at the same time, "Oh gee, that's rough, ah, we only broke one arm between us, there were lots more to spare."

Emma caught on instantly and jumped in before he could add any more to the worst excuse she had ever heard. She used that pleading voice that worked so well on her mother, "Gazza means that we did a good job, accidents happen all the time you know."

Jack added, "Can't we just promise to use the mobile more often or something?"

The act was starting to work. Jamie and Penny realized their mistake as soon as Emma joined in but their part was already done, so they left the other three to 'bung it on'.

Lucky Break

The legend of the Valley is only a couple of hundred years old. The battle of wits between kids and parents is much older. Sometimes the parents win, sometimes the kids. This one was a dead heat. They all put their points in a very civil manner, no raised voices, just a discussion where the parents allowed the kids to put their case as young adults. The parents then discussed the views of the children and made the decision that they had arrived at long before the discussion.

The kids managed to argue long enough to convince the parents that they were listening to what they were told. They appeared to be 'put out' enough for the parents to be comfortable. Both sides had a win and both groups left the meeting knowing that the other side would have to be watched closely.

The good news was that Jamie, Jack and Gazza had already been out looking for a site that would suit the parents and thought they had found the ideal spot. Now what they needed to do was find it again under the new rules and get the parents to approve it. The other trick would be to make the trail to the spot difficult enough for the parents not to turn up uninvited when the gang was at work.

QuintX had their own meeting the week before the folks. They knew what was on the joint mind of the parents. They got through the rebel stuff like "Who cares, we'll show them, etc." fairly quickly. Really, they all knew their parents were pretty cool and they knew that this was all about "Take care of the kids," type stuff. So that meant that their own plan had to make sense because the parents would work it out in a while. They were parents but they weren't dumb with it.

Jamie led the way, across the road and up the rocks above Jack's place. It was one of the easy tracks that they had used when they were all younger. The track wound up through the steep hillside but it was all walking, no need for ropes or climbing gear. As they made their way along the face of the rocks, Jack remembered that they had stopped coming this way because it was too long and too easy. After almost an hour of walking they had climbed over, around and down the other side of the rock that stood behind the 'Old Stone House' built by the Kerrys so long ago. The track was good enough for the mountain bikes but that would have to wait until Penny's arm had healed. Where the track bottomed out there was a spring, it came out of the ground a little further up, ran like a stream for ten or fifteen metres, then disappeared into the rock and probably found its way to the river. On the other side of the spring a clearing about the size of a tennis court ran up to the sheer cliff on one end. It was surrounded by low scrub running into a mixture of trees and bushes then up to the steep hills at the other. There seemed to be no other way into the small clearing. It looked like a good place to camp and there was even a mobile signal from the southern side of the cliff. This is what they would show the folks.

They did not think that the parents needed to know that if you went to the right instead of the left at the start of the track, you would be on a very interesting climb across the face of the cliff and be up and over in about fifteen minutes. Another ten minutes down the other side and you would be standing in exactly the same spot. There was a need for a little more exercise which involved climbing a short section on one of the knotted ropes they had installed a year or so ago. Actually, there were two rope sections if you were counting everything.

The ropes were no problem. They were 20mm polypropylene mainsail sheets left over from one of the sailing projects that Jack's father had been on, they had a twenty year UV life and were mounted with marine grade stainless fittings. He kept them in the shed, you know, just in case, along with a whole lot of other good stuff that Jack's mother was always wanting to clear out. She didn't want to use the space, it was just the sort of thing that a good woman should do. She should object to the storage of anything 'other than money' for any length of time over, say, two months, or even less if she happens to see it too often in between times.

Jack had heard that story being told to Penny by G.P. one day, he never did know if she was serious. He mentioned the theory to Granddad Kerry one time and he said it was true, "It's been that way since the cavemen used to try to keep the odd elephant tusk in the back of the cave, just in case he needed it later. Exact same thing, that's why blokes started to build sheds, women don't go into sheds, well - they didn't used to."

"Derrrr! We don't have elephants here Granddad."

Anyway, the point is, if you come in the short way and out the other, you can see that you have made a full circle around the piece of cliff that stands behind the Stone House. That was pretty good since it looked like the only way in was long slow and boring.

If you knew where to look when you got there it got even better.

Keepers
In the Forgotten Valley

Chapter Seven

Show Time

Just above the clearing where the spring runs, there are two giant gums. They have dead straight trunks for about twenty metres, not a branch on either until about thirty metres up and they look like they have grown as one with the cliff face. From the clearing you would think they were hard up against the rock. When you come down from the high side however, you can see that they have been put there to guard the entrance to a secret place.

The only way in is behind the gums. There is a gap between the uphill tree and the cliff face, just about wide enough for a small car and if there were bears in this country, it is exactly what they would be happy to call home. It was exactly what QuintX would call home from then on. Although they did not bother to show the folks the real cave, they did find a small sort of washout in the cliff on the low side that looked like a good place to store lots of stuff. They told their folks it was the new headquarters of QuintX and it was not far from the truth: about thirty metres to be exact. So two Sundays after the big meeting, Jack announced that they had found the site as instructed. The whole lot of them set off for a walk up and around the cliff to the pleasant little spring, with the little cave and no ropes or cliff climbing anywhere in sight.

The kids had thought this was an easy and boring walk. However after about twenty minutes it started. "Are we there yet?"
It was mostly Mr. Corndiff (out of condition).
Mrs. Wilson (wrong shoes).
Then after another half hour: "Are we there yet?"
Mr. Walker (wrong shoes)
Mrs. Walker (out of condition)
So they stopped for a rest while the kids went on to check the trail. About twenty metres ahead they huddled up and Jamie said, "This is great! My folks might not even get there this time, let alone come back on their own."
Penny added, "Yeah, I think Dad is just about over it and Mum wasn't much of a problem anyway."
Gazza mused, "My old man is in terrible nick. I don't know where he gets that from."
The others looked at him waiting to see some sign that he was joking. There was none.
Emma said, "I don't think we will lose ours," looking at Jack who continued for her.
"No, Dad's fairly fit and Mum's got the right shoes on," he said, smiling at Em.
As they broke up laughing and headed back to pick up the parents Penny said, " It's all good, stay with the plan, most of them are over it and we can handle any that aren't."
The rest of the gang murmured their agreement.
By the time they arrived at the clearing, almost an hour after the first rest, and ten minutes after the last, they had drifted into three groups, the kids, who kept getting ahead then stopping to wait, the

"not-well, bad-shoes, are-we-there-yet?" group and then the Kipleys with Mrs. Corndiff and Mr. Wilson.

This group looked like they were on a Sunday walk, (derrr?). They could probably have kept up with the kids but were being politically correct by supporting their peers, (example to children: are you watching? type stuff) and they were nice folks enjoying the walking and talking as well.

The parents were all impressed with the site. The water in the stream was fresh and cool and the bush grass in the clearing was soft and green. It seemed that there were no introduced weeds in the area, that gave the place a real old-time feel, it was still the way that it would have been if Hamish Kerry or any of the Ancients had found their way to this hollow over the last twenty decades.

Kate Kipley pointed out evidence of that as she stared at the two magnificent gums that were growing against the cliff just above the clearing. She spoke mostly to her husband but everyone heard, "Alex, look at those two incredible trees, they must be hundreds of years old, they are so straight and tall. Think of all the things they have seen while they have grown here in the hollow out of the sight of loggers and woodcutters." She moved up the hill toward the Guardian trees. Jamie and Jack looked at each other and shrugged helplessly.

Penny nodded to Emma, they moved together to pass Kate and arrive at the first tree before her. They went past and both wrapped their arms as far as they could around the huge trunk of the second. "Yes, I knew you would love these," said Emma as Kate put her hands on the first tree. She stood with her eyes closed, feeling the life of the tree, feeling The Place. With her eyes still closed she watched time in fast forward, the tree as a sapling the hollow in dry times and in the wet, the passing parade of Goanna, Wombat, Wallaby, possum, snakes large and small, birds of all types. She even heard their calls and she knew the kids would be safe here, The Place was all around and they were one with it.

For an hour or so they sat around the clearing, it was about then that Mr.Corndiff calculated if they moved a little more quickly going down than they did coming up, it would be just on lunch time when they got back. So with he and Mrs. Wilson leading the way, they hiked back down to the Kipley's for the BBQ.

All in all the event was a success, for now the folks would always know where the kids were and the kids would know that the folks were happy and Jack was still keeping an eye on Mrs. Corndiff and his father to see if they were buying the story, so far so good.

It turned out that Mr.Corndiff never did make that walk again, nor did Mrs. Wilson or Mr. and Mrs. Walker, but neither did Penny .

Chapter Eight

Out of the Mist

One battle for the rest of QuintX had been to keep Penny under control while the show and tell day was on.
She had been like a chained up dingo ever since she had heard someone say that she and Emma should be looked after or taken more care of. WO!! Was she going off when the gang first discussed the bush walky, show mummy and Daddy thing.

She apologized to Emma in advance, " Em, you know I love you dearly and I do in fact agree that you should be looked after. BUT, if they think that I am going to rely on this bunch of clumsy drongos (sorry boys) (Not) to look after me in the bush or anywhere else for that matter then they better think again. Just because I broke one bone in one arm and it was only a hairline fracture anyway."

You have to believe that it went on and on, and on. The rest of the gang did the usual, when Penny was off the air. They would take turns being in front of her, sort of like target practice. It didn't matter much who was there, she would rant on about the same things over and over, although Emma didn't seem to work well and Gazza seemed to work too well. So the other two just rotated around until she wore herself out. Then about half an hour after she stopped you could usually talk to her. Well for Gazza that would be an hour. (at least)

The outcome from this 'Penny event' was mostly good. She made two promises to the gang. First, she would do her part at the show day. Second, she would not go to the headquarters by the bush track, on foot, ever again. In fact she would not go there at all until she could go by the shortcut across the cliff face.

There did not seem much point in further discussion on the matter. At that time the fracture was about three of the required six weeks into healing. Then there was usually physiotherapy to regain movement in the wrist because it had not been used for so long. So that would make it about another five or six weeks before they had to worry about this cranky climber making her way up the cliff.

The week after show day, the three boys arrived at headquarters with some gear to start fitting the place out. They were talking about how the climb got easier each time and how they might have to add a rope or two for Penny when the time came. As they approached the guardian trees, the three of them stopped in their tracks. Around the base of the trees there was a mist rising, they could see it coming from the floor of the cave. They stood looking at each other and at the mist. Was this a sign from the ancients? were they going to see into the past?

Jack led them slowly forward. At the edge of the entrance they could hear a hissing sort of noise, like Hssss, then Hssss, it was regular but faster than say, normal breathing.

Could it be the Snake Spirit in the cave waiting for them?

Jack moved a little further toward the mist. In his dreams the mist had a pleasant smell of earth and river and once you were in the mist you could see and talk to the Ancients. He took a deep

Breath, Jamie and Gazza were right behind him. They all started coughing and spluttering at the same time and stepped back away from the mist. It smelt and tasted just like dust.

The hissing stopped as soon as they started to cough. Through watering eyes they watched as a figure with no face came to them through the settling mist. They heard Penny's voice clearly.

"About time you lot, there are brooms over there, lets get stuck into it. I brought more of these paper dust masks, they're inside," she looked at the boys and wondered for the hundredth time, "What is wrong with these blokes? They are standing there crying, looking at me as though I am a Ghost or something. Mum is right, there is no way to work them out, just keep them busy and let them think everything is their idea."

They swept the smooth floor of the cave until the dust stopped rising. Then they swept some more until Penny said it was clean. The cave was much bigger on the inside, the roof rose sharply after the entrance and the sides curved around like a bowl.

Gazza said, " Wow, It looks like we are inside a bowling ball, like, sort of, oh you know."

The others looked that, "Gazza be quite," look and he sulked off to the back of the cave while they talked about furniture.

The back of the cave was not as rounded as the rest and it was rougher, much rougher. As Gazza started to climb up the sloping rock of the back wall he realized that this wall was not solid rock. It was mostly huge boulders but they were all separate, like they had been dumped on top of each other about a trillion years ago. He got a fair way up when he realized something else. He could see, he was at the back of the cave, about twenty five metres from the entrance but there was plenty of light. Gazza sat on a rock shelf about five metres up the wall of the cave, about half way to the top.

There were plenty of hand and foot holds to use to get to the top but he sat and studied the light.

After some clever deductive reasoning, he called to the others who were still chatting near the entrance. "Yoo Hoo, I can see you," It was Gazza, they ignored him.
Once more, "Yoo Hoo, I can see you, can you see me,"
They could tell when he was not going to stop until someone played his game.
Jamie looked up and called back, "Yes'y we can see you,"
Gazza waited, nothing, " WELL, !!, you can see me,! !"
The penny dropped for Jack first, then as soon as he started looking around the roof of the cave the other two realized what Gazza was on about. Now that he had their attention Gazza started to tell them what he had found. He began to make his way further up as he spoke, his voice echoing off the sandstone walls. "There is daylight coming in over the top of this back wall. We didn't notice because as the light hits the roof of the cave it is spread out evenly all over because of the shape."
Jack agreed. They had been so busy making plans that they didn't realise how well they could see. Now he looked at the almost perfect dome shape of the roof and how it spread the light all the way around the cave. Jamie was on his way up to join Gazza, they arrived at the top of the wall at the same time. Gazza looked at him and not for the first time, he marveled at the way Jamie seemed to move like water flowing up hill or a spider with extra legs. He traveled over the rock so smoothly, it was amazing. Jamie returned his stare, " What?"
You don't tell a mate how good he is, "Oh, no, nothing, just thinking."
That day they decided that the cave probably used to be longer but at some stage its roof had collapsed. That meant the top of the

mountain fell into the hole and when it settled it left a narrow slot along the top and that was where the light was reflecting from. It was way too narrow to try to fit through but there was really good air flow as well as light in the day time. Excellent, that meant they could have a good safe fire anytime without worry about bush fire and even without being seen, perfect for QuintX business.

Jamie said that he would climb to the top one day and see what the outside looked like. That wouldn't happen too soon, lots of other things happened instead.

To begin with there was gear to be stored, firewood to be cut and stacked. Over the years they would carry, drag, push or pedal all sorts of things up to their cave. Penny carried an amazing array of things across the cliff face. That first time when she had come across with four brooms tied to her back pack just like an over size archery set with her arm still in a cast, was nothing. Gazza was really happy that she did not play the piano, cause if she did, well, she would have a go at it anyway.

Jamie did find the time to blaze another trail along the back of the cliff which meant there were now three ways to reach or leave headquarters. The most recent followed the back of the cliff for about fifteen minutes then cut into the rocks through some gullies and about twenty minutes later it came out just above the main road 3ks west of the Kipley place.

Almost all of that trail could be ridden, there were only two places where you had to lift the bike over pretty deep crevices and one where you had to drag it over a big round boulder that just looked like it was put there to block the track.

It seemed like headquarters was really meant to be their place.

Keepers
In the Forgotten Valley

Chapter Nine
Who Am I

Once they got to high school it meant early starts and the hour long bus ride up the mountain to Galston High. That was a real bummer until they got in to the habit of bringing articles or books about the river or the Valley or other places where there were environmental issues. Some of the other kids on the bus thought they were weird but some of them joined in the discussions too. Jamie was a freak for Australian history, he had aboriginal ancestors somewhere, maybe that was part of it. For him there was a comfort in the bush, it was where he could breath. He knew that one day when he had learnt enough, he would be able to help clean out the feral animals and introduced plants and let the bush look after itself in the way it was meant to.

Then there was Penny. Her folks way back on her mothers side, were Chinese but she was as keen as the rest to learn what it would take to keep the planet alive, starting with their own valley. It seemed to be like one of the things Jack's Granddad was always saying, "It has taken all sorts of people a long time to make the world the way it is and it will take all sorts of people a lot longer to fix it."

While Jamie was wrapped in learning about wildlife, bush craft, nature and a mad soccer player. Penny was into the philosophy of martial arts. For her it was about the mind controlling the body and the self discipline to make the perfect form.

With or without the perfect form, the boys had found out early that Penny was fast and fierce when she needed to be. So the games had sort of drifted away from the 'boy saves girl thing' pretty quickly. She found that she had a real talent for archery and headed the state junior competitions from when she was eleven through to thirteen. There was even talk that she might qualify for the Olympic games in three years time. As well as the archery club and the martial arts training, Penny wanted to learn the law. The law that allowed big business to take over the land when ever it suited them. It was her ambition to learn how these laws could be changed in time to save the endangered parts of the country and keep it alive for ever.

Gazza, what could you say about Gazza? You have to say that even in a strange place, Gazza would still be weird. He was into science, electronics, computers and prawns. There was a fish tank in his room and in it he had a family of prawns. He says that he can tell the males from the females and that eventually he will have a breeding program to restock the lower reaches of the river, who knows ?.

His father is a big wig contractor to an electronics research group and his mother is a truck driver. Mrs.Corndiff drives the water tanker that works the Gosford side of the river. There was a story about a 'sea change' or a 'tree change', or something similar a while back but now it doesn't seem to bother anyone and Gazza has upset a few teachers over the years at those show and tell type things. "What do your parents do Corndiff?"

"Well sir," says Gazza, in his most serious voice. "Dads a research scientist and Mums a trucky."

A long unsure look from the teacher, then on to the next kid.

Until recently Gazza was, how to say nicely, fat, yeah that would be it, his mum would say, solid or "He has big bones". There was a time when he just never seemed to move, he would sit at the computer all day. Then when his mum was not watching, he would get his exercise. He would walk to the fridge then jog back to the computer. By the time the Kipley kids were 'called' , there was a lot more of him to love.

These days he is out with the gang. Bush walking, camping, mountain biking and the blubber is dropping off but he still needs to watch himself, especially around things like that cheese cake that Mrs. Walker brings to the Sunday barbys.

Both lots of Gazza's grandparents have the same serious money problem, too much of it.

They get into like, a bidding war on his birthdays and Christmas. If one finds out that the other is planning, say, a remote control car, then a remote control plane will appear. Next time it will be a helicopter, an awesome BMX will get topped by a 125cc trail bike and on it goes. That's how he got all the stuff that he has. Then his Dad gets in to it. He and Gazza work on the control systems to extend the range or add some functions. Not all of them are successful. There has been one plane which just kept flying after a control failure, they chased it in the car for a while but it just kept flying. "Heading for Tasmania," says his Father.

One chopper that would only fly upside down, that was Okay until it had to land. And a submarine that just never came up again. They all got replaced bigger and better than before. Jacks mum say's it is because he was a late child, his brother is twenty three. Jack say's, "Whatever."

Gazza is happy to share his gear and Jack is pretty good at the chopper flying, that is, with the unmodified controls.

For Gazza the ultimate future project would be to build a remote control 'King Prawn' so that he could steer it around the trawlers net and all the others would follow. Then they would not get caught and another species would be saved.

Oh ! good one Gazz, where to put the batteries ??

Jack had a fair bit of bother with school work, not the actual subjects, he just didn't seem to have a hook sort of thing. Like it seemed that the others had their special interest and the rest of their school work seemed to flow from there. He had no special interest although playing lock with the school Rugby league team kept him tough and fit. He was big for his age and he enjoyed the game, he wasn't a fanatic about it. He couldn't even tell the others what his interest was because he didn't know how to say it. It was like he was interested in so many things that he couldn't keep still long enough to finish learning about one of them. Some stuff came easy when there were tests at school. Maths wasn't a problem although it took a long time to find a use for it. That started to happen when his Dad was showing him some of the ways to work with navigation charts. When you use a sextant and protractor to calculate your position at sea it really does help if you are not scared of numbers.

It happened again when his Granddad was calculating the volume of rock that he needed to cut at his rock quarry to fill an order for paving stones. A cubic meter is pretty heavy when it is made of Hawkesbury sandstone, you certainly do not want to cut more than you need.

The rest of the subjects were alright but he always felt that he needed to learn more and faster. He felt somehow that he would not be ready in time but he had no idea of what he needed to be ready for.

He and Emma had both learnt to read early. The stuff that you could find in books was almost enough to stop them being out in the bush or on the river learning, " like sponges", Their father would say, just letting the spirit of The Place soak in so that they could 'feel' what was right as well as 'knowing' what was right. Jack thought he might one day be a marine designer like his father, although his Dad had to travel a lot. It had a connection with the water and he loved to be on the water. He also thought he should fly, a plane or a chopper. It was like he was meant to be part of the water or maybe part of the air. He would do whatever he could to stay a part of the River or the Valley, it did not matter which, everything is connected.

Emma was different to the rest of the ten year olds at school. Most of the time she was a ten year old but some times she would just surprise everyone. She was really keen on gardening and growing things but she seemed to know a lot more than she should about plants and animals. Usually if someone asked her how she knew so much she would just say Mum or Dad must have told me. If she was at home and Mum said "Where did you learn that?" she would say her teacher must have told her.

She did not have a life plan but she did have frizzy hair and mostly if you asked her what she wanted to be, she would say, "Bald". Her mum had tried all sorts of things. Cut it short, grown it long, layer cut, straighten it, curls. It did seem to keep them occupied. Whenever any of the other women in the family came by they would always ask about Emma's hair. "The poor little thing", they would go on and on.

Emma had already decided that whatever she did in life she would wear a hat. Maybe that was it, she would be a racing car driver or maybe a nun, either a helmet or a habit.

Her mother did worry when she came up with those ideas. "Don't worry Em," she would say, "You will grow out of it, everyone does." Emma knew her mum would not lie but there was no harm checking out some helmets anyway.

Because she was still at the junior school in the Valley she missed the meetings that were held on the coach as the rest of QuintX traveled to high school but Jack always told her any news when he came home. Sometimes it worked the other way. Because any news in the valley is big news, the mothers at the school were quick to swap stories and information. If there was something happening in the valley the mothers would know first and not long after that, Emma would know.

That was how she knew that someone had been using the old Pearson property out on Settlers rd.

It was not old Mrs. Pearson, she was still in the home, had been since she took that nasty turn last year. It was probably the son of her sister or one of his kids. They used to visit a bit after she lost Burt, that was four years ago now. They seemed to be stopping in there once or twice a week recently, maybe they were doing the place up for her, it certainly needed work.   boring !!!

Keepers
In the Forgotten Valley

Chapter Ten

Sub-Conscious

It was two weeks before end of term when they first saw the truck.
The school coach had picked them up as usual and turned on to
Old Northern road heading for Wisemans Ferry. The coach driver
(Barry) was in the same happy mood as always and he was
running on time. The road is not too bad in places but the
overtaking lanes are a bit short sometimes. Most of the kids were
in that after school coma that happens while you try to forget what
you were taught and remember what you are going to do when
you get home. Gazza had been picked up by his Dad to go to a
computer shop across the gorge in Hornsby and Penny was at Tai
Chi class, so Jamie and Jack found their seats in the middle of the
coach and began to chill out.
The coach had built up a bit of speed but Jack noticed the driver
keeping to the side more than usual. There was a small white
truck slowly coming up alongside the coach, it looked like it would
not have the speed to get past before the overtaking lane ended.
He was looking down into the back of the truck which had high
timber sides, from ground level you would not see what it

was carrying. A tarpaulin had been tied over the top but the front left hand corner had come loose and was blowing back in the wind. Jack was sort of looking but not seeing, in the gap under the tarpaulin there was a heavy looking, bright yellow drum and the outline of others behind it. More important to Jack was the fact that the coach was not slowing and neither was the truck and they were rapidly running out of room.

The overtaking lane ended at the start of the first climb just ahead. Both the coach and the truck wanted to maintain their speed for the run up the hill but there was only one lane on this side of the road and the truck was not going to give way. The coach began to edge out slowly. The truck held his ground even though it was up to him to pull back. The coach driver new that with a load of kids aboard he could not play dangerous games with this clown. So at the last moment he backed off and hit the brakes allowing the truck to pass. The rest of the trip was normal as Barry followed the winding road over the hills that surround the valley.

Sometimes Jack wondered if he was the only one to always be impressed with the view of the river junction from the top of the ridge. No matter how often he saw the junction of the Macdonald the Hawkesbury rivers just upstream from the Ferry he felt the same comfort, he had come home again.

The original road had been a dirt track for horse drawn coaches. Over the years it had been widened and sealed but it still followed most of the same ridges and gullies that were used by the settlers that came from the Sydney side in the 1800's.

When you reach the bottom of the valley at Wisemans Ferry there are two places to cross the river. The main ferry, or the one called the Webbs Creek Ferry, both carry vehicles, pedestrians, horses, whatever. If you want to cross you just get in the queue and drive, ride or walk on when the ferry master gives the signal. If you just miss it when you first arrive, then you will be there for about fifteen minutes before it comes back after loading on the other side. When the first ferry went into service it was run by a man called Solomon Wiseman that was in the 1800's. Now it is run by the main roads dept. you don't have to pay and it is always there, except for floods and breakdowns.

After all that rush and hurry, the truck was still in the queue for the main ferry when the kids got off the coach and switched to the local bus to cross the river for the last part of the trip home.

As they settled into the smaller bus, Jamie started telling the driver(Jock), about the incident with the truck. "We were watching and waiting, we thought Barry might have run him off the road." Jock was laughing, "No I think it is against the rules to run people off the road with a school bus," then he went on. "That truck is a bit later than usual. He started turning up a couple of weeks ago but he is usually on the other side before I come across, don't know where he goes but he's not a local." Jack broke in "How often have you seen him Jock?" The driver thought for a moment, "Pretty often now that you mention it, probably every second day or so for the last two weeks or so."
The truck was two vehicles ahead of them when the ferry landed on the other side and as soon as the boom gate lifted it was off and away in the opposite direction to the bus.
Jack watched it drive away and said to Jamie, " Where do you reckon he's going?"
Jamie watched as the truck disappeared over the hill, "No way to know, there are a few properties out there, just a sec." Jamie turned to the driver, "Hey Jock, have you seen that truck coming back at all?"

Jock liked to chat with the kids, "Well that's how I know it's every second day, he goes back the following morning, he is always there in the queue when I come back on the second run with the primary kids for the local school."

Jack joined in again, "Any idea what he's carrying?"

"No idea, he comes down loaded and goes back empty, the way he shoots up the hill on the other side, that's an unloaded truck."

Jack said "I saw some really solid heavy drums in the back. They were yellow."

Jock turned suddenly serious, "Oh wow, now I see the problem, big drums you say, yellow drums eh, several trips you think," He was speaking softly now and looking to see who was listening, "That means, somewhere in the Valley, where no one can see--
He looked suspiciously at the kid sitting in the nearest seat—
piece by piece, those guys are building-- a yellow submarine."

Jock had pulled to side of the road as he finished Speaking, it was the stop where both Jamie and Jack got off.

He turned their way as he pressed the lever to open the door for them and started to sing an old 'Beatles' song, "We all live in a yellow submarine, a yellow submarine," -----then he started that cackling laugh, the one that made everyone think that someone else should really drive the school bus. He was still cackling and singing as he drove away. The kids still on the bus were looking quite uncomfortable as Jamie and Jack watched them head down the road with a singing maniac at the wheel

"Well" said Jack, "What do you think?"

"Oh no doubt" replied Jamie," He is as silly as a two bob watch."

Jack laughed, "No, not Jock, the truck."

Jamie was smiling as they wandered along to his driveway. "I don't know, it's just a truck isn't it?"

Jack was more serious, "I don't know, something feels strange about it."

Sub-Conscious

As Jamie turned into his drive he said ,"Well I'll do my homework while you work out what's strange about a truck on the ferry and tell me all about it, see you tomorrow."

When Jack got home Emma was out in the vegie garden with mum. They spent a lot of time together growing native plants as well as European types of food. Emma understood the different way that native plants used water and which ones were best suited to local conditions. She called when she saw Jack, "Hey what's happnen bro." trying her U.S. rap talk. (and not doing it very well) Jack, joined the game, " YO big mama , yo, little mama", Kate responded, "Come here, I'll give you 'big mama'," waving her secateurs as she said it.
Jack ran for the back door as they all laughed.

Later when he heard them come inside, Jack called, "Hey Em, come here for a minute," around the doorway of his room popped her frizzy head of hair.
"Yep?"
"I want you to keep your eyes open, well your ears really"
Emma perched herself on the edge of his bed as Jack sat back in his desk chair and continued,
"There is something going on but I don't know what."
Emma was on the case, "What sort of something?"
"Well I don't really know, it's more a feeling than anything,"
"Hey that is strange, I was having feelings last week, I spoke with mum about it. There wasn't anything definite, it was just some sort of feeling, like I was scared or something, it was coming and going so Mum was saying just relax and let it grow if it was real."
"So, what happened?"
Emma was a little uneasy, "That's the problem, nothing happened, or at least nothing changed. I am still getting these weird feelings

80

every couple of days then it stops then it does it again. So I don't know if there is anything there or not."

As soon as Emma said, "Every couple of days" Jack felt a shiver down his spine. "When was the last one?"

Emma looked nervous, "Today, about an hour or so ago, why?"

"And the first one?" ignoring her question.

"I don't know, two weeks or so, what's going on Jack?"

"Look," he started "It probably isn't anything. Let me do some checking for a day or two, then we will talk. If I say the wrong thing to you now it might change how things work, so just relax and see if there are any more feelings, ok?"

Emma understood what he meant, sort of, "All right, but just a couple of days, then we talk, yeah ?".

Jack ruffled her boofy hair, "OK Em,"

It was Wednesday. That meant if the routine continued the truck should show up again on Friday. If that happened and Em got that feeling again, well, Jack did not know exactly what it would mean but it would mean something.

Chapter Eleven

False Alarm

Friday at school dragged slowly by for Jack. He was anxious to check with Jock and Emma to see if his feelings were justified. At lunch he caught up with Gazza and Penny, Jamie was away at some orienteering training.

Jack spoke to Penny about Emma, "Don't you think that it's too much coincidence for her to be sensing trouble at the same time that truck comes into the valley?"

Penny had heard the story on Thursday and was still undecided about it. "It is possible that something is going on but you and Em. are too new and the rest of us are not feeling anything. The legend always say's, you have time to learn the way, that's what they told us."

Jack had already thought about that part, "Yes I know, they say the 'Keeper' is always called at thirteen but it might be any time before he is needed,"

Penny poked him in the ribs with stiffened fingers. "Ouch, yeah Okay !, ten, and she ! Okay ?".

Gazza joined in, "What about Em, are there any rules about when

she should see things or whatever it is that she should be doing?"
Penny answered, "There aren't any real rules there's only stories about what has happened, not what will happen."
Gazza came back, " The Ancients said they can see the future,"
Jack quoted his Grandfather, "The Ancients told Hamish Kerry that they could see the future in the same place that he could see the past, that was more than two hundred years ago."
Gazza looked lost, "Yeah?"
"Oh !!", said Penny, "You're thinking what if they saw the future like, this far or one hundred years or something like that."
Jack was nodding, "Yeah, that's the problem, maybe the Ancients are sort of worn out or are out of date or something."
Gazza got a grip, sort of, "Struth. So we might be Keepers just on our own or sort of like a DIY deal."
Sometimes Jack wondered about Gazza, "Something like that, yeah. I don't know how they were going to help us anyway."

The coach ride to the ferry that afternoon was normal. Jack was not surprised, the truck was not usually there at this time anyway according to Jock. As soon as the coach pulled in to the stop, Jack was off trotting to the local bus. "Hey Jock, how's it going," he greeted the driver.
"No worries," came the usual reply.
Jack looked around. The others were almost at the bus. "Say Jock, did you happen to see that truck again today," he queried.
Jock was instantly into the game, "You mean the one with the submarine parts?" he said with a smile from ear to ear.
"Yes, that's the one," said Jack, he knew that if he did not play Jock's game he would get no information.
"Well," The driver started in a serious voice. "I got down here right on time and while I was waiting, what do you think I saw?"
Jack was hoping, "The truck?"

Jock was still serious, "No. I saw the submarine. It went past while the Ferry was on the other side, I saw the periscope, though I don't know how it got past the ferry cables," the cackle started.

By now the rest of the kids were on the bus and ready to go.

Gazza had waited to hear the story, now he was laughing and waving goodbye. He was the only gang member living on this side.

Penny was first "Oh good one Jack, now you have wound him up".

Ben Taylor from further down river at Gunderman cut in, "Yeah it's all right for you Kipley. You get him going then you get off just up the road and we get stuck with him singing and laughing all the way home. Just don't talk to him, right!?"

Jack took the point, "Alright I'll be quiet, maybe he will calm down," The three QuintX members got off at their stop, the bus took off with a highly suspect maniac doing the submarine song again and Ben and the others looking daggers at Jack out the back window.

Jack was looking for Emma as he walked up the drive, She was not in the garden, neither was mum. He found them in the kitchen they were right in the middle of building what was probably dinner, Jack looked at Emma.

She looked back. "What?"

"Well, any feelings today?"

"Oh, that, no nothing today" Emma answered brightly, "I feel fine."

Emma felt fine the next day and seven more after that. Then the school term ended and it was time for the last day of fishing before they all went off on their holiday activities.

Emma did not usually fish with the other four, She thought it was cruel on the fish, although she liked to eat fish and meat for that matter. She just did not want to know what had to be done to provide the food, that made her a 'user' but GP said most of us are. She did like to ride in the boat and since Jack had been given the new one for his birthday she wanted to be in it as often as she could. That's why she was on board when they picked Gazza up, his place was up stream past the ferry, the other two were down stream so Jack had to come back past home anyway, so she could go for a ride, mum said so, 'nah'.

Gazza was ready with his gear as they approached the jetty. The boat hardly stopped at all as they used the QuintX high speed pickup technique. In went his back pack and his rod then he followed, it got better each time they tried it. Jack eased the boat back out into mid stream and they headed back to drop Emma off and pick up the other two.

They were about ten minutes away from the ferry when Emma suddenly turned to face Jack with a strange expression on her face. "I've got that feeling again, the one I had last week."

For a moment he did not understand, then he realized what she meant and started looking around.

Chapter Twelve
Overboard

Through the trees and scrub up above the river he caught a glimpse of something coming down the road from the direction of the ferry. He yelled "Hang on" wound the steering wheel hard to the left and swung the boat one hundred and eighty degrees.
Gazza had no idea what was happening until jack sent him aft and told him to keep that truck in site no matter what, pointing to a white four tonner up on Settlers rd.
"Aye aye capan," was his best seagoing reply.

He was driving his boat as fast as he dared and they were just able to keep the truck in sight. The road followed the river or visa-versa for the next few kilometres, so they might be lucky and see where these guys were heading. Jack was happy that his father could not see him now. Running at this speed on the narrow Macdonald river was not only dangerous and against the law, it was also against the agreement he had with his parents not to take chances, Emma was crouched in the bow, she was on lookout.

Excited as usual to be in on adventures with Jack and although he did not invite her along there was no time to be rid of little sister and she knew it.

Jack did not really mind, he had a soft spot for her and it was her senses that found the truck.

Gazza was in the centre on the back seat of the tinny. He had enough sense to keep his weight balanced so that Jack had maximum control. It was lucky that Gazza had been in the boat when the chase began, this way Jack could concentrate on driving. Jacks tone had seemed a bit intense but Gazza knew that Jack could be an intense sort of kid so he just hung on, watched the truck and enjoyed the ride. The others would not be happy when they found out that he was the first to be in Jack's new boat when he opened her up, oh yeah !, man this was moving

Although the river and the road ran parallel to each other in places, there were sections where they separated, like where the mud flats were on the bends in the river at low tide. At those parts, the road and the river could be one or two hundred metres apart and you can't see anything from the river, then on the straight sections they come back together and it is no problem.

On the bends Jack had to drive even faster to make up the extra distance. He new he shouldn't and he new it was dangerous but he thought it was important to find out more about this truck and the people in it. He was hoping for some luck and he was hoping that the chase would not last too long.

The boat was broad in the beam and almost flat in the hull with deep chine's making it an extremely good river boat. It had been his grandfathers and Jack had been helping to recondition it for the last few months. He did not realize that it would be his own birthday present.

Overboard

His grandfather had insisted that everything on the boat was in good condition. It would carry up to six adults, had a fold down canopy, life vests, marine band two way. There was no requirement for a tinny on the river to be so well equipped but Reg Kerry was one who believed in being prepared for anything. It had a ply floor and even with a shallow vee there was still room between the floorboards and the hull to store the first aid kit, flares, fishing gear a small esky and some water proof clothes just in case, along with the other bits and pieces that make a boat a home, there was a fish finder and GPS mounted in the centre control console.

Yes he was very pleased with the boat and it was topped off with the motor, which was not too big for the style of boat but gave it too much speed in theory. Under sixteen in New South Wales you can only get a restricted boat license in, that means limited speed.

Jacks father had no problem with Jacks ability to handle the boat. They had been in and around all sorts of craft since they were born. His concern was the usual for parents, young boy fast boat.

Every year there are injuries and deaths from boating 'incidents', he would not call them 'accidents', most of them were the result of someone doing the wrong thing, that is no accident. It's usually ignorance or carelessness what ever the age of the driver. "You don't have to be young to be dumb," was one of his favourites.

He took a chance and said alright when Reg told him that he planned to give Jack the boat and so far it had all been no problem At the moment Jack estimated their speed at about 25 knots , well over his agreed speed limit but from what he had seen he thought it was worth it. They were skipping lightly over the smooth river surface, wind in their faces, pleasant afternoon sun still high in the clear northwest sky and Jack was the only one thinking of anything other than a good time.

Keepers

Emma was only ten but she new her job in the bow of the boat was to watch for floating debris that might damage the hull or motor, especially at speed. Jack could see fairly well in this little boat but Em had gotten into the habit on some of the bigger craft that their Dad had ferried up and down the river. So it was always her job and he had to admit she had good eyes, so it was sort of comfortable to have her there this time.

There had been heavy rain in the previous week, that meant there would be more than the usual amount of flotsam to be aware of. Some of these things went through his mind as Em's left arm shot up pointing at the 11 position and before he could react, her right arm sprang to the 1 position. That meant dead ahead was obstructed. Now both arms were chopping the air with some agitation meaning "do something and do it now' !

Jack could not see the problem but he did not hesitate. His feel for the river said go starboard, so he did. He brought the steering wheel sharply right about fifteen degrees, backed the throttle off about ten percent and kept his eye on Em. She was well balanced and had sensed that he would go starboard.

Gazza however was not so prepared.

As the boat answered the helm with the alacrity that Jack and Emma expected. Gazza, with his attention on the truck ahead and his grip on the seat loosening as time passed, was first thrown to the left and forward a little but he caught himself just in time and reached to the right to secure his grip. He turned, looking over his shoulder to see what game Jack was playing.

As he did that, Em's right arm swung over to three with her left dead ahead and they were chopping at the air like a butcher making mince meat. Jack hit the throttle hard slammed the wheel to the left and watched Gazza leave the boat.

Overboard*

She was right, no doubt about it, just below the surface was a massive island of floating rubbish and Em had steered them through it perfectly. Jack saw as they passed that she had found a channel about two boats wide which zigzagged through the debris for half the length of a football field. They were out of it now but Gazza was not.

By pushing himself to reach the right side of the boat to regain his grip, Gazza was entirely unprepared when the right side of the boat came to meet him as Jack swerved around the tangle of logs. The outcome was a sort of hunched up cartwheel up and over the low gunnels of the boat and feet first into the river. He landed beside one of the submerged logs that made up the jam and as he hauled himself up into a sitting position he understood that Jack was not playing a game at all. Had they hit one of these at the speed they were doing, it would have been nasty.

He could see Jack, now at a much more appropriate pace, swing the boat into a one eighty and reverse course to pick him up. No harm done, he would dry off soon enough. A real shame there wasn't a camera handy to pick up that action, it would be a natural for one of those funny video shows.

Jack was relieved to see Gazza perched on the tree trunk as he eased the tinny back along the passage to pick him up. Thoughts of explaining to panicking parents about how their son was last seen flying (clumsily) over the Macdonald river had flashed through his mind straight after he was sure that Emma and the boat were out of danger.

Gazza was full of intelligent questions as they helped him struggle back into the boat, "That was mad, how high did I go? How far do you reckon? What speed were we doing?" he stopped to breath.

Jack jumped in, "Gazz, we have to get you dry, then you have to shut up. If you tell any one about this, the olds will find out and I will get shot, OK?"

"Yeah, that's cool," Replied Gazza, " but how far did I go, I reckon twenty metres maybe more ---

Jack let him go on. He signaled to Emma with his finger to his lips and she nodded, no problem. Then he pointed a finger gun at Gazza's head and pulled the trigger. Emma laughed and nodded her agreement again then turned back to her look out position.

They motored down stream at a pace much closer to the eight knot limit. Jack began to explain to Gazza what the chase had been all about, Gazza sat on the center seat listening and drying. Emma could not be moved from her post after being praised and credited with their survival by the two boys, she was determined to stay on duty.

Chapter Thirteen

Speak Your Mind

Jack was being intense again, "That was the truck that I was telling you and Penny about the other day," he told Gazza. "And this time Emma got that feeling at the same time that the truck appeared,"
"Yeah, OK" answered Gazza, "It does seem like there might be something there, but we lost them, so we don't find out this time."
Jack was still intense, "I know we lost them but we have narrowed down the search. If they come this far up stream there is only three more properties before the common and they won't be storing anything on the common,"
Many many years ago a section of land up in the back of the valley had been set aside for the use of livestock farmers to run their stock for agistment if they needed to. They called it the common, it was still open for use by any of the local folk so if these guys were up to no good, they would not be doing their thing

(what ever it was) on public land. The road through the common ran for about six ks, after that it turned into a pretty rugged track for a while. Then it came good again as it headed further north, Jack was pretty sure that the truck was not going that far.

Gazza agreed, "That's right, there is The Woodbury's then the, ah, oh, who's got the place between them and the Pearson's?"

Emma could not hear them from her position in the bow but at that moment both Jack and Gazza heard her voice say, "They are at the Pearson place."

They looked at her. She had been facing away from them when they heard her. Now she swung around and simply nodded her head, then turned back to lookout.

"Whoa," exclaimed Gazza, "did you hear that?" still staring at Emma in the front of the boat.

"Oh yes I heard her," He was staring at his little sister also.

They had arrived at Jamie's jetty by that time. Jack ran the boat in against the pontoon while Emma threw a bow line to Jamie. Penny was at it before the line was tied. "Where have you lot been? Jamie and I could have swum to your place by now," she interrupted herself, "Oh Hi Em how are you," she wasn't really cranky, "Now where was I, oh yes, we've been here long enough to breed fish, let alone catch them."

Gazza jumped in while Penny took a breath, "Put a sock in it Pen, we've been on Keeper business."

"Say again", said Jamie as the three of them climbed up to join him and Penny on the pontoon.

Jack began to tell them about the truck, "I don't know if this is Keeper business but it is something."

Gazza Butted in, "Of course it is, how else would Emma be doing that talk without speaking thing?"

After Penny and Jamie had heard the whole story. Including Gazza's swimming lesson, they all decided that it must be Keeper business after all.

For once Gazza was not alone when he said, "So what now?"

They decided to stay more or less with the plan for the day. They loaded Jamie and Penny's fishing gear, then loaded Jamie and Penny and headed back the way they had come.

Just two small changes to the original plan,

(1) They were heading in the opposite direction to their intended fishing spot.

(2) Emma was still with them.

Emma did not usually go fishing with them, but this may not be usual fishing. Jack opened the locker in the centre console and took out the mobile phone ready to pass it up to Emma who was still on forward lookout, along with a message, "Call mum, tell her you are coming fishing with us."

As he looked up to hand the phone along, Emma turned around and looked back at him. He heard her voice, "I have already called mum, she said Okay."

Her lips had not moved and she was not yelling over the noise of the motor. He heard himself answer her, "What do you mean you called her, can she do that too?"

Emma was smiling now, "She answered," She sure can, we've been practicing for weeks,"

Jack was dazzled, "Is mum a Keeper too?"

Emma had turned back to lookout position know but answered anyway. "No mum is not a Keeper but we think she might be the new Guardian, She really is part of The Place,"

"You know what is really good?"

"No, what?" thought Jack in reply,

"You are doing it too," Emma turned to look at him over her shoulder, she was laughing.

Jack started to laugh as well. The other three looked at them both, then at each other, then started laughing with them. It was certainly a happy crew heading upstream that morning.

Keepers
In the Forgotten Valley

Chapter Fourteen

River View

Five of the newest Keepers in The Place motored up the
Macdonald river, at a speed which was much safer than the earlier
run. Emma was still the spotter and again she guided the boat
through the log jams with no trouble. Everybody stayed in the boat
this trip although Gazza made things difficult as he jumped up
three different times to point out the log that he had landed on.
Finally Penny said through her teeth, "If you rock this boat one
more time by jumping up and yelling, it was that one, then it will be
that one again. Understand?"
Gazza looked sooky, "Yeah, he mumbled. Then without getting up,
he pointed and said brightly, "But I really think it was that one,"
Penny kicked him, Jamie slapped his head, Jack just laughed.

About thirty minutes later Jack and Jamie thought that they had
reached the right part of the river. They were looking for some sort
of land mark. As the boat drifted back with the outgoing tide
Penny pointed to a jetty on the northern bank Jack looked from

Penny to Emma. Emma was pointing past the jetty to somewhere further back in the bush, the three of them were mind talking.
Emma thought, "The feeling is coming from up there in the bush."
Penny joined in, "I can feel something about that jetty."
Jamie tried, "Man, can you guy's really hear me?"
Emma, Penny and Jack all smiled in response.
Gazza was looking around the group, he spoke out loud, "You lot look like you are all on drugs, what's the grinning nodding thing?"
They all started speaking out loud after that, none of them wanted to explain, now was not the time.

There was a 8mt cruiser with twin 150's moored out in the channel off the mud flats and it looked like there might be just enough water for the smaller tinny tied to the jetty when the tide was out. Further along there was a small beach starting to show as the tide slipped away.
They motored back up past the beach. Jamie pointed to a pair of giant ghost gums standing inland and a scar on the steep hillside behind them shaped like an arrowhead pointing down. It must have been a rock slide that tore out the trees and made the shape.
As the boat lined up with the two gums the arrowhead pointed at the beach, Jack agreed it could be a useful land mark.
They drifted past the beach and the jetty two more times, there was nothing and no one to be seen.
Jack asked "Do we go ashore?"
Penny answered, "I don't think so, we don't even know why we are here,"
Jack was edgy, "What about the feelings?"
Jamie's turn, "Look, it is only feelings, if we get sprung on someone else's property we'll get hung or shot."
Gazza interrupted, "Probably both."
Jack was not convinced, "So what do we do?"

Jamie continued, "Look, we can't see anything from here, let's have a look from the other side, we can check out the driveway."
Penny joined in, "At least that way we can just go a bit at a time instead of getting caught in the middle of the jetty."
That sounded better to Jack, "Right, we'll do that then," he said as he started the motor and pointed the boat back down stream.

On the way back, Jack was talking to Jamie about how they would take their bikes as far as the driveway, then go in on foot, spread out so that they could hit the dirt if they had to.
Penny had been listening, "When do you think this grand plan might take place?"
Jack answered quickly, "I'll pick Gazza up in the morning, bring his bike across in the boat and pick you two up on the way."
Penny cut him off and said, "In the morning?" she had that, I am about to call you stupid look on her face.
"Yeah?"
Without looking around Penny called loudly, "Hey Gazz, where will you be on Monday?"
Gazza sensed a trap, "Derrr, like you don't know, at grandma's, first week of vacation, same as usual, why?"
Jamie half smiled, "Oops, I will be heading for that four day camp with the climbing club."
Penny still looking smugly at Jack said, "I have three days at the sport institute."
Jack realized that he had been a little hasty as he admitted. "Oh, yeah, I've got two day's away with the footy team."
Penny liked to catch the boys being dumb, "So," she said, "Is there a plan B?"
Jack and Jamie laughed, "OK," said Jack, "We will make plan Z when everyone is back," then he smiled at Penny and said,
"I knew all that".

Keepers

Penny splashed a hand full of river water in his face.
Jack splashed back and hit Gazza, Gazza got Jamie, everyone got Emma. By the time they let Gazza off there was as much water in the boat as out, Jack hit the bilge pump switch and the water was pumped away as they motored on.
"See you next week" Gazza called as he squelched along his jetty.

Next, the boat pulled in to the Walker's pontoon again. Jack looked at Penny. "What do you think about Gazza and the mind talking? Like, on the way here the first time this morning he was hearing Em, no problem, then when we were all into it, he missed the whole thing."
Penny Shrugged her shoulders with her palms in the air, "Well, really, that's just Gazza isn't , I mean, sometimes he's there and sometimes he's somewhere else, you know."
Jack could tell she was not being funny.
Jamie joined in, "Penny is pretty near it you know, I can never figure out how he can be so clever and so thick at the same time"
Emma threw in her two bobs worth, "Remember G.P. saying some were better than others at it, maybe he hasn't been practicing or something."
"So you don't think we need to talk to him about it?"
Penny was shaking her head, "No, I think leave him be, he does everything else his own way, he'll catch up, eventually."
Jamie agreed, "Yeah, don't start him thinking that he needs to work at it or you will have him hearing all sorts of weird stuff, I think he already does anyway." they all laughed.
Emma finished it, "I think it is about were your head is, for us it is working without stress, maybe for Gazza it will work if there is a need or something." The other three looked at each other, it wasn't mind talk, it was what their folks were always saying, "That girl is ten going on forty sometimes."

Jack pulled on the front of the boof covering cap, that she was wearing, "OK 'Doctor Emma Kipley' ! We will leave it be. Now you two get out and we will see you next week," as he tugged the boat back against the pontoon.

Penny and Jamie hopped out, Jack passed their gear to them, unhooked the line and started the motor as the boat was picked at by the current of the ancient river.

He watched his friends or relatives or whatever they were, as they walked along the jetty and wondered what next week would bring. He heard Emma thinking, "No problem, QuintX will dominate," she was laughing again.

Keepers
In the Forgotten Valley

Chapter Fifteen

School is Out

As they motored back to their own jetty, Jack was thinking about the rest of the vacation. He would usually spend a couple of days up at Granddad Kerry's stone quarry. That's where he had learned to ride dirt bikes, drive tractors and most of the other excavating equipment.

His Dad used to worry a bit when he was younger. Like when he was about nine, Dad came to pick him up and found him driving the old Ford tipper around on the floor of the quarry.

It was a little weird. Jack had to stand in front of the steering wheel because he was too short to see over the dashboard if he used the seat. That meant he couldn't use the pedals to start the truck moving. Granddad fixed the motor so that it would stay at a steady speed, then he showed Jack how he could sit on the floor to push the clutch in, put it in first gear, release the hand brake, slowly let the clutch out, then when it was moving slowly ahead he could jump up and steer around in circles. He would do that for hours. If he wanted to stop he would turn the ignition key off. These days he could use the seat and the pedals and his Dad figured that if the 'Old bloke' had not killed him yet then he should be alright.

Granddad said, "As long as you know how to stop a machine, you will be alright, always find out how to stop it before you start it."
So, Jack learnt how to stop every machine in the place, some had a key, some had a lever or a cable. As he got bigger he learnt how to start them and drive them. He still preferred his boat but driving a twelve ton bulldozer through a huge pile of rubble and pushing it up into a heap as big as a house was good fun too.

Emma's vacation was different to Jack's. Usually she would spend some time with their Dad's parents, the Kipley's. They had moved to the far north of Queensland a few years ago and both Jack and Emma enjoyed their visits there, often together. This time it would be just her, she would even be on the plane on her own for the first time, that made her a bit nervous but she didn't tell anyone.
On the Monday morning both Kate and Alex took her to the airport. Jack was away at footy camp. Kate was nervous about Emma being on her own. Alex was saying, "Don't be silly, the attendants will look after her and they are not allowed open the doors while the plane is in the air so she can't fall out and Mum and Dad will be there to pick her up, relax." He was nervous too.

When they finally called for boarding her flight there were hugs and kisses all round. Then Emma, with her frizzy red hair under a baseball cap, her backpack, which was almost as tall as her, and her thumbs jammed in the straps, strode through the boarding gate, like the worlds smallest soldier heading off to war.
With her Mum and Dad left behind for the first time ever she was feeling pretty tough, scared and little, but tough too. She knew that when she got back, the mystery of the Pearson property would continue but for now she was on her own personal adventure.

School is Out

From books and movies she knew that these planes often carried, smugglers, robbers, secret service agents, movie stars and sometimes they got high-jacked and flown to far away places. She decided that she would keep a close eye on everyone on the plane just in case there was some QuintX work to be done, yep, she was busy being ten again.

Penny was keen to get to the Sports Institute in Canberra. She had been invited by the coach of the national archery team after her success at the last regional competition. Her own coach had explained that the institute was about general methods for fitness and motivation as well as archery. All sports people have some things in common, once you have found that you have some preference for a particular sport you need to learn how to use your body and mind to achieve the best result. The other thing that all sports people need, is to always enjoy their activity.
This first visit to the Institute would give her a look at their methods and give them a look at her. Many talented kids do not go on to national level for all sorts of reasons, one of the most common is lack of competitive enthusiasm. That is not a bad thing, it's just one of the differences in people of all ages and types. Someone who is good at something, it does not matter what, may be as good as the best on one day and not so good the next day and good again the day after. That's pretty normal, if you really want to be at your best long enough to get through a competition that might go for ten days, then you need to train in more ways than just your sport. It takes a lot of commitment to train at that level and if you do not want to put that much in, if you just want to do it for you, that is fine, but the only way to find out is to have a look.

Penny really did enjoy archery and she was very competitive, just ask the boys, so she was interested to see if the training methods at the Institute would work for her. The common thread for all elite athletes is what they call, mental toughness. That is what lets one archer make the perfect shot while the other gets nervous or fatigued or lose their confidence. Penny thought she could handle it and it would not be long before she would find out for sure.

Jamie was a member of the Galston climbing club. Although he was a junior, he had been training with the general members because there were simply not enough juniors to make up their own class. In fact there were only two other juniors in the club, Ashley Whyte was about Jamie's age but she trained on different days and Gerry Kenney, he was older. In fact he would soon be a senior but he was not very good and often missed training.
On week nights the training was indoors on the rock wall, which was in the same building as the 'Power Pack' Gym and sauna.
On weekends and holidays the club moved around the district, there were plenty of good climbs nearby. The escarpment topped the Galston Gorge which actually ran all the way back down to the Forgotten Valley, which most people forgot.
Then down in the Valley and all through the national parks were lots of opportunities for climbs.
The climbing was good fun and learning how to do it better and faster was something that Jamie really enjoyed. The real buzz for him was where it could take him. There was so much of the district that was rugged and steep that most people just did not bother to make the effort. Jamie and the other real climbers were there so that they could take their skills out to where most people did not go. To find yourself out on top of a ridge or a cliff where you knew that no body had been, or to see The Place from an angle that most never would, was what they were about.
This four day camping trip was planned to be out in the Lithgow valley about eighty kilometres away by road. The Lithgow area

is part of the trailing edge of the Blue Mountain range which circles Sydney and was a major challenge for the early explorers who had to find a way across the range to connect Sydney Town to the rest of the inland country. If you followed the Lithgow valley long enough and it would be very long, guess where you would come to, 'The Forgotten Valley', yes the path can be long but it is all connected.

Gazza had spent the first week of this vacation with his mum's mum for as long as he could remember, it used to be with Grand dad too but he died three years ago. They had a property in the southern highlands of NSW, not far from a town called Bowral. They had built up a dog training business back when Granddad retired from the commonwealth police. Then, they trained drug dogs, bomb dogs, attack dogs, security dogs, trackers, rescue, all sorts of dogs, now that Nan was on her own she only did specials. From the age of four 'Gareth' (that made two) had been working with dogs, German Sheppard's, Labradors, Pit Bulls, Rottweilers, Dobermans, Kelpies, any breed for any job. Some dogs, like 'bombers' could take years to train properly.
The owners or the handlers had to be trained as well, some of them took longer to train than their dogs.
One of the many things that Gareth learnt about dogs is that a lot of it is about people, if don't understand your dog then your dog will not know what you want. Dogs are pack animals, they need a strong and clear leader, that is when they are comfortable and happy, that's when they do their best.

Chapter Sixteen
Drive Time

Plan 'W' was in place. All of the gang were back in the Valley. Everyone had stories to tell and experiences to share from their vacations but that would have to wait.

They would each bring enough gear for a two day camp, (at headquarters of course). Emma would come with them, that was not always the case, she was a bit small for some of their expeditions unless they were heading for their headquarters, so since that was their story, she had to be with them.

There had been no more talk about Keepers among the families, it seemed that all of them believed one thing or the other, either the whole thing was like a big coincidence or as the legend says "They have time to learn the way". Almost none of them thought anything would be happening until all the kids had been to Keeper school, whatever that was.

Keepers

Kate Kipley felt that the kids were not going to have a lot of time before they would be involved in the business of the Keepers. She had no real reason, the feelings that Emma had, the interest of Jack in those feelings, it just seemed that something might be on the way.

They had to meet at the ferry this time since they were traveling by mountain bike, and Penny, Jamie, Emma and Jack lived on the same side of the river, Gazza lived on the other.

The ferry runs non stop 24-7 all year, except for the first Thursday of every month when it is stopped for two hours for refueling and maintenance. It is the biggest of the six vehicular ferries still running in the Sydney basin. The others are on the Hawkesbury river at Webb's Creek, just around the corner, Lower Portland about ten K's upstream that is where the Colo river joins the Hawkesbury. One at a place called Sackville and the others are West on the Nepean and south on the Georges River.

They are run by the Department of Main roads, in places where a bridge is not considered practical, mostly because of money.

It was about 9am. So the work crowd had gone and the ferry was less than half full each way, they could see Gazza walk his bike on and about eight minutes later he was walking off after the 150mt crossing, QuintX were assembled and ready for action.

The road that follows the river to the Pearson place is long, winding and narrow, nobody likes to ride on it if they can avoid it. The locals and tourists are lucky to miss each other in cars let alone looking for push bikes on the blind bends that make up a lot of the road. The gang planned to use one of the historic features of the Valley, it is called 'The Old Great North Road' and it was built in and around 1830 by convict labour. That road was a bit like some current government projects, by the time it was finished no one wanted to use it. They had found it easier to travel north by steamship, steam power was a new gadget back then.

All that did not matter to the kids. The good news was that the road was open to mountain bikes, it was in good condition and it made an excellent way to get to the top of the ridge on that side of the river. Then if you knew the tracks, there was a point where the Old rd. was just above Settlers rd. again and at that point it was a short distance to their destination.

They set off single file heading for the start of the 'Old Great North Road' and another QuintX adventure.

The 'Old rd' had some pretty steep sections and the climb was a bit hard for Emma, so it was nice of Gazza to stay back with her and tell her, "Just take it easy Em, enjoy the ride. You don't have to keep up with those lunatics. I'll stay with you so that you don't get lonely." Emma was a little mischievous, she said, "Thanks Gazz, but I will be okay, catch up with the big kids if you like,"

Gazza was a little red faced and sweating when he answered, "No, really, its fine, I'll stay with you,"

Emma started to peddle faster, she was a little mischievous.

At the top of the first climb Jack, Penny and Jamie were making plans when Emma rolled up beside them and a couple of minutes later Gazza was puffing and panting alongside them. No one said anything until Gazza had caught his breath. Then he was the first to speak, "The boat." He said hoarsely.

"What?" asked Jamie on behalf of everyone.

Gazza looked at the group and said accusingly to Jack , "It's your boat. Ever since you got that new boat we haven't been out of it, we haven't been on the bikes or hiking or anything. It's no wonder a bloke has lost a bit of condition."

The other four just stared at him as they usually did when he was being Gazza, then slowly, Jamie, Jack and Penny turned their heads in unison looking from Emma to Gazza and back again until Emma got the message. "Its alright Gazz, I'll stay back with you so you don't get lonely."

Gazza replied in his serious voice, "Why thank you miss Kipley but this is bloke stuff I will take the lead from here." He was already pushing off as he spoke leading the way along the next section of the Old road, it was flat. The others passed him about three minutes later, Emma caught up to him at the start of the next hill and at the top they all waited until he arrived. When he did and had caught his breath again he said quietly, "It's my grandmother, her cooking ----

Jamie calculated that they were at the point where the two roads were the closest. It was midday so they picked a clearing by the side of the Old road and settled down for a lunch break.

Emma noticed a few clumps of wheat growing wild in between the rocks, it was a strange place to see European crop in the middle of the bush she got up to investigate. Jamie saw what she was looking at and started to poke around as well. Jack realized that the clearing they were in was not in keeping with the contours of the immediate area. Penny started to see things as the others pointed them out. Gazza fell asleep.

They were on a flat section of the road running along the spine of the mountain ridge. As Jack paid more attention he could see that the point of the ridge had been cut off to make it flat enough for the road. Looking back the way they had come and ahead as well, he could see the hollows in the natural line of the ridge that had been filled with the excavated rock. Because all this had happened nearly two hundred years ago, now it was weathered and looked almost natural, unless you knew what natural should look like.

Jamie and Emma had worked out that the clearing they were in was in fact an old quarry site, maybe a major camp for this section of the road building crew. It was the nearest point to the river below and after the stone had been cut and used to build the road, it was level and clear. The convicts who worked on the road had to have food and water so they would need these sorts of sites every few miles along the way. The wild wheat was like the Keepers, Emma announced,

"Leftovers from two hundred years ago, almost forgotten but still going strong."

They woke Gazza, who mumbled something about his Aunties mud cake, then they packed up their gear ready to set off down the hillside. Jamie was in the lead, he had already tried to ride down the track on his 'Viper', he made about 20mts before he stacked it.

If he could not handle it the others stood no chance, it would be a bad idea to ride down. It would be a lot worse trying to ride back up, the bikes would be stashed up on top near the clearing but out of sight.

Going down hill suited Gazza, almost. While he was waking up he only bounced off two different trees, then he started to look where he was going, stupid place for trees to be anyway.

QuintX were right on target. They came down through public land between the two properties and hit the main road about half a K. from the driveway into the Pearson place. Jack took the lead as they walked single file on the edge of the asphalt. At the start of the gravel drive where the old letter box said. B and R. Pearson, he turned off into he bushes and the others followed. While they stashed their packs out of site they went over the plan again.

They would spread out on each side of the driveway. Using their eyes and ears, at any alert they would each get off the drive and under cover. If anyone was sprung, the story was that they lived just up the road and were looking for wild mushrooms, that's why they each had a canvas carry bag on their shoulder. The aim was to get onto the property and see what was happening.

Jack, Emma and Gazza, started down the right hand side. Jamie followed Penny on the left. Penny had left her archery gear with the bikes, it might look strange if she was hunting mushrooms with a bow and arrow. About twenty five metres in they came to a single bar swing gate across the drive, it was locked and meant to stop vehicles, not kids. They carried on, progress was slow and they were all nervous, because they were walking so quietly they were sure to hear any vehicles approaching.

They would not hear a bush turkey scratching in the leaf litter beside the drive. Jack passed it by and Emma saw it as she approached, the turkey did not see anything until Gazza stepped on a dry twig. Gazza did not actually see the turkey, he did hear it squawk loudly as it took off startled into the bush with great flutter of wings. Since he was already a nervous wreck from tip toeing down some evil doers drive way, he took off as well, in the opposite direction with a bit louder squawk but no wings.

The turkey disappeared quickly and was quite. Gazza took four quick steps across the drive looking over his shoulder and ran directly into Penny who reacted instantly, side stepped and instinctively used her foot and her elbow combined with his own momentum and sent him off the driveway down the shallow embankment and into the native grass and bushes below.

Gazza disappeared like the turkey but he was not as quite.

The rest of them joined him in the scrub, Penny sort of apologized to Gazza, "It was just a reflex Gazz."

Gazza was plucking small splinters from his forearm "Oh yeah, of course , just a reflex, I'm being attacked by some bloody great monster and you throw me over a cliff, yeah reflex, ha!"

Jack cut in, "Chill out Gazz, it was a bush turkey and a two foot hill, settle down."

Jamie joined, "Yeah, look , we are all way too tense on this thing, everyone needs to breath deep and chill. If all that commotion didn't attract any attention we can say there is no body nearby."

Emma added, "I can't feel any danger, I think we are okay too,"

She checked Gazza for any real injuries, there were none so they took up their positions again and started down the driveway once more. Gazza was still rubbing at bruises as he said to Penny, "If you have to throw me any where else, pick a softer spot will you."

Jamie cut in, "Yeah make sure he lands on his head."

Jack added, "Too right, that's really soft."

Gazza made a disgusting noise and everyone laughed.

They rounded a bend in the driveway about thirty metres on and up ahead they could see the next problem for the day. Across the drive was a double chain wire gate about two metres high with four strands of razor wire across the top. Stretching off into the bush on each side was a run of fencing in the same material. Same height, same razor wire, the lock on the gate was as new as the rest of the security fence.

"Wo", said Jamie, "This is some serious fencing."

Jack had been checking the fence, he came back out of the bush. "You are not wrong, it must run right up to the cliff on this side."

Penny appeared from the other side, "Yep, all the way to the river here and even out into the mud down to the low tide mark."

Gazza said what they were all thinking, "You don't go to this much trouble unless you have something that you really don't want people to see, I guess that means we really have to find a way in."

Chapter Seventeen

Dogs Day

Penny called for them to follow her along the fence line, about half way to the river she stopped at a big old paper bark tree standing just inside the new fence. She pointed to a branch about eight metres up, the branch was growing out almost horizontally over the line of the fence. "If we get a rope up there we can get down on the other side no problem."

"What about the other one?" asked Gazza.

Forty metres away stood an identical fence with the same gate across the driveway.

While they were all talking at once about the cost and the trouble for two fences and how important it was to find a way through, Emma suddenly stiffened, she raised a finger to her lips, "Shh, they're coming."

Jack quickly checked their position. They were out of site from the driveway but they would be easy to see from inside the compound.

No more talking, just a quick signal and all of them melted into the scrub, settling down to wait, hearts pounding, nerves on edge.

The noise of vehicles came from the driveway, it sounded like a truck and something else as well, maybe a car. They slowed and stopped. Jack whispered something to Jamie, he nodded and moved silently deeper into the bushes.

Penny's thoughts came to Jack, "Good idea, looking for another way back to the bikes."

As the truck moved through the gate and into the compound it came into view from their position. It was the same white Isuzu that they had chased along Settlers rd., a black Rodeo ute with a canopy on the back followed it through the gate. One man got out of each vehicle. The man from the truck was big and rough looking, wearing bright Day-Glo green overalls, sunglasses and maybe hadn't shaved for a few days.

The one out of the ute was not quite as big and looked like he washed more often. He had sunnys on as well but he was wearing farm gear and a stockman's hat. The big fella opened the second gate, came back and drove the truck through, "Are you sure about this?" he asked as the other one opened the back of the ute.

The farmer type replied, "Just relax, they can smell fear, don't get them excited."

The big bloke spat back with some sort of accent, "I'm not scared. I'll just shoot them if they give me any trouble."

The farmer closed the tailgate that he had been about to drop, he turned on the big man, "Gunther, if you hurt my dogs I will have the RSPCA, the coppers, everybody out here in a flash, so make up your mind. If you want to hire them like we agreed, I will show you how to use the whistle, and they will do just what they are trained for, so make up your mind."

The big man stood his ground, "How do I know they will behave?" he asked in a nasty voice. The farmer seemed exasperated, "Look, you have done well with the enclosure, you have spent all the money on the fencing and the kennels, the dogs are trained, I had them out here two days ago so they know the area. They will not harm you while I am here and two blasts on the whistle they go straight back to their kennels while you close the gates, that's all there is to it."

Jack took his small binoculars from his canvas bag and swept the compound. At each end he could see smaller enclosures and on one side he could just see the top of a kennel.

The big man backed away from the ute, "All right let them out but you don't even think about sending coppers or anyone out here, clear, no one, that's why I pay you so much cash, no one knows about this place."

The farmer turned back to the tailgate, "I only care about my dogs, you leave them alone and there is no problem. I don't care what you are doing, two weeks hire, pay your money, no one knows nothing," with that he dropped the tailgate and lifted the top section, he stepped back pointed at the ground and called, "Down Hammer, down Claw".

Two huge Rottweilers leapt from the back of the ute, they stood where they landed waiting for instruction. The farmer spoke to Gunther , "Go on, one blast of the whistle."

The big man pulled on the lanyard around his neck and found the large silver gadget at the end. Gazza recognized the gadget, a dog whistle, so high pitched that humans can not hear it, only dogs and a few other animals. It was the same as the one that his grandma used at her training center. The same as the one Grand dad gave him before he died. The two dogs were immediately on alert, they each went to one of the fences and started to trot along it's length. The farmer closed the gate that they had come in through, Gunther stood and watched the dogs.

One of them, Gazza thought it was Claw, trotted along the fence opposite where they were hiding. He was almost past when he stopped, he sniffed the air and began to growl softly, then he started to bark, he was staring directly at their position.

They were about six metres into the bush behind a big fallen log. Jack was pretty sure they could not be seen but it looked like they could be smelt. There was a slight breeze from behind them and that was all it would take for dogs like these to know they were there. If that one was Claw, then Hammer stopped his tour and trotted across the enclosure to join the fun, soon they were both barking and growling at the unseen kids.

Jamie had just returned when the growling started, he sort of arrived, saw what was happening and left again almost all in the same motion. By the time the two men had walked down to join the dogs he was back again only now he was holding the top of his canvas bag closed.

"What are they doing?" Gunther asked in a suspicious voice.

The farmer answered, "They are on to someone who should not be there, let's have a look."

The farmer spoke to Hammer and Claw "Hold", just one word, spoken clearly and the dogs settled down but they maintained their position staring directly at the invisible group.

Gazza was impressed, these dogs were young but they were well trained, that was not really good news for the gang.

The farmer had gone to the ute and was coming back to the dogs with two heavy chrome chain leashes. Gunther was behaving like a giant third dog only not as good looking, staring into the bush and growling, "I can't see anything out there."

The farmer answered, "There is someone there, that's for sure."

As the farmer bent to hook the leads on, Gunther turned just a little to watch him, QuintX made their move.

Dogs Day

Jamie was so quite he almost seemed to float forward with his carry bag held in front. The rest of the team did their best to move as smoothly as him but in the opposite direction. At the last stand of scrub, he would have been seen if they were looking, his timing was perfect. He reached into his bag and took out the Peahen that had been nesting just behind their hiding place and threw her gently over the last bush and toward the fence. In the same moment he was gone, back into the brush.

The Peahen was most upset, she had been plucked from where she had been nesting her eggs on the low branches of a paper bark tree and suddenly it was dark. In the dark she was confused and quite, then it was light again and she was flying toward a bunch of big ugly things, this was no time to be quite. The Peacock family of birds can make a wide range of sounds, honking like a goose, screaming similar to a Cockatoo and a lot of others, she tried all of them as she landed a couple of metres from the fence. She landed with her wings flapping and making all the scariest sounds she could think of.

Jamie was mind guiding Penny, Penny was guiding the team. The trail he had found which would take them back to the hidden gear was a fairly well used animal walk ,so once she was focused it was not too hard to follow. By the time they had reached the third fork in the trail he had caught them up and took the lead in person. Gazza was in the rear crushing gum leaves and dropping them on the track, there was no need to talk. They were soon into their backpacks and away with Emma in the lead followed by Gazza, there would be no stragglers this time.

Penny was at the rear sensing for danger, Jamie told Em to go straight across the dirt shoulder and turn left after she was on the asphalt, that will leave less tracks, that's what they all did.

Hammer and Claw were disgusted. They were the only ones to see what happened and they were trying to tell the story but the boss and the big bloke were not listening.

When that young human popped out of the bushes with that dumb bird, Claw went ballistic. Hammer was already on the leash but he went off as well. Claw jumped up on the fence barking like a mad dog, Hammer was growling fit to burst. Their target was right in front of them and the boss is saying, " Stay, sit, hold," all that stuff they had been learning, but Boss, ! look ! ! there they are , look ! ! just there, come on you guys get real, ! ! !

The farmer was surprised when his dogs flipped out.
Just as he hooked the leash on Hammer, they both went insane. He looked up to see what had stirred them up and all that was there was a scrawny little chook of some sort making weird noises and flying at the fence, that should not bother this pair, they were trained to react only to humans.
He got the leash on Claw and it still took a couple of minutes to settle them down. He looked at the man who was paying to hire the dogs and wished he had a third leash handy, the big fellow was not happy. The farmer cleared his throat and started to say that they had better get outside and see what was there, he did not get to say all that. This customer was not happy and really, the farmer had found he did not seem too bright either. It took a long time to explain things to him and this looked like it would take a lot of explaining. Gunther had seen the whole thing he did not need an explanation, these two useless hounds had gone bananas
about a chook in the bush, they were hopeless. He saw the bird fly out of the bush, he saw the dogs freak out. How could this bloke come up with a story about them only reacting to humans after that. Was he blind, stupid or just greedy?

And so that was the sort of thing this pair were going on about for probably fifteen minutes. It took the farmer that long to convince Gunther that they had to go out there and see what was going on.

Emma made good time for them on the sealed road but it got pretty tough for her once they hit the trail back up into the National park. They struggled a little way up and as soon as Jack thought they were out of sight they stopped to rest.

Jamie went back to the edge of the road and did what he could to cover their tracks. They had gone in and out in single file, he did a little brushing of tracks and a little transplanting of a couple of bruised bushes and it seemed okay. He made his way further along parallel to the road, crushing leaves as he went and hoping Gazza was right. When he came out of the bush about twenty metres from their actual track, he made sure that he did some damage. As he walked back along the edge of the bush in the tall native grass where his scent would last the longest he went past the original track about twenty metres again, crashed through some scrub leaving a clear trail. He went in about ten metres heading away from the track, then turned and headed for the gang, crushing leaves as he went.

By the time he got back they were ready to go.

It was a hard slog up the rest of the track and by the time they reached the top the sun was starting to set. It was time to make camp, Jack and Jamie thought they were safe enough for now so they set up in the same clearing.

Chapter eighteen

Bite Me

Claw and Hammer were getting pretty bored with the boss and the other one, it seemed like they were barking the same sounds over and over. As they sat side by side waiting for orders Hammer said, "I thought boss was the leader of the pack."

Claw growled, "Yeah, he is."

"How come he is still barking with the other one then? why doesn't he just bite him and settle it?"

Claw didn't really care much, "I don't know, although if you watch them they don't seem to bite often, that's probably why they bark so much, anyway be quite I'm going to sleep."

The farmer needed to save this job, he needed this customer to have confidence in his dogs. Business was hard enough without word getting around that he trained 'bird dogs'. He finally convinced Gunther that they should go out and check around.

"Fine, whatever, you and the mutts can go and play, I am going up to the house, if you find something, call me. If you don't find something, make sure all of you are gone when I come back, ten minutes, understand?" The farmer understood alright, he tugged on the leashes and called the dogs, "Come on boys, lets go."

Hammer jumped up and barked, "Okay we are off,"
Claw yawned, shook his head and growled, "Shut up, I hate morning people."
The farmer and his dogs went through the gate and back along the fence on the other side to the point where Claw had first picked up the scent. The dogs realized that they were back at work and started to strain at their leashes. At the spot, the farmer stopped and gave the dogs a little slack. The scent was no where near as strong as before.
Claw whined, "That would be right, they are gone, they were over there and now they are gone."
Hammer said, "Yep there were four, no, five of them, right?"
Claw agreed as they tested the air for more evidence.
"Well what do you want to do, will we have a look?"
Hammer was not bothered, "The boss seems to think we should be doing something, let's wander over and poke around until he comes up with an idea."
The two dogs moved into the brush, as they came to the place where the kids had been they started to whine and growl. The farmer held them back while he studied the ground, he took the dogs around the site and came back across on the other side. As they crossed the trail used by the kids, the dogs started up again.
The trainer held them back while he looked carefully at the track. Then he said to them, "Hammer rest, Claw rest." The dogs relaxed and followed him back to where Gunther was just driving back to the gate.
The farmer called , "Come over here, this will interest you."
Gunther was still not his happy little self, "Yeah, well it better."
The farmer led him to the edge of the hiding place. "Just have a careful look in the dirt behind that log over there."
Gunther wandered over to the area, at first he could see nothing, then, as he concentrated he noticed some shoe prints, a couple of

different shapes and sizes. His mood changed a little, "Well, well, it looks like there was someone here after all and there was more than one."

The boss answered, "Yes it looks like maybe three or four."

Claw barked, "Five."

Hammer sighed, "Yeah I know."

The farmer told Gunther, "We found their trail heading off that way," pointing toward the road, " What do you want to do?"

Gunther was still examining the shoe prints, he rubbed his unshaven chin as he thought, "Some of these prints are small, I reckon it was kids."

"Bravo," barked Claw.

"Genius," whined Hammer.

"Yes, so, it's up to you," said the boss.

"Okay, I agree the dogs are alright," conceded Gunther, "Can they follow these tracks?"

The Boss considered the idea, "This pair are not trained for tracking. They will follow a scent while it's strong enough but they might get distracted if it is left too long."

"All right," Gunther cut in, "Let's get going, start them up. I want to find out who made the tracks and what they were doing here."

As the boss pulled the leashes to bring the dogs to their feet he said, "Gunther, I already said that I don't care about what you are doing here, but I don't want to get involved in anything either."

The big man stared at him and spoke slowly but it was not a pleasant tone, "Just follow the tracks and I will look after the rest, you are not involved, in fact you and your dogs don't even exist as far as I am concerned, lets just do it."

The boss took the dogs back to where they had found the trail.

"Here we go again," Claw was whining, "Did we get lunch?"

Hammer thought for a second, "Yeah we had a feed in the ute but I could go some tucker myself, it's getting to be a long day."

Gunther moved the truck, locked both gates and started off down the driveway in the ute. About half way to the road he caught up with the posse, they were in the bush just off the edge of the drive. "It looks like they came in from the road," boss answered, "Yeah the boys have gotten a bit vague just along here, they might have lost it."

After about six or eight minutes the dogs had started to slow down and hunt around the edges of the trail. "Hey I'm having a bit of trouble with that scent," Hammer growled.
"Wo, that's a relief, I thought it was only me," answered Claw.
Hammer went on, "I think we are 'tracking', that's what one of the Labradors back at the kennel said it was called. We are supposed to follow the scent until we find the target then we stand and point."
Claw looked at him sideways, "We what?"
Hammer repeated, "We point."
Claw was getting stressed, "How do we 'point', what is 'point' and why don't we just bite, that's what we do, we bite remember?!"
Hammer was getting edgy as well "I don't know what is 'point', the Labrador didn't tell me, probably because I bit him, he was really annoying, just like you."
Claw growled quietly.
"Oh Yeah," Hammer glared.
"Yeah," Claw barked, "bring it on."
Hammer snarled, "Come and get it dog face!"

The farmer knew his dogs were tired and probably hungry, they were starting to get distracted and snarly, "Settle Claw, settle Hammer," he told them as he loaded them back into the ute, there was water in there, that might quiet them a little.

Down at the road the men got out to look around, they found the spot where the kids had stashed their gear. "No need for the dogs here," said Gunther, "look they had something stashed here, see where the grass is flattened."

The big man had followed the bent bushes out to the road, he called the farmer, "Come on they headed off that way, I can just see some dust from their shoes, lets see if we can catch them."

The farmer climbed in to the ute, he said, "We would have had a better chance if you had listened to me half an hour ago."

The big man just glared at him. The farmer was not the type to get scared easily but he decided to be quiet anyway.

They drove back along Settlers road for about fifteen minutes. They drove way too fast and the farmer was convinced that Gunther was spending more time looking in the bushes than watching the road. Twice they nearly ran off the road, it was just lucky there was nothing coming the other way.

Finally Gunther pulled into a driveway on the left and got out of the car, while he was checking in the dirt for foot prints, the farmer swapped seats. Gunther came back, the farmer said, "I have had enough of this nonsense, get in, this is my car and you are not going to kill anyone with it, especially me."

Gunther got in the passenger seat, he said in a very calm voice, "They could not have gone further than this and there are no tracks here, we have only passed two other driveways lets go back and see which one it is."

The farmer was weary, "All right but that's it, we check the driveways nothing else, I have to feed the dogs or you will be their next meal."

Gunther grunted," Yeah right."

There were no tracks at either driveway, as they headed back to Pearson's Gunther was confused, on a bend about half a kilometer before the drive he noticed for the first time that a section of bush sloped down to the road in between some pretty steep country, "Pull over."

"What now?"

"Just one last chance," said Gunther as he climbed out of the car, slowly the big man paced along the edge of the asphalt. When he stopped and waved at the ute he had gone about one hundred metres back the way they had just come. The farmer swung the ute around and drove up to where he was waiting. They both studied the dusty road shoulder. "All right," said the farmer," It looks like they went off here so ?"

"So now we track them, if they went up the mountain they are not locals but maybe they just went through here as a short cut to one of the properties."

"I'll give it a go." said the farmer," But remember, these are not tracker dogs, oh and by the way, they are now hungry dogs, so keep out of their way."

The tailgate opened . Hammer and Claw blinked in the light, they had been trying to sleep while the ute was bouncing around all over the place.

"FOOD" barked Claw.

"YEAH, FOOD", barked Hammer.

The farmer was firm, "Down Hammer, down Claw."

The dogs followed orders, they were on the leash again, being dragged along the road side and they were not happy. At the point where the tracks had been brushed away the dogs picked up Jamie's scent. "One of them was here," growled Claw.

"Yeah, but he went this way," barked Hammer pulling to the right.

"No he went this way," snapped Claw, pulling to the left.

The farmer ordered them "Settle," as they barked and snarled in opposite directions.

"What's wrong?" Gunther asked, still keeping his distance from the clearly cranky Rottweilers.

"It looks like they split up, the trail goes in both directions."

Gunther looked up and down the road, there was only bush as far as he could see, "So what now?"

The farmer said, "Look if you really want to do this we will have to be quick, it's close to sunset already ,I am going to let the dogs off, they will each follow a trail. You follow Hammer I follow Claw, stay out of his way, if he finds something, just say firmly, "Rest Hammer rest," Then he added, "I will give it about fifteen minutes then call him back with the whistle, so just follow him okay?"

Gunther might have been nervous,"What will they do if they find someone?"

"They are trained to attack, that's what they do."

Claw went right Hammer went left, hungry and cranky they were both hoping to find somebody to bite. About twenty metres along they each found the scent went off the road and into the bush. "I've got him going into the bush," barked Hammer as he headed into the scrub, the big man following at a distance.

Claw barked back," Me too, I hate this bush.".

Both dogs went in about ten or fifteen metres then turned again to go parallel with the road for about four or five minutes then stopped sat down and started barking.

The big man checked his watch, fifteen minutes had passed as he stood watching the dog who sat watching him and growling in between barks. He turned toward the sound of the other dog barking far away and yelled, "Can you hear me," there was no answer, he tried again, still no answer.

Hammer Barked, "I've had enough of this, what are you doing?"

Claw barked back, "Sitting in the bush, doing nothing, I can smell lot's of stuff every where, I don't know where to go, where are you? I can hardly hear you."

Hammer answered as he stared at Gunther,

"Don't be stupid, I don't know where I am, I'm in the bush with this big bloke, I think I am going to bite him, where's the Boss?"

Claw barked again, the boss is here, you're lucky, I can't bite the boss, I'm going to sleep."

Gunther decided to head back, as he turned to leave Hammer stood up growling.

"What's your problem you stupid dog?"

Hammer growled and stepped toward Gunther.

The stand off lasted about a minute, to Gunther it seemed a lot longer. They stared at each other and then Hammer stopped growling, he tilted his head from side to side and took off at a trot. He went straight passed Gunther, back the way they had come.

Gunther stumbled back to the road, by the time he made it to the ute, the dogs were in the back.

Gunther flopped into the passenger seat. "I've had enough, If those kids turn up again I'll let your dogs deal with them, that Hammer looked like he was gunna have me for dinner back there."

The farmer smiled for the first time that day, "That's what they do." he said as he turned into Pearson's Drive.

Chapter Nineteen

Two Scents Worth

Just before dark Jamie was sure he could hear dogs barking somewhere down below but they were a long way off. The rest of the gang heard nothing. Jack built a small, safe, camp fire in among the stone that had been cut by men that worked in this spot two hundred years before.

There had been lessons at school which simply said, "There were roads through the valley which had been built by convicts and times for them were tough but some of their work was good."

That part was fine but when you where here, on the land, even resting in one of the scars that men had cut across the place, you can see that the land is still recovering after all these years.

The men are dead and gone, the road remains as a monument to mankind and its pursuit of poorly planned destruction, then they call it heritage. As they discussed the days events, each one of them was becoming more convinced that the Pearson place was the site for another monument to mankind and some form of pain for the planet. They each decided that it was up to them to find out what was going on at Pearson's and somehow, that's what they would do.

As they set up their sleeping bags for the night Jack remembered something, "Hey Gazza, that idea of yours with the gum leaves, where did that come from?"

Gazza continued to look for a soft rock to sleep on as he answered, "Grand dad used to say that a dogs sense of smell is so strong it could be used against them if they were not trained especially to pick up a particular type of scent. When we crushed those eucalypt leaves the scent of the leaf would mix with our scent and then, for an untrained dog in the bush, everything would smell pretty much the same, that's all it was."

Penny was listening nearby, "That might be all it was but it's sure handy to have you around sometimes Gazz."

Gazza was poking at one rock which seemed just a little softer than the others. "What do you mean 'sometimes' ! I am the permanent ' HandyGazz'," with that he made a theatrical bow.

Jamie threw an empty water bottle at him and they were all still laughing as they settled down for the night.

Their breakfast was the usual for one day camping, dried fruit, muesli bars and water, Gazza studied his water bottle, he thought about the fridge at home but he did not say anything.

"Alright let's get down to business". said Jack. "We have tried the river and the driveway, what's next?"

Jamie in an unsure voice said, "Do we really need to get in there, that big bloke looks like he could be a serious problem if we get caught on the property."

Emma added, "Yeah, can't we wait till we see the truck again?"

Jack was about to speak but Gazza got in before him, "That big bloke has got a plan, he told the dog bloke that he only wanted the dogs for two weeks. Whatever he's doing, he will be finished and probably gone by then, we might not see the truck again."

Two Scents Worth

Penny spoke slowly, "So are you saying wait or don't wait?"
Gazza was hesitant, "Well, I guess, don't wait, I guess, if he's gone maybe we won't find out what he's doing at all."
They all went quiet, each with their own thoughts.

"All right," started Jack again after a few minutes, "What about this, Gazza, you know that camera plane system that your Dad was working in on for the electricity company?"
Gazza was thinking, "Yeah, that was a drone, a mega drone, like half the size of a real plane, flown by remote control to check power lines in the outback, but we can't get that."
Jack explained to the rest, "That drone was only big because it needed heaps of fuel and it had it's own on board computers but the idea was to send it out without a crew so they could just fly it on and on. It didn't need a landing strip, just a bit of driveway or flat paddock, fuel it up and off it went again."
Jack continued to Gazza, "We don't want that one, it's too big anyway. What about rigging up one of your planes with a camera. If we could get some pictures of the property we might be able to work out what they are up to."
Jamie joined in, "That sounds pretty good. It seems that whatever they are up to is something big, like easy to see, that's why the gates and the dogs and stuff."
Penny agreed, "Well 'Handygaz' what do you think?"
Gazza had been thinking through the idea while the rest were talking, it made sense. There were plenty of companies around doing Ariel photography with remote control planes. All he had to do was adapt some of his own gear and it should work.
He was doodling in the dirt with a twig when Penny tried again, "Hello, earth to Gazza, are you receiving over?"
They all watched as he sketched a control diagram in the dust, completely unaware that they were talking to him.

Keepers

Jamie said, "Well it's not hard to tell what the answer is, I think you have got him going Jack. Now all we have to do is get him back in to this universe so that we can get it done, any ideas?"

Emma wandered over to Gazza's back pack as his mud map was becoming more and more intricate. No one could work out what it was that he was actually drawing but it was obvious that he knew. She fished around in the pack until she found what she was after, "I thought so," she said as she pulled something from the pack then walked around to Jack and asked for his hunting knife. As she stirred the ashes of the fire back to life Penny worked out what she was up to and sat back laughing quietly. Jack and Jamie woke up to her plan at about the same time.
Emma sat by the fire, a small pan with a fold up handle heating on the flames, she was waiting to see if the others agreed. Penny nodded, Jamie too. Only Jack held his hand up as he was watching Gazza who was now mumbling as well as drawing.
As he completed a section of his sketch and sat back a little to check it, Jack dropped his hand and with a quick flick of the knife Emma did it.

It must be how sleep walkers are. Like eyes wide open not seeing anything but their dream, that is how Gazza looked. When he finally lifted his eyes from his drawing he said to no one in particular, "What a brilliant idea."

Penny said slowly, "So you think it will work?"
Gazza sort of looked at her dazed. She pointed to his drawings.
"Oh that," He started, looking more awake by the second, "that's no problem. We can do that easy, who's cooking bacon and eggs, that smells excellent!"
Emma said, "It's just rolled ham actually," as she shuffled the

pannikin and sliced another piece from the roll.

Gazza was a little confused, "I thought we weren't cooking in case the smell traveled."

As Emma passed the pannikin and a fork to Gazza, Jamie said, "It's a special occasion Gazz, enjoy."

Penny was packing the last of her gear, she said over her shoulder, "Yeah we are celebrating because you smell."

The others laughed, Gazza looked a little sheepish and sniffed at his shirt, the rest of the gang cracked up. Gazza was on his feet now stuffing his gear into his pack, as he swallowed the last of the cooked ham he said, "It's on Dad's side. Mum said it is."

Penny could hardly stand, she was laughing so hard now, Jamie had tears in his eyes.

Jack was holding on to his bike so that he would not fall over,

Emma could not help herself, she felt sorry for Gazza who was looking confused and red faced but it really was funny.

Gazza was first on his bike after all that and as he headed back the way they had come he said, "You lot can be very weird sometimes, and it is not nice to talk about people smelling while they are listening, Dads brother now he is bad --------

That was all they heard as he rode away mumbling, Emma followed but it was a few minutes before the other three could mount their bikes and head down to catch up. "Some one has to tell him before he gets home," Jack coughed between laughing fits.

"Yeah, just a bit longer but," begged Penny, wiping the tears from her eyes and trying to ride straight.

Gunther watched them pass.

Chapter Twenty

Don't Look Back

The big man had planned to leave the property in the morning anyway. Now that the dogs were there permanently everything should be Okay, he drove the short distance from the house to the first gate. Claw and Hammer paced the fence as they heard him coming. At the gate he took out the whistle that the dog trainer had given him and from under the seat, he took out his shot gun, he did not like dogs.

Two short blasts on the whistle and the dogs separated as each one went straight to his own kennel and sat inside looking out. He opened the gate, the dogs stayed put, he walked across and opened the other gate, they stayed where they were, he came back, drove through, not a move. He left the inside gate open, locked the outside gate, put his shotgun back under the seat and blew one long blast on the silent whistle. The dogs sprang from their kennels, ran each way along the fence then trotted back to the gate and stared at him.

"Not today boys," he half smiled as he climbed into the truck, he didn't like dogs.

He had almost passed the section of bush again when he suddenly decided to stop. The night before had been a bit of a mess and although the dogs did not do any good out here he was sure something had been going on. He remembered where the dogs had entered the bush in different places and on a hunch he picked a place about midway between. As soon as he moved some of the scrub he could see it had been repaired. A little further up he could see where they must have stopped and sat down, either hiding or resting.

He made his way up the hillside, in some places he could see tracks, in others he was just guessing. It took him a fair while to get close to the top, he had not seen any tracks for a while and decided that they would have kept going last night anyway. The buttress of the old convict road was in sight above him when he decided to stop for a spell, leaning the shotgun against a tree trunk, he was thinking that he should have brought water instead of the gun.

There was a light breeze blowing along the edge of the road and on it he was sure he could smell cooking.

Alert now, he started to make his way along the edge of the road but the bush was too thick. He would either have to go back the way he came and try to find the track again, or go up to the road , in the open.

Gunther climbed up on to the road and was moving in the direction of the breeze, there was no smell on this side so who ever was cooking must be below and ahead of him. He was planning each move along the high side of the road. In the books it would say he was 'Darting' from one position to the next. This bloke was so big and clumsy that you would have to say he was 'charging' more like a bull than a Dart. He had made about sixty metres in this manner along the old convict road, he had no interest in the history or the place, he just wanted to find out who had been on the property and decide if it was important enough to tell his boss.

He stopped at a large boulder to catch his breath and as he was about to make his next run he stuck his head out, then pulled it back in. There was a kid on a push bike, one of those cross country types, he had his head down and as he went past. Gunther could hear him mumble something about, ' stinky'.

If the kid had looked up he would have seen Gunther look around the boulder but he was busy talking to himself.

Gunther watched the first kid go and within seconds another one, a little girl with frizzy red hair went past. She looked like she was trying to catch up to the first one. If either one turned around they would see him standing against the boulder with a shotgun in his hands, he put the shotgun down out of sight. Nothing wrong with a bloke out walking, is there, he sat down and made himself relax, just out for a walk, that's it.

He expected two more, if his bush tracking had been right but there were three. They came through together about a minute behind the first two but you could tell they were all together. Gunther did not hear what they were talking about, the girl in the second lot was riding all over the place and giggling like a real sheila but none of them looked back so there was no need for his bushwalking story.

After about five minutes he decided there were no more to come. He left the gun in the bushes just in case and walked up the middle of the road just like any bush walker in overalls, bright green day-glow vest and work boots.

Thirty metres ahead he found the camp site, the blackened stones around the fire place were still warm although the fire had been thoroughly extinguished, and there were a whole bunch of symbols

scratched in the dirt.
"Graffiti anywhere, kids nowadays."

He found two or three shoe prints at the site which he was sure
were a match for some of the ones back at the fence. His mood
lightened, it was only kids, that was a relief. He had been in this
game for too long to get sprung now and this last job should set
him up nicely, so if all he had to worry about were a few kids out
camping and doing kids stuff, then he was Okay. Those dogs
probably scared the pants off them, no need to bother the boss.

In a way it was good that the dogs did not catch them yesterday,
he had no idea what he would have done with that bunch anyway.
He was sure they were heading home after their big adventure and
that was the last he would see of them.

Chapter Twenty One
Plane and Simple

Gazza did not see the funny side of the smelly joke when Jack explained it to him back at the ferry, it was probably a good thing that they separated for a while. Gazza headed home to sort out the surveillance plane, Jack and the team took off to headquarters to work out the rest of the plan.

Later, when he thought about it he did admit it was a bit funny, the smell and the smelling Ha,ha, but he would not tell Penny that. Gazza went straight to the shed when he got back, he was sometimes a little embarrassed about his shed, it was huge.

He told most of his friends that it was his fathers workshop just so they would not think he was rich or something. He knew that he had lots more stuff than some kids but most of it was from the Gramps so it wasn't his fault.

That did not matter today, there was a job on and he liked the idea. He had already worked out most of the method, now he needed to match up the hardware. First things first, establish the payload, that would be which camera, how heavy and how to mount it. The job had him so interested that he almost worked through lunch time, yeah right.

It took most of the day to work out which plane and which control set would do the job. The next day was taken up with setting the camera position and the operating method, on day three he was ready for a test flight. The plane he was using was one of his favourites, it was a test model from a survey project that his father had worked on two years ago, the one that Jack had remembered.

Just over two metres span, fuel tanks in the wings, heaps of control options, like fuel dumping valves in case it was going to crash, cut out section in the belly for the camera mounting, duel controls on most functions, a beacon navigation system, but the one he liked best was the electric start engine. Most model planes can not carry enough weight to have the battery power for remote starting but this one had it all.

Jack came over for the test flight, Gazza gave him a run through on the features of the package, Jack was impressed like he always was when Gazza was fully functional.

The plane lifted off in the space between the house and the shed, nowhere near as much as Jack would have thought. Gazza explained that it was built with S.T.O.L. design, that is, 'Short Take off and Landing', it's the way that planes are built to fly from bush tracks and mountain strips, it's been around for a long time.

They took turns at practice runs over the house trying the same run at different heights to check the best picture quality. The camera that Gazza had fitted was a digital sports model, water proof, shock proof, 6mg res., movie or still frame option with 10 times optical zoom. It was his fathers field camera, Gazza had intended to ask permission but thought he might as well test it first. He had thought that he might be able to transmit the pictures to a computer while the plane was still in the air but that was a bit too tricky. The equipment to do that sort of thing was big league stuff and although the working model for the electricity company could do it, Gazza's Dad had not left that sort of stuff lying around.

The QuintX surveillance plane would have to cross the target area probably in two directions, take the pictures, then land so that the camera could be removed and the pictures down loaded in the normal way. That was what they practiced, they picked the height on the third attempt, tried it with the motor running and with it off, no difference. They tried the setting for movies, single shot, 1 second interval and auto repeat sequence. Single shot at about sixty or seventy metres was the best combination.
They played around so that each of them was comfortable with the controls and practiced using the second set, swapping between each other, that was the biggest risk. The plane would receive signals only in line of sight or from the beacon, so if you could see it you could fly it, if not, it would simply fly home and circle until it ran out of fuel and crashed.

It was four days since the gang had discussed the aerial surveillance idea, now they were ready.
Because of the line of sight thing with the plane, they had worked out an idea to keep the plane in sight from two positions. One of them would launch the plane from the river side and fly it up to where the other one could see it from the cliff behind the property. After the job the remotes would be turned off and the plane would fly back to Gazza's place following the beacon signal, it should have plenty of fuel to circle until one of them got there to land it. Good plan.

Small problems.

(1) The cliff behind the Pearson place was called 'Rogues Ridge', nobody had ever climbed it.

(2) If someone was going to climb it, Gazza did not want it to be him.

(3) If anyone was at the property while they were doing this they would surely get suspicious about the plane going back and forth overhead.

Solutions.

(1) Jamie had already been back and thought he knew a way up.

(2) Bad luck Gazza, it would be you with Jamie and Penny making the climb.

(3) Jamie again, he would be ahead of them, duck down the driveway, check the gates and meet them at the back of the ridge ready for the climb.

One other solution that did not even have a problem before it. Gazza would carry another camera, one with a telescopic lens in case they could see enough from the ridge to get pictures without launching the plane. They went over the plan several times, checked the gear several times, ropes, two way radios, batteries for the remotes. The plane was fuelled and its batteries were charged, the climbers had food, water and first aid kit, using bike helmets instead of climbing helmets made just a bit less to carry. Everything was in place, QuintX would be in action tomorrow morning, day five.

Nothing could go wrong.

Chapter 24

Mountain High

Jamie moved much quicker when he was on his own, he made it down the hillside, checked the gates at Pearson's, they were both closed, and was back up on the convict road before Penny and Gazza had arrived. They rode about a hundred metres past their last camp site then stashed the bikes in the bush again.

It looked like a tough climb, Jamie made sure that the gear was all in order. Each year that his team entered the orienteering competition for state schools their coach insisted that preparation was the key. It was not just about safety, when you are well prepared, free climbing , repelling and abseiling were heaps of fun and as well, it was always good to finish in front of the city schools. To climb Rogues Ridge, do their business and get back down to base would take teamwork and effort, it was an early start but there was a big day ahead.

Penny and Gazza shuffled their packs to settle them into a comfortable position. They were heavy but this was Jamie's gig, if he said all this stuff was needed, then all this stuff would get there. Jamie showed Penny how to sling her bow so that it would not be in the way while she climbed and he tied the top of the quiver so the arrows would not spill out if it tipped over too far.

The first hour was pretty cool, mostly following animal trails, down into the small valley behind the ridge then winding up through a cool climate rain forest, that's what Jamie called it. Gazza was not all that interested in the names of the plants and stuff, he was working on walking, using his energy for the best result. The others seemed to move so easily, he hadn't told anyone but it was all he could do to keep up with this mob although it was getting a bit easier. Climbing things, riding bikes all over the place, swimming across rivers when the boat was too noisy and the rest of their mad carry on over the last couple of weeks, had been the best fun he had ever had, so he was going to stay at it no matter what. Not only that but the gang was great, they made their plans together, they let each other have a say and through Jack, the Ancients recognized that each of them had a use that could work to keep the valley alive. How cool, Ancient elders talking to kids about keeping the world working and he was in it.
As they climbed more steeply the rain forest in the gully gave way to the more familiar bush and eucalypts that covered the hills and plateaus in the valley. The climb became more and more steep and soon they were at the foot of what looked like a sheer rock face with no way up.

Gazza looked at Penny, Penny looked at Jamie, Jamie laughed and waved for them to follow him.
About 30 paces along the face, Jamie disappeared into the cliff. When the other two got to the same place, he was standing in the bottom of what he called a 'funnel', it was a vertical gap in the rock, more like a three-sided chimney really. Jamie was digging in his pack, he told the others to pull out their crampons as well, this

was the first time for Gazza and Penny to wear the spiked metal gadgets over their boots but with Jamie's help they were soon ready for their rock climbing instructions.

The gap in the rock face was not very wide and it was no where near as smooth as the walls in their cave, Jamie was explaining how all this was formed about a trillion years ago but Gazza was busy making sure each time he dug these spikey things into the soft stone of the side wall that they would hold him while he lifted his other foot for the next step.
He felt sure that if he missed one and fell on Penny's head they would give him a really hard time. Penny had no trouble, she was into yoga and dance when she wasn't practicing archery so her balance and her leg strength made her comfortable as they climbed. She did not look up but she could tell by the strange noises that there was a fair chance she could be wearing Gazza as a hat some time soon.

About 20mts up, the vertical sides began to lean deeper into the cliff and the higher they went the more the slot they were in laid over and became closer to horizontal. It wasn't long before they were on their hands and knees and soon they could stand and lean forward as they walked out on to the top of 'Rogues Ridge'.

The three of them stood on the slightly rounded rock were nothing grew for about 20mts in all directions, they looked out on their valley from an angle that very few people had tried before them. All of them were blown away by the beauty of The Place, it was about two years ago that Jamie stumbled on the funnel but he had not made the climb before. Now he felt like he always did when found himself in a new part of this age old valley. It belonged to those who could see it most clearly, from here the valley was his, though he did not mind sharing with the gang. They understood his feelings, they knew that there was no one in the valley who knew as many tracks, and climbs and caves as Jamie. He could take you to water any time, he knew about bush tucker, he was already well on his way to being a real Wildlife Warrior and he was loving it.

This part of the job was easy, they made good time along the top of the ridge, the scrub was light and Jamie made sure they did not follow any of the little side trails which he knew would eventually lead nowhere. Gazza could not help but remember that just a little while ago he would have had no chance of being in on this sort of adventure, until he joined the gang he thought his computer was the only place to have a good time.

Soon they had covered the distance from the funnel to a point that Jamie was sure was directly above the old house on the Pearson place. The three of them were happy with their performance, they were ahead of schedule. There was plenty of time to get the pictures and call Jack to cancel the plane, then get back down the ridge and home.

All according to plan.

Keepers
In the Forgotten Valley

Chapter Twenty Three
Rock Hopper

Jack and Emma had a little more trouble than expected when they tried to load the plane on to the boat for the run upstream to the Pearson place.

When Jack and Gazza had practiced the day before, there had been nearly no wind and Gazza was almost as tall as Jack. Today the wind was stronger and Emma was shorter, shorter than Gazza anyway.

Handing the plane down to Emma was really tricky, the thing was so well built that it kept trying to take off each time the wind blew. Jack actually thought that it could probably lift the little red head if it got enough wind. They finally got it down from the jetty and into the boat, or at least, on to the boat. Jack got the straps over the wings to hold it down and off they went to catch up with the rest of the team, it was already an interesting day.

Keepers

Up on the peak, Jamie held on to Gazza's feet as he wriggled forward to get his head and shoulders over the edge of the rock. Gazza had the strap of his digital camera around his neck, he had his cap on backwards and as soon as his head stuck out over the edge-- he had his heart in his mouth.

"AHHH !" he screamed in terror.

"Shut up" growled Jamie in surprise.

Now Gazza couldn't speak any way, he just lay there watching the world change shape. It was spinning, it was blurring, it was coming to meet him and it was rushing away all at the same time. He was sure he was being pulled over the edge by something strong and there was nothing he could do about it .

He had no problem on the climb and he could stand in the middle of a paddock and look out into the valley, not a worry. But he had just found out that he could not casually stick his head out over a 70mt sheer sandstone cliff and do anything other than be petrified. Jamie had heard about alto phobia, as he started to drag Gazza away from the edge, he told Penny to be ready to help once he had him far enough back.

They sat him against a burnt out stump and made him drink some water. He was shivering, his face was white and his eyes were so wide it looked like they would never close again. Penny and Jamie were doing all the talking, stuff like, don't worry, you'll be OK, no problem, happens to lots of people, all of that sort of thing.

After about ten minutes Gazza started to breathe again, at least breathe normally, his stomach was climbing back down to it's own space, his arms and legs felt like they might work again and he did not think he would have to change his undies after all.

He looked over to where Penny and Jamie were sitting on a

boulder. "Now what do we do?" he asked in a voice that was a lot more squeaky than usual. "I didn't know I was like that".
Jamie answered as though he was reading from a text book, remembering the course they did on alto phobia in his climbing classes. "People who know they have alto phobia stay away from high places and don't confront the issue. When someone discovers suddenly that they are scared of heights it can leave them with a permanent and serious neurosis which can impair their performance in a range of activities."
Gazza looked at him blankly and said "What are you on about? speak English."
Penny cut in, "He means we don't know if you will be more weird than usual after the shock you just had."

Gazza got to his feet, stamped them on the rock, lifted his arms above his head, turned his head from side to side and said, "All systems are go, I am simply never, ever, at any time, ever, going over there again, ever." as he pointed to the precipice.
Jamie jumped up, "Yeah we get the idea, let's go, I'll try the picture, Penny hold my feet, Gazza, just sun bake buddy".

Through the view finder, even on full tele. the only thing that Jamie could make out through the trees was the roof of the old house. There was no chance of a shot of any people and too many trees on this side to see much at all. He wriggled back from the edge. The three of them sat on the rock, "Looks like we gave you a fright for no reason Gazz, we are going to have to do it the hard way, at least it still didn't look like there was any body home. Let's get sorted, we should have lift off in a little while."

The run up to Pearson's had been a lot slower than planned.

Jack had to keep the speed way down. The wings of the plane were catching so much breeze that he was worried about keeping the boat stable. Emma had received a mind talk from Penny almost an hour ago saying that they were in position and ready, now that she and Jack were nearby she was trying for contact again.

There was no luck this time so Jack turned on the two-way and tried their call as planned.

"Water bird to rock hopper, over." he spoke into the radio.

Emma screwed her face up at the 'boy stuff' , water bird, rock hopper, how dumb.

On the second call Jamie replied, "Rock hopper to water bird, go ahead, over."

"Rock Hopper, what is your situation, over."

"The water bird must fly, do you copy, over."

It was pretty likely that Penny would throw one of the radios off the cliff at about the same time that Emma threw the other one into the river if the conversation went on much longer.

Luckily for every one it did not need to.

Jack said, "Understood, stand by for lift off." and put the radio down.

"Okay Emm," clapping and rubbing his hands, "Up she goes."

Keepers
In the Forgotten Valley

Chapter Twenty Four
Plane Dumb

Emma looked around, looked at Jack and said, "Where?"

They were still about 2km from the beach on the other side where they had planned to launch the plane.
Jack said, "It's Okay, this thing has so much lift that it will take off as soon as I untie it, we can launch it right here."
Emma was not convinced. "Are you sure?"
"Yeah, no worries, you take the wheel, hold the boat steady into the breeze and I'll fly it off just like an aircraft carrier."
Emma was not keen, Jack was her big brother and very clever and all that, but this didn't feel right.
Jack tried again, "Come on Emm, we are already late, we have to get this done so that the crew can come down off the cliff, it's fine!"
Jack was getting that stressed thing going again.
Emma moved around to change places with him. "Better get it over with," she thought.
"Get what over with?" asked Penny
Whoops.

Keepers

The new plan was simple, untie the plane, get under it, hang on to the landing gear, set the camera to the auto position, prime the engine, turn on the power circuits, start the engine, run it up to speed, keep the plane steady until it started to lift then let it go and take over the controls. No problem.

Okay, maybe one or two.

As soon as he untied the wings the plane started to rock from side to side in the gusting breeze. Getting under it was not a problem, hanging on to it with one hand certainly was. From that point on there was no way back, Jack realized the trouble he was in and he realized that Emma was at the control console directly behind the plane, if he let it go now she would be caught between the plane and the boat motor. He would only have the one chance.

He tried to concentrate on what he had to do, he could call himself stupid some other time. The plane was too hard to hold, he could feel himself losing his grip and that was with two hands, if he tried to do any settings he would lose it for sure.

Emma's thoughts cut through his panic, "Hey bro, chill, use your head, adjust the plan."
Jack felt a calm come over him, he took a deep breath, "Yeah, right Em, slow the boat down and turn around so that we are running with the breeze instead of against it," he thought.

The boat reacted as though he were driving it himself, as soon as the direction changed, the affect of the wind changed. Rather than trying to fly, the plane was now being pushed down by the breeze. Jack made the settings, the camera, the circuits, the fuel. alright, ready to go.

Plane Dumb

"Alright Em, swing back around into the breeze, after I start the engine we need to get the boat up to take off speed for the plane and keep your head down just in case."

This time he was ready for the buffeting of the wind, as the plane pointed back into the breeze he hit the starter button. The engine fired up first time and as soon as the propeller was turning the airflow over the wings became steady and the plane was much more stable.

That was the good news.

The bad news was that the plane was not built to have people under it or even near it when it was running. The noise from the engine was amazing. When a petrol engine runs it makes an enormous amount of noise and the heat at the exhaust pipe where the burnt fuel comes out as white hot gas, is incredible.
The exhaust pipe for this engine was directly under the plane, the noise was deafening and the exhaust pipe was pointing straight at the arm that Jack was using to hold the plane. In a few seconds he would be deafened and severely burnt if he did not let it go or shut it down.

Emma felt the pain of the burn, she did not know exactly what it was but she knew he was in trouble. She heard Jacks thoughts, he was icy calm, "Bring the boat speed up gradually Em, if it's too fast we'll lose control."
As the boat began to pick up speed across the water, the flesh on the inside of his forearm was boiling and beginning to cook.

The plane began to feel comfortable and stable as the boat speed came closer to flying speed. "Just a little more Em."

Keepers

The plane came into balance, there was no weight, it was floating in mid air just above the boat with the engine roaring and the propeller spinning at a hundred miles an hour. "How could he have gotten them into this?" –

"Chill Jack, nearly there."

He braced his feet under the centre seat in the tinny, brought himself to a sitting position and continued the motion smoothly to standing, as he reached full height he gave the plane a final shove straight up.

The thing went up about two metres and stayed there just hanging above them. Jack sat down and grabbed the control box, Emma backed off the throttle of the boat, the plane began to draw ahead. Jack pulled back just a little on the remote joy stick and the plane began to rise slowly but steadily, it was climbing.
He applied just a touch of right rudder, now as it climbed it began a very slow circle. He had no idea how far from the proper position they were but at least if it was circling Gazza might be able to see it before it was too far away.

Jack put the control box down, lowered himself down on the floor between the seats and passed out.

Chapter Twenty Five

In Control

Up on Rogues Ridge the rest of the team were not happy, Penny and Jamie kept receiving parts of thoughts from Jack and Emma. Gazza was still trying to find a place were he could see the plane without getting near the edge of the cliff.

Jamie lost contact with the radio, Penny picked up pain and confusion then, nothing.
Jamie tried the two- way again, "Jack, Emma, what's happening?"

No call signs this time, he was worried.
"Jack, come in, come in, over." still no reply.
Penny moved away from the boys, she leant against a stunted old gum, she could feel the strength in the tree, it was one of the many up on the ridge line that had been watching over this part of the valley for a hundred years or more. The power of the place wrapped around her, she felt calm and safe but she knew there was trouble down below.

After a couple of minutes she came back to Jamie and Gazza who were on the starting to panic. "It's cool," she announced calmly. "Jack is hurt but he is alright. They will be heading back soon, to wait for the plane at your place Gazz."
Gazza said, "What plane, where is it?"
Jamie pointed to a small speck in the sky slowly climbing and doing lazy circles about 2ks south of their position.
He pulled out his binoculars while Gazza turned on the control unit. "Keep your eye on it Jamie, it must be nearly out of range, tell me if it responds,"

Jamie watched while Gazza worked the controls, nothing happened, the plane just kept flying in circles and the breeze was taking it further away from them.

Penny and Jamie looked at each other. Gazza put the controls down and picked up a stick, he started scratching in the dirt.
"Here we go again," thought Penny.
"Jamie, give us a minute mate," said Gazza as he drew what looked like a game of snakes and ladders in the dust.
"If we are here," he made an X, "and the river swings around like this." he made another snake," Where is my place, is it here?" he made a dot on his map.
Jamie looked at the map, the sun, then back along the river. "No" he scrubbed out Gazza's map with his boot, took the stick and drew a new river with a new X and a new dot. "Your place is here," Gazza studied the new map, "right, so where is the plane?"
Through the binoculars Jamie looked for landmarks and tried to match up the position of the plane as it circled higher and higher. He came back to the map. With the stick he extended the river and included a circle on one of the new bends.
"It's not over the river any more, the wind is pushing it south east.

In Control

I reckon it's already past Peats Ridge road behind Spencer, about there." He stuck the point of the stick into the middle of the circle.
Gazza took the binoculars and watched the plane for a few seconds. He came back to Jamie's map and scratched a straight line between the outer edge of the circle and the Dot.
"All right," he made another X on the line opposite their position, "How far apart are the Xs?" Jamie looked for a moment, then he turned and pointed across the river. "The second X is about one K that way, across the river."
Gazza had one more look through the binoculars, checked his watch again and said to them both. "We have got about twenty minutes so we better go over the flight pattern again."
Penny did her shrug with her hands up thing, which this time meant, what are you on about, the plane is gone, it's out of range, the party is over, derrr ! .

Gazza was already explaining, "In about three minutes the plane will be above the valley walls, at two hundred metres it will pick up the homing beacon, the on board computer will point it in a straight line to my place where it will circle until it gets more instructions. If our "bush tucker man" here is right, it will go past us over there," he pointed, "That will put back within range of our controls, I will override the beacon signal, regain control and away we go."
Penny was not entirely convinced, she watched the plane while Jamie and Gazza worked out the pattern that it would need to fly to get pictures of the whole property. They figured three passes in each direction at about fifty metres altitude should do the job.

After about three and a half minutes, Penny shouted," It's Coming, it has stopped doing circles and it's coming this way."

Gazza checked his watch, said, "Yep," then picked up his water bottle and rehearsed the flying pattern, memorizing each of the turning points that he and Jamie had decided on.

As the plane approached it seemed that the line of flight was actually a little closer to them than their mud mapping had indicated but that was still pretty good for scratches, dots and crosses in the dirt.

It was passing their position about six hundred metres away when suddenly, it banked to the left and dived sharply from its cruising height. It leveled out at exactly the same height as them, Penny still had the binoculars, she had been trying to see any signs of life down in the valley. As she swung them back up to check on the plane, she jumped in surprise, it looked like it was heading straight at her and not far away either.

Gazza pretended not to notice when she spun around to give him the death stare, he guided the plane across the river and down to about the fifty meter height. As it crossed the property heading toward they're position on the cliff top, he started the picture run.

With the engine speed reduced and the flaps and ailerons set for landing, the big toy plane was able to fly at an extremely slow speed, she behaved beautifully. It drifted a little on the air currents down in the Valley but Gazza had no trouble keeping it under control. As it neared the tree line at the foot of the cliff Gazza pressed the button for the last picture, pushed the throttle on full, reset the control surfaces to a neutral position then pulled back on the joy stick.

She soared upwards in a beautiful climbing turn parallel with the vertical face of the cliff and about ten metres short of it, at the top of the turn the plane was ten or fifteen metres above the cliff top and about twenty metres to the right of their position. Gazza cut the throttle, let it fall into a dive, then pushed the power back on and took her swooping down across the property on the next run.

Penny was not a fan of the whole 'boy toy' concept for this job but she watched Gazza and the plane for the next ten minutes as he guided it gracefully back and forth over the property, she had to admit the boy knew his toy, it looked pretty good.

Gazza was still having a good time but as the plane cruised over the property for the last run, he adjusted the trim and set her into a spiraling climb, the same as Jack had done about an hour ago.
"That should do it, any word from the other two?"
Jamie and Penny both shook their heads.
"Well," continued Gazza, "I have to send the plane home, she has covered a lot more ground than we planned, I don't want her out of fuel before she gets there but some body still has to be on site to land it and we won't get me there in time."

Chapter Twenty Six

Dreaming ?

Jack found himself at the meeting fire with the elders. There was no pain now but his arm bore the design of the snake spirit. Like a raised red tattoo on the inside of his left forearm was the shape of the serpents head flattened in anger and the body trailing off toward his elbow.

One of the Ancients spoke to him. "You were chosen to lead the others but instead you take them into danger, this is not the way of the Keepers."
Jack responded calmly," There is danger in the Valley, some men are doing harm, we must discover what it is." As he spoke he had a disturbing thought, now not so calmly he asked, " Why am I here, am ,am I dead, is Emma alright?"
The elder waved toward the fire, in the flames Jack could see Emma leaning over his own body still on the floor of the boat.

As soon as her brother started to lower himself to the floor of the boat Emma could feel that he was becoming faint. By the time he had closed his eyes she had turned the boat for shore and shut down the engine. From the storage lockers in the floor she quickly pulled the first aid kit and the fresh water container. She knew that the first thing to do for a burn was to get the heat out of it, so she poured the water slowly on to the black and red raw wound, then she called her mum.

Again and again Emma called for her mother to respond, there was no answer, with tears in her eyes she kept doing the only thing that she thought was right for her brother. She had never seen him helpless before, she had never seen such a serious burn and she had never felt so alone.

The old tribesman spoke again to the young Keeper. "Your sister and the others are well and you will suffer but also survive this time but you will forever wear the mark of the Serpent because of your foolishness. You are correct, there is danger in the valley but unless you can take more care, you will not save the valley or yourself from disaster."

Jack understood the risk he had taken and he knew that by changing the plan, he had put Emma in serious danger. Only dumb luck and maybe the spirit of the serpent had got them out of it. He would never risk his sister again. "What should we do now? about the Pearson place."

The Elder smiled as though he had read his thoughts. "Do not loose your nerve but use your head more often. You are learning the way but now time is short, soon you will have some help."

Jack wanted to ask more questions but he could feel himself drifting toward the fire and as he came out of the flames and back into his body only his arm felt the heat.

Emma clapped her hands with joy when Jack screwed his face up in pain, shook his head and opened his eyes. "Hey Emm," he said through clenched teeth as the pain shot up his arm as he sat up. "How long was I out?"
Emma was wrapping some gauze bandage over the burn, it did not look like a Serpent, his forearm just looked like something that came off the BBQ too soon.
"Oh, almost half an hour I think," she said as she wet the bandage with more water.
Jack looked around to get his bearings, his plane launching event had taken them about a kilometer past the Pearson jetty. With his free arm he pulled the binoculars from the covers and scanned the sky in the direction of Rogues ridge.
"Have you seen the plane?"
Emma emptied the water container onto the bandage, "Yes, about fifteen minutes ago it came from down that way, crossed over and dived down behind the trees."
"Excellent, Gazza must have caught it."
As he was taking his place at the controls, Emma stowed the bits and pieces. "This is the last one," she said as she sat beside him with a full water bottle and began to rewet the bandage.
He tugged the front of her cap, "Thanks Emm, sorry about all that."
Emma looked up and their eyes met just for a moment. Suddenly they both felt something like fear and relief. "There is more trouble coming, we will need to be a lot more careful," she thought.
Jack agreed.
Emma stayed near her brother so that she could keep the bandage wet. With the boat moving the breeze made the water feel even cooler and the pain eased a little. As she became more relaxed she could hear Penny trying to make contact.

Emma explained that they were heading back up river and Penny said that the flight plan was complete and the plane would soon be circling to pick up the homing beacon.

Up on top of the ridge Gazza was talking softly to himself, "Fuel, I don't know about the fuel. Can you hear me, over."
Penny had just finished telling him and Jamie what Emma had said, "What on earth are you mumbling about?" she asked Him.
"I am trying to talk to Jack, how come I am the only one that can't do that stuff?"
Jamie cut in "We don't always get it to work Gazz, maybe it's about all that other stuff you have in your head or something."
Gazza was offended, "What stuff?" he demanded, "I don't have any stuff in my head."
Penny could not let it pass, "There you go Gazza, who said you and I would never agree."
Gazza realized what he had said and they were all laughing while they got set for the climb down the funnel.

Jack did not receive the message.

Keepers
In the Forgotten Valley

Chapter Twenty Seven
Last Shot

The plane was just climbing above the top of the cliff, it would need another hundred metres of height before it could pick up the beacon signal and head back to base.

Gazza turned for one last look before they started the trip down the back of the ridge, Jamie and Penny followed his gaze so the three of them saw the piece of wing break off at the same time. It was the tip of the wing really, and it exploded off, like it just shattered into little pieces and blew away, half a second later there was a sound like thunder from down in the valley.

Gunther was annoyed. He should have hit the thing dead center, probably trying to get too close, shooting straight up is too difficult, get further back for a more comfortable angle.

Emma did not hear the shot over the noise of the boat but she did feel herself jump and look up at the same instant that Penny did. Jack saw her stiffen, he shut the motor down immediately and waited.

Jamie and Gazza realized what had happened. They both ran back toward the edge of the cliff as the plane began to wobble, the graceful climbing circles became a sort of crooked step up then a slip to the side of the damaged wing.
Gazza was trying to loosen his backpack on the run, Penny was behind him. The rough ground that they were on was not the place to running flat out without watching where you were going.

Penny yelled, "JAMIE", just before Gazza's foot rolled over on an uneven rock, he was off balance and there was no way he would do anything except land head first on the rocks of the ridge. That is unless, like a weird ballet dance Jamie spun around and lifted him under one arm as Penny at full speed hooked on to the other, so almost before it happened it was over, he was still standing. They all understood what could have happened, Jamie pushed the air down with both hands and said what they were all thinking, "Yeah, OK, just chill."
Gazza had the control box out now and while he tried to save the plane Penny spoke to Emma. "It looks like they are on to us, they have shot the plane, Gazza is trying to steer it now."
Jamie was relieved, the plane responded to the controls and although the reduced lift of the damaged wing made it uneven, Gazza was able get it steady and keep it flying.

As soon as he knew he had control Gazza looked at the other two, "So what now?"

Penny answered, "Jack says to steer it straight out to the river, that will get it out of range of the guns and he will fly it from there."

"No problem," said Gazza as he swung the plane on to a heading that would take it over the trees and out to the river.

Jack had turned the boat around as soon as Emma told him about the gun shot, now they were approaching Pearson's jetty again, this time at full speed.

Emma was using the binoculars and had just sighted the plane, Penny was watching from the other side. They both had an excellent view as the tail of the plane disintegrated and the fuselage spun out of control toward the trees near the river.

Gazza surprised himself. Almost instantly he hit the engine stop and the fuel jettison control, if the engine could cool off even a little, before impact and there was no fuel in the tanks, then there was a good chance that the plane would not burst into flames when it crashed. Without the tail section there was no hope of control, he watched as his big toy plane spin like a corkscrew into the trees and out of sight.

Gunther was much happier with his second shot, especially since his boss was in the truck with him when they drove up and heard the plane on its last run over the farm. They did not know how long it had been there and they had no idea who owned it but it was pretty clear what it was doing. As they watched it falling from the sky on the far side of the property Gunther smiled and said, "Good shot eh boss?"

The boss was busy thinking, "Yeah, yeah, nice going Daniel Boone, now get these two drums in there, pull the cover over and let's get out of here. Someone is way too interested in this place."
"Yeah, sure thing, what about that plane?"
The boss had started to walk toward the house.
"I'll get one of the bikes and find the plane, unless it fell into the river, you get done here so we can get out of town, and hurry up."
On the way up to the house the boss was going through a mental list of what needed to be done to make sure that they did not leave a trail for the authorities to follow. He had been at this caper for a long time and he did not want to get caught now. He wondered about the plane and he wondered what had made any one so interested in the Pearson's place. They had not had this sort of trouble on any of the other dumps.
In the shed beside the house were two trail bikes, he threw his leg over one of them, was just about to start the engine when he had another thought. He stepped off the bike, went to an old tool box in the corner of the shed, moved some farm tools, lifted one dusty floor board and took his rifle from its hiding place. He liked to be prepared.

Chapter Twenty Eight

Down and Out

Penny and Jamie were standing staring at the spot where the plane had gone into the trees, Gazza was on the radio to Jack.

"Hey Jack did you see that?"

"Yes we saw it go down was that another shot?"

"Too right it was, sounds like they are using a cannon or something,"

Jack spoke again, now Jamie and Penny were paying attention, "This is getting dangerous, if these blokes are shooting at things maybe we better just head back and tell the coppers."

Jamie took the radio, "Jack, whatever these guys are up to is important enough for them to start shooting, it must be important to the valley, we have to find the plane and salvage the camera."

Penny took a turn, "He's right Jack, we know they were leaving this week, now that we have stirred them up they might run early."

Emma took Jacks radio, "Look you guys, Jack is hurt and it's bad, we need to get him to a doctor or something."

Jamie answered, "No problem Em, take him back by river, we will go down the front of the ridge, find the camera and head home the way we came in."

While Jamie was speaking it occurred to Gazza that he was talking about climbing up and down that bloody great cliff. Maybe Jack was right, maybe they should just go home.

Jack was back on," OK, if we do this, we do it together, Em and I will run the boat down to Spencer, we need fuel and some other stuff. By the time we get back you lot should be down, if you find the camera, good, if you can't find it, just head down to that little beach between the two ghost gums and we will pick you up, clear?"

Penny and Jamie nodded to each other, they both looked at Gazza who was hanging on to the remote control box with both hands, his knuckles were white.

He realized they were waiting," Oh yeah, right, great, let's jump off the cliff. Lets go play hide and seek with the mafia down there, lets leap a tall building while we're at it."

Penny could tell that he was going to go on and on, she nodded to Jamie. He pressed the send button and said. "No problem, we all agree, QuintX are on the job, see you at the beach, over and out." Gazza was still going on and on.

It took a lot longer than they wanted to, convincing him that he had to come down with them or starve to death up on the ridge.

Jamie had taken them about half a K. further along to where the rock shelved down and the Valley floor was rising against the side of the cliff face, that way they only had about twenty metres to get down to where they could scramble over the loose rock to the real floor of the Valley.

Gazza knew they were right and he knew they were running out of time. "All right" he said "I will go down, but if I die of fright on the way, you two will have to tell my mother that you scared all the shit out of me, then, when there was nothing left, I just blew away."

Jamie was impressed with the way that Gazza let himself be fitted up with the abseil rig. Penny fitted her own, she had been abseiling a couple of times with the school.

Jamie set himself up and anchored the ropes, making sure there was no chance of them rubbing or cutting on rocks near the edge. He checked each set of gear one more time and they all walked backward over the edge, Jamie loved this stuff. Penny enjoyed the view and Gazza was sure he could feel something wet running down the inside of his leg, he tried to listen to Jamie. How to feed the rope, how to keep tension on to control the speed, how to do this, how to do that, he never, shut, up. Then they were down.

Gazza stood on the loose stone with shaky legs, he unhooked his gear and said. "That was easy, let's go again", then he fell to his knees and started kissing rocks.

Penny un slung her bow and loosened her quiver, she had time for a quick laugh at Gazza then she motioned for him to be quite and get moving. Jamie was already making his way down the scree toward the valley floor, from here on the danger was real.

It was about a twenty minute run down stream to the little town of Spencer. There was a fuel bowser on the wharf, a general store where Emma replaced their stock of bottled water, and in the short street behind the store was a place that she had heard about in one of those boring mothers meetings after school, or maybe G.P. and her mum were talking, anyway the house was there.

The small sign at the gate said 'Natural Medicine', Emma knocked at the screen door. A lady opened it and for a moment she just looked at the little girl with the boofy red hair, then she smiled, "Come in," she said, "I know who you are," Emma walked in to the front room of the small house.

Keepers

All along the wall were shelves with bottles and jars set out under labels. "My name is Loraine, how can I help you?" said the woman. Emma did not know where to begin or how much to say, she stood nervously in the middle of the room.

The woman was still smiling, she sat in a chair in the corner of the room. "I know your Great Aunt Pearl," she said quietly.

Emma took a deep breath and felt the fear leave her, she thought about Jack, Loraine sat still in the corner.

When Emma's thoughts about the last couple of hours caught up with where she was now, Loraine stood up, "I see," she said although now she was not smiling.

"Just hang on a minute," she said as she went to an adjoining room. When she returned she had a dark coloured jar with no label.

"Put this on then wrap it up again, but don't be silly, he will have to get to a doctor soon or he could have serious trouble, right?"

Emma nodded and pulled out her money.

Loraine waved her hand, "This is not for sale, I know Pearl, just get it on and get him to a doctor soon."

Emma nodded, smiled and left with the jar.

On her way back to the wharf Emma realized that she had not said a single word to the woman in the house. Today that seemed only a little bit strange.

At the wharf she opened the jar, it was full of a shimmering silver liquid, they looked at each other , Jack said, "We better do it,"

As soon as Emma had applied the silver and wrapped the wound, she told Jack what Loraine had said.

"No worries, we'll all be home in an hour or two, but I will need longer than that to think up a story to get me out of this one,"

Emma laughed but she knew he was right, when their folks saw that burn he would probably be grounded until he was thirty nine.

Keepers
In the Forgotten Valley

Chapter Twenty Nine

Follow Me

It was convenient that the mud flat on that bend of the river near Pearson's was a popular spot for the locals to catch some good size Flathead and the occasional Bream. One more little tinny with a couple of kids in it would attract no attention at all as it drifted with the tide, then motored back down stream to come drifting back again on the last of the run in.

Jack knew they would be early for the pick up but he was hoping his team would call soon.

The first time around the bend and on up to Pearson's beach it was about 2pm. the tide was still running in.

About 40mins.before it peaked they would have enough water to run in over the mud and after the peak there would be another 40mins. or so before it became too shallow again. That should be a big enough margin for the crew to make it out. It meant that they had to clear the beach by 3.40 at the latest. They motored down to a little cove on the western bank, Jack dropped the anchor into about 5 fathoms of slow moving water, let the boat take a swing on the line then cinched the rope. They would be out of sight there but could still watch the beach through binoculars.

———————

Jamie led them back toward the old house, he had not been in this area before so he was careful to keep his bearings. When he and Jack had worked out the rendezvous point they had done it looking from the river at the ridge. Now Jamie was looking from the valley floor to the river and things were very different. For a start he could not see the two giant ghost gums that were so obvious from the river and he could not see the vee shape on the side of the hill where the rock had slipped and taken out the trees.
He did not mention this to the other two, but he had no idea how to get them to the beach. Time was short, they had to get what they needed and there would only be one chance to pick the right direction, once the tide turned there was not much more than half an hours worth of water to work with. He knew Jack would be there but if they ran out of tide, well -------
Probably because he was looking so hard to find a land mark, Jamie almost walked them in the back door of the old house. The other two were following him trying to walk as quietly as he did and not having much luck. They both assumed that he was seeing the changes in the track since even they could see them, then suddenly the shape of the house came out of the bush up ahead.

It was Penny who laid her hand on his shoulder and motioned both he and Gazza to be quite. About 15 paces away through some light scrub the back door of the house was clearly visible.

Jamie froze, he realized his mistake and looked all around for any sign that they had been seen , then remembered to breathe again.

They turned on the spot and tip toed back along the track which Jamie now noticed was very well used. After about 50 nervous paces Jamie took the lead again and now with his mind on the job, led them around to the side of the house using tracks that only the local wild life would know.

When they were a safe distance from the house he called a halt. They sat in a small clearing and Jamie apologised for his mistake and he told them about his navigation problem, for a few minutes they all sat quietly with their own thoughts.

Gazza was first to break the silence, "I reckon suicide is the only answer, like we all just sit here till we die of old age."

Jamie looked at Penny, Penny looked at Gazza, Gazza spread his hands and shrugged his shoulders like to say "what?" Then Penny pushed him over and they all laughed a little nervous laugh.

"Yeah fine" Penny said, "first things first, lets find the plane, then see where we are."

They jumped up, settled their packs and deliberately started to walk, each in a different direction. This time the laughter was quiet but real. "OK, OK I get the message, first things first, follow me you goons". Jamie said, he was happy with this crew, he would make no more mistakes like that one.

Funny how things work out, now that they were sitting up near the scree line above and to the southern side of the house, they could not only see both doors but Jamie could see what he was sure was the upper parts of the two ghost gums. He pointed them out, now to find the vee and they would have their bearing.

Penny had noticed some activity in a lean-to on the far side of the House, she nudged Gazza and pointed. He aimed his camera and pulled on full zoom, into focus came the man they knew as

Gunther but with him was another man about the same size and not pleasant looking either. The famous truck was just behind them, the side boards had been taken off, now you could see what was in the back, nothing. Penny was watching through the binoculars, one was mounting a trail bike and they were both waving their arms around, it looked like an argument.
"Do we need pictures of these guys," asked Gazza in a whisper.
"It won't hurt to have some pictures when we get back," replied Jamie -- "why are you whispering?"

Gazza realized that the zoom had taken him closer to these blokes that he wanted to be but he said nothing.
Penny checked her watch and wondered about the tide.

Jamie checked his watch and wondered how to find the plane.

Gazza checked his watch and remembered that he had food in his back pack.

Out on the River.
Jack checked his watch. It was time to move.

Chapter Thirty
Bush Ballet

Gunther took one last look around the paddock, he had taken more than half an hour to get finished but being slow was better than being wrong. He and Marty had found out a few times how cranky the boss could get if they made mistakes. They arrived at the house at about the same time, the boss did not look happy.

"I've been up and down that stretch of the river half a dozen times, I can't see any sign of the plane, get the other bike and give me a hand," he grumbled as Gunther stepped out of the truck.
Gunther was pointing at different sections of the property, "Have you tried over there or over there," he asked.
The Boss did not want a discussion, he pointed to the area that he wanted Gunther to check, "Just get down along the bank over there, don't worry about looking in every tree, if it broke up there will be pieces on the ground. If it is stuck in a tree in one piece then no body else will find it either until we are well away, and check the edge of the river as well in case it landed in the mud."
Gunther knew better than to try talking to him any more so he climbed on to the bike and rode off to follow orders.

Watching the men, Jamie realized that they must be searching for the plane, they rode off in different directions and that left three kids wondering what to do. If they tried to make it to the river while that pair were hunting around on the bikes they could end up being caught, if they waited too long to make a move they could miss the tide and not be able to get away at all.

As Jamie dug around in his back pack to find the radio he noticed Penny scratching lines in the dirt with a stick he moved closer to have a look. Penny finished her work, "Right," she began "This is where we were when the plane went down, this is where we are now and this is where the plane should be," she announced as she made crosses and dots in the dirt.

Jamie and Gazza joined in and after a few minutes they had a 'mud map' that they all agreed with, more or less.

Once they could see the relative position of themselves, the bad guys and the probable position of the plane, as well as the beach that they had to reach, things looked pretty bad.

"Hello Jack, are you there, Over." Jamie spoke quietly into the radio, "We have a bit of a problem."

Jack listened to the report from Jamie then answered, "I got all that, stay under cover, we still have a little more than an hour so wait till you know where those guys are then head straight for the beach, don't worry about the plane, just get out of there, Over."

Jamie, looked at Penny and Gazza, they both nodded, "No problem, over and out."

They moved around trying to get comfortable for the wait.

It wasn't long before Gazza got restless. "Look, we know where those guys are, let's check the house out, there might be some evidence there that we can use."

Penny agreed, "Yeah we will hear the bikes when they are coming back, it should be alright."

Jamie was wary, "Yeah, maybe, we can move down closer to the house, if it is still clear then, you two duck in for a quick look. I'll keep watch, if you hear the Currawong call, get out fast, I mean it, don't muck about, clear?" The other two nodded their agreement and Jamie lead them back toward the house.

Gunther didn't care about the plane, he wanted to be gone. Spy planes, those kids the other day, something wasn't right. He did as he was told, poked around in the bush looking here and there, he figured to give it about twenty minutes then head back and tell the boss that he couldn't find anything.

The coast was clear, now they were back almost where they had stumbled on to the house earlier. Jamie climbed up into a small paper bark tree so that he could see more of the surroundings. When he was comfortable he looked down at the others, "All right you two, five minutes, that's all, and make sure you don't leave any sign that we were here."
Penny and Gazza had already dumped their back packs, now they each gave Jamie the thumbs up and took off in a crouching run toward the back door of the old house.
Penny was in the lead, she had her carry bag over her shoulder and she held it to her as she ran.
Gazza was close behind, he had his camera over his shoulder and held it the same way that Penny held her bag, that was all they had in common as they ran for the house. Gazza could not help but be impressed by Penny as she moved across the ground, she had such 'easy grace' (he had heard his mother say that once

about a Ballet dancer on TV) he on the other hand felt a bit like a three legged dog as he sort of tip toed, tripped and thumped along behind her.

They made it to the door, it was unlocked, Penny pushed it open, there was no noise inside. She stepped in with her back against the door frame, her heart was pounding. She was trying to breathe slowly, Gazza stomped in behind her. There was no one there, they knew that, it was a research thing, if you were sure of your facts then there was nothing to worry about, research was his thing. He walked casually across to the old wooden table in the center of the room, there were empty mugs, a jar of instant coffee, half a jar of vegemite, and a bunch of keys lying on an old newspaper, nothing interesting there.

In the cupboards there were some cans of baked beans, a bag of sugar surrounded by little black ants and some empty jam jars.

There were only three other rooms, Penny got her breathing under control and walked slowly off to the left. Gazza went to the right, he had been through both rooms on that side by the time Penny came back. Gazza had been sort of aware that she was not moving around the house with that 'easy grace', now he noticed that her face was shiny with sweat and her breathing was strange, "Hey are you alright?"

"Yeah , I just want to get out of here, this place is spooky and I don't like feeling closed in."

Gazza understood straight away, "Sort of like me and those cliffs eh," he said kindly.

"Yeah, sorry about giving you a hard time,"

Gazza smiled, "Hey that's cool, you turned out to be human that's all, who would have thought, let's get you out of here before you have a heart attack or something."

Bush Ballet

As they walked back past the table Gazza noticed the bunch of keys again, one was a truck key, it had the brand name on it. On the same ring was a long silver steel tube, he had an idea.

Jamie was on full alert in the paper bark tree, he could hear one of the bikes a fair way off to the right but that was all. After about four minutes he saw Penny step out through the back door, look both ways then do that gliding run of hers back to where he was, he looked the question at her.
"He's OK, he said he would be ten seconds behind me," she leant against the paper bark, "You know he's not such a complete goose,"
Jamie was only half listening, he was still on look out, he thought he heard what she said but it did not sound right, " Eh! what was that, I didn't hear you,"
Penny was breathing normally now, she was back in control, "Oh no, nothing, can you see anything?" she said as she busied herself in her backpack.
Jamie was a little confused but just then Gazza came bouncing out the door and across to their position, he had a jam jar with sugar and black ants in it and was smiling around his fingers as he licked the last of the vegemite off them.
Jamie fired up, "Did you pinch food in there you maniac."
"Hey chill out, I got some good pictures from a two year old newspaper and I just have to duck down to that truck. Are we still clear?"
Jamie often found Gazza to be a bit disconnected from the real world, "What are you on about now," he said in frustration.
Gazza was moving off to the other side of the house where the truck was parked, "back in two minutes," he called softly as he did his delicate three legged dog thing around the house.

He was back within two minutes minus the sugar jar and minus the smile. He ran at full speed past the other two, picked up his back pack on the run and said "Get out, they're coming," he had suddenly picked up some 'easy grace' as a result of great fear.

Jamie jumped down and he and Penny followed the flying Gazza back up the track away from the old house.

Keepers
In the Forgotten Valley

Chapter Thirty One
Just Us Trees

The boss was fuming, he had told the other two to keep the bikes fueled and ready, so what happens, he gets almost to the furthest corner of the farm, cough, splutter, stop, out of fuel.

If there was no spare petrol in the shed he would shoot them both.

Had he not been busy with evil thoughts he might have been looking ahead instead of kicking at the dirt as he approached the house. If he had looked up when he was about fifteen metres away, he would have seen a young man walk out from behind the truck, look to the left, then to the right, see him coming, look left, right, up and down almost all at the same time, mumble something like, "So much for research," then take off around the corner of the house without much 'easy grace' but a great deal of speed.
As it was, that did not happen and he was inside cooling off when he heard the other bike arrive a few minutes later. Gunther sort of realized his mistake as he made it, "Where's your bike Jimmy?" he asked then wished he hadn't, about four minutes was the usual rant and rave that the boss went on with whenever he or Marty stuffed up, this one was a bit above average.

Keepers

No there was no spare fuel, no they did not think they were so low, no he had not found the plane and no the mobile phone would not work unless he climbed part way up the hill behind the house.

Jimmy sent Gunther to climb the hill, "Ring Marty make sure he has extra fuel for the bikes and make sure he is on time, if the tide is out when he gets here you will have to put those dogs away so that we can use the jetty."
He yelled at Gunther as he went out the back door, "And ring that dog bloke, I want them gone today or he won't get his money." that was just one more detail to mark off the list as he went around the house removing traces of their time there.

Penny, Jamie and Gazza watched Gunther leave the house and walk straight over to the trail they had used to escape. They heard the boss yell the last order, Gunther was heading their way.
It was too late to make another run for it, they had gone to ground about thirty metres up the hill behind the house. The bush around them made for good cover if anyone looked from the house but as the big man got closer the bush seemed to feel thinner.

Jamie was blaming himself again, he should have taken them further from such a well used track. Although there was no reason that he could see for them to come this way, there was something making this bloke plough his way toward them. Penny was calm, they were about ten metres off the main track behind a Black butt tree and among a growth of Wattle and Bougainvilleas.
She motioned to the boys to relax, breathe, feel The Place, "Easy, just take it easy," she thought to them both.
Jamie got the message, he let himself relax, he felt the bush become more dense, he felt himself become part of where they were, they would not be seen, there was only The Place.

Just us Trees

Gazza got a message also, something about , "Be a tree, or join the club," it was something like that anyway but he did not want to be a tree, people cut trees down for fire wood. He wanted to be at home or at least somewhere where this big bloke was not.

Gunther was walking with the phone held out in front of him like a diviner looking for water, closer and closer he came to their hiding spot. Just as Gazza decided he would like to be a tree after all, or a duck or a wombat, the big man stopped and from about six metres away he started to dial some numbers. He didn't bother to look around there was nothing up here but trees and bush.

———————

Jack knew that he could not risk using the radio to contact the crew, they would have it turned off any way to make sure that it did not make a noise at the wrong time. Emma had been trying to contact Penny and was having no luck. The tide had turned, if they could not reach the beach in the next forty minutes they would be stuck on shore, unless they could get to the jetty.

They were still at anchor in the little cove on the opposite bank, Jack reckoned he could up anchor and reach the beach within about four minutes if he had to, so it was safer to stay out of sight for now.

———————

"What do you mean you are half way from Spencer? Jimmy thinks you will be here any minute," Gunther said into the phone. "Marty if you don't get moving we won't be able to get the stuff out to the cruiser before the tide is gone, he said to bring fuel for the bikes but if you haven't got any don't waste time, just get that boat moving and get us out of here." now he was stressing. "Yes the truck is here but we are leaving early. There's been some action here today, we need to get down to Brooklyn to pick up the car, just get here !"

––––––––––––––

Emma finally found Penny, she sat calmly in the bow of the boat while Penny explained what was happening, then she repeated it to Jack, they had about thirty minutes left.
So some one was coming in a small boat to take them out to the cruiser that they had seen anchored in the channel on their first trip past Pearson's. Who ever that was needed to get in there at the same time that the crew had to be out. Jack told Emma to tell the gang that they had to move now ! they could not wait any longer.

Jamie had the same thought, he signaled the other two to follow him and moved away parallel with the track where Gunther stood having an argument on the phone, this time with the dog man from the sound of it. He was concentrating on his argument so they probably could have been noisy, but they weren't.
He led them along the hillside then down through the bush heading around to where the two ghost gums were. They got to the base of one giant gum which stood about twelve metres from the other. Jamie went ahead about twenty metres, he turned to look back hoping to catch a glimpse of the Vee shape on the cliff behind them but he could only just see the top edge of the escarpment.
To change the angle and see more of the cliff he would have to be further away or higher up, there was no chance of climbing the Ghost gums. They were old trees and the first branches were fifteen or twenty metres up. He noticed that he had come to the edge of a well used track leading toward the river. He gave the Currawong signal to bring Gazza and Penny to him, he had almost decided that the track was the quickest way to the beach when

they all heard Emma thinking loudly. "Jack says get out of sight if you are near the beach, one of them is heading your way."

They quickly retraced their steps away from the track, after about ten paces Jamie motioned for them to slow down, move more quietly. Over their own sounds he heard heavier steps. The man had no need to be quiet there was only him and his mates in this place. The only way to get here was by river and there was nothing on the river bar a tinny or two fishing the flats. He stomped on past the kids who were hunkered down in the scrub hardly daring to breathe, and went on toward the old shack.

That was enough for Jamie, time was running out. They had all three bad guys accounted for and that track must lead to the beach. He led them quickly back to the track then all three started to trot, thinking they would soon be safely away.

Chapter Thirty Two

Safe at Last

Jack ran his boat past the beach and the jetty. They set the drift and made a show of casting lines etc. then drifted for about ten minutes back toward the beach. The drift took them between the jetty and the cruiser anchored in the deep water channel, twenty metres past the beach they wound the lines in and motored back to the starting point. Emma's eyes were glued to the shore line, the water level was dropping, they were almost out of time.

On the second drift over the flats Jack heard a powerful outboard approaching. He looked down stream as a rig similar to his own came into sight, it had centre mount controls and steering but the motor sounded bigger, maybe a 70 horse. As Jack ran his boat back for the third drift the man drove the boat directly to the jetty and tied onto one of the pylons. He glanced in their direction but did not seem very interested. The man walked along the jetty until he was inside the line of the mangrove trees then he turned left and jumped off. It seemed a bit weird for this bloke to jump into the mangrove mud.
The boat was drifting in the same direction as the man and a moment later Jack and Emma saw him picking his way through the

mangroves along the river bank toward the beach, that was when Jack told Emma to send the alert to the crew.

They watched the man get almost all the way to the beach then turn right to follow the trail that they wanted their own gang to use. Emma received no response from Penny so she did not know if the message got through. The tide was still falling, the gang needed to be nearby and needed not to be seen by this villain.

Jack knew that they had to continue pretending to fish, on the next drift he stood up to clear an imaginary snag on his line just as they passed the jetty. Now he could see further up into the mangroves and at the far end of the jetty he could see the silver colour of a new wire gate. He looked at Emma, she understood, it was the dogs. The area covered by the two fences that they had seen included the jetty. They must have some duck boards set up over the mud so that they can come and go without putting the dogs away each time. If you did not know they were there you would probably not see them and the dogs would make a fair bit of noise if you got as far as the gate. That might be a way out for the gang if they could get the message through.

Emma was trying to contact Penny, Jack had an idea and cut that drift short. He started the motor and ran the tinny slowly up behind the cruiser on the opposite side to the jetty. He took one of his spare ropes and leant over the side of the tinny. From the shore it would look like they were just passing by on the way for another Drift, no one would see what he was up to, Emma was still trying to reach Penny. She kept telling herself to relax, to breathe, to use the power of the place but she was having a serious attack of being ten. Her brother was burnt, her friends were lost, there were bad guys coming from everywhere and she really needed to find a bathroom.

Safe at Last

Almost another ten minutes went by. Just as Jack was ready to start up for what would be their final run, he heard the 'come here' call of the Currawong. He brought the tinny in to the beach in a straight line, he wanted to get in as close as possible for the pick up. As he cut the motor and raised the outboard the other three broke cover from the bush and sprinted toward the river. Emma scanned the line where the bush met the beach and tried to use her ancient senses to see beyond.

The boat was beginning to run aground as the gang came together in the shallow water, no need for discussion. The three of them grabbed the bow and the gunnels and fed her around one hundred and eighty degrees without actually coming to a halt, and then kept running with her, through the sticky mud, toward the channel.

First one over the stern was Gazza (shortest legs) then the lightest (Penny) she handed her bow ahead of herself and leapt nimbly over the side. As soon as there was enough water to lower the motor, Jamie pulled himself over the transom with a hand from Gazza. She fired up first hit and Jack fed the throttle on steadily while the crew spread themselves around to balance the boat. Within fifty metres they were under full power. By the time that they were out of sight of the beach the boat was up on the plane.

Emma was smiling as she gave Jack the thumbs up. She thought they had not been seen by anybody on the shore line and she thought a bathroom should not be too far away.

One thought was right one was not.

————————

Marty was half way to the house from the jetty when he remembered that he was supposed to bring fuel for the trail bikes, he hesitated for just a moment, then he turned around to head

187

back to the boat. He had one 20lt.drum on board, that might be enough to settle Jimmy down, he was pretty scary when he got fired up, not that Marty was scared or anything.

He was almost back to the small beach when he heard some noises up ahead. At first he thought it must be some wallabies thumping through the bush but then he caught a glimpse of a person through the trees. From the noise he could tell there was a few of them and he knew that they weren't there just a few minutes ago. He turned back toward the house and started to run, he had only taken two steps before he ran head first into Jimmy.

They both went sprawling in the dirt as they collided. Jimmy recovered quickly, "What's all that noise up there you fool?" he growled as he dusted himself off.

Marty was still surprised at finding the boss in his face when he turned around, " I, I don't know," he stammered, " It's people, I was just coming up to tell you someone was here."

Jimmy was moving toward the beach as they spoke, Marty followed. About 30 metres off shore they could see an aluminium runabout with a bunch of kids in it.

"Come on," Jimmy barked as he led the way to the jetty. He was still carrying his rifle and decided not to go back for the bag he had dropped in the collision, it would be there when they came back.

By the time they were on Marty's boat, untied and under way, the other boat was almost out of site.

"Get this thing moving, I want to know where this lot are going."

Marty didn't like something in the tone of his voice but did what he was told. He saw the gun stowed on the floor boards, he didn't like guns either.

Meanwhile on the QuintX boat, it was high fives all round and with the power trimmed back for the run to town, they started to fill each other in on the parts they had missed over the last few hours.

When they got to the part about number three (Marty) arriving to load the cruiser, Jamie and the others started to worry whether they might get back with the police in time. Jack did not seem concerned at all, he did wonder about the police though. Without the camera from the plane there was nothing to talk about, as far as he could see they were the only law breakers in the deal.

Penny agreed, trespassing, break and enter, probably something about unauthorized spy cameras and no evidence from any of it.

Gazza was smiling like a cat full of canaries, "Just get me home, I have some pictures in this camera that will interest the coppers, and by the way, let's not tell too many details of where we have been today, I don't want to end up in Long Bay or somewhere.

He would not show them the pictures, "You will see them soon enough."

He said that he would down load and email to each of them and make hard copies for the police.

Well, that is what he said.

Chapter Thirty Three

Gotcha !

Gazza's jetty was the first stop, which should work out, he had to down load then print the pictures and be ready for Jack to pick him up again after he dropped Penny and Jamie on the other side of the river. Penny would jump out at Jamie's jetty since her place was nearby and she was the only one without a jetty.
Jamie would double her home on his trail bike, she could dump her pack and gear, jump on her old peewee and follow him down to the ferry. Gazza's place was on the same side as the police station so they would just tie up at the public wharf and meet the others at the ferry when they came across.

By the time Gazza was climbing onto his jetty the other boat had caught up enough for Jimmy to see that he had a camera with him. They could see the rest of the kids still in the boat when it cast off heading up stream.
Without hesitating Jimmy signaled for Marty to run his boat in along side the jetty where the kids would not see it if they looked back. On the way up to the house Jimmy explained in detail, how

he wanted that camera and how Marty had better do exactly as he was told.

No body looked back.

There was no one home as Gazza let himself in, that probably saved lots of questions. That also meant Dad's computer would be available, it had nearly twice the speed of his own and for some reason he had a feeling that speed would be important. His Dad's office was in the middle of the house, so was the kitchen, M'mm food. "Just start the down load first". that was brain to stomach talk. The machine was on and the web was active, Dad must not be far away, he would have shut down if he was gone for too long. Gazza put the camera into the dock, downloaded and saved the images, on the bigger screen they were even better than he had thought, then selected 'best quality' and hit the print function.

There was a loud bang at the front and back doors simultaneously. His instincts exploded, this was bad, he heard pounding foot steps through the other rooms, things being thrown, furniture crashing. He moved the cursor up to email, the contact list came up, they were close now, he clicked a contact, selected 'all pictures', hit 'send' and jumped up trying for the window.

They grabbed him from behind, blind folded and tied him so quickly that he hardly had time to breathe until he was thrown across the room landing awkwardly in a corner.
"Well he had a camera alright." Voice one.
Voice two, "Shut up, grab it, cancel the printing and clear those pictures from the memory."

Gotcha !

This was real. They had used a plastic zip clip to tie his hands, it was already cutting his wrists, the blindfold was so tight he thought the top of his head would come off and when he landed his face hit the chest of draws cutting his bottom lip against his teeth.
Gazza lay dazed, tasting blood and shaking all over from shock.

"I don't know how to do that, you do it." voice one was not happy.
voice two was really not happy. "Get out of the way idiot."
voice one "Why don't you just wreck the thing?"
voice two "They could salvage the hard drive, I want to make sure those pictures are gone."
The printer was buzzing and clicking in the corner, it started to push out the pictures as ordered, voice two cancelled the command before any more printing was done, took the one that was done and stuffed it in his pocket.
He selected 'all pictures' and tried 'delete', a notice came up saying "email transfer incomplete' option 'cancel or continue'.
He hit cancel and swore loudly. Two strides to cross the room and his right foot swung against Gazza's bum. "Who did you send the pictures to you little mongrel?"
"I, I don't know. "Gazza stammered."
Another kick, this time in the muscle in the back of the left thigh.
"Don't try me on kid, I'll rip you apart."
The pain from the kicking had strangely stopped him shaking and when he spoke again his voice was calmer. "I just hit send when I heard you coming. I don't know where I sent them." that much was true and there was no way he would tell them that the list of contacts only contained four options.
Voice one went off, "What are you saying, has he sent the pictures somewhere?"
"It looks like he has" Barked voice two "We need to get out of this district and fast."

"What about this one and the others?" voice one sounded like he was tearing the computer apart, pieces were going everywhere. Gazza knew that 'This one', meant himself, he knew that voice two was the one that Gunther had called Jimmy or boss and he was pretty sure that he was in a lot of trouble.
Voice two sounded nervous, "We can't do anymore about them, there was this one and four more, we have to run, we can't get them all and we don't know where the pictures are !"

Gazza had found his voice, "Run where you like, the coppers know what you're up to you won't get far." He really wondered why he said that at this particular time, but he still said it.
His wrists were really hurting and he could feel the blood running down his hands but he could not get the leverage to push himself over to a sitting position.

Just then there was the sound of a car in the driveway.
Voice one in a panic "What now?"
Voice two in a rage, "Grab him, lets go, move!!"
Voice one, more panic "That's kidnapping, you'll get us hung."
Gazza could picture the dangerous face that went with voice two.
"Pick him up or I'll be up for your murder and his and whoever is out there, do it now."
Gazza knew it was his Dad's car and a different fear started in his gut and spread through his whole body. He did not want his Dad to be attacked by this pair. He did not struggle or call out even when it hurt, as Voice one heaved him over his shoulder like a sack of spuds and took off for the front door.
His head was starting to work, he was trying to figure out three things, how these blokes had found him, where they were taking him and how could he contact the gang.
He did not know that he had already done the last.

Chapter Thirty Four

The River Knows

Penny and Jamie had just climbed up onto his jetty, when Emma cried out in pain. Jack heard the cry and saw a look of fear on her face, "Em what's wrong?"

She was shaking, "I don't know, someone is in trouble."

Jamie was holding Penny who had doubled over at the same instant.

Jack felt a calm come to him, he realized that they could work it out together, "Bring her here," he called to Jamie.

They helped Penny into the boat, Jack took Penny's hand in one of his and he took Emma's hand in the other. He felt the pain, he tasted blood, he could feel the stubborn determination.

"It's Gazza" he cried as he scuttled back to the controls.

Jack started the engine and wound on the power, QuintX came about and headed back to Gazza's jetty.

The boat was skipping on the slight chop and coming in to the jetty at high speed. Emma recognized Gazza's father as he ran to the end of the jetty, looked up and down the river, turned toward the house, then turned back as he realized who was in the boat.

He was in a state!

"Have you seen Gazza?" he called as they neared the jetty.

"Yes we just dropped him here about ten or fifteen minutes ago. What's wrong?" Penny called back.

Jack tied the boat off while Mr. Corndiff went on about the house being wrecked and blood all over his office and no sign of Gazza any where. They ran back to the house with him and found everything the way he said.

"I am calling the police and I want know exactly what you kids have been up to." He said, "Do you lot know what this is about?"

They told him the truth, they had no idea, at the moment.

While he called the police they went back outside.

Jack told Emma to call Gazza, she stopped and lent against the old Gum beside the walkway and closed her eyes, Penny and Jamie stood nearby, Jack walked on toward the river.

A few minutes later they found him at the end of the jetty staring into the water. They waited, eventually he said "They have got him and they are heading back to the old house."

Emma said, "How do you know that, I couldn't reach him?"

Jack simply said "The river told me."

"Em, you will need to wait here, explain to Mr. Corndiff where we have been and tell him what we have seen and what we think has happened to Gazza. Then call Mum, she will let Dad know, when the police turn up tell them the same thing. I will talk to you through Penny but you both have to stay calm, "He looked from Emma to Penny, they both nodded. "I will talk to the folks on the marine band two-way, Jamie, Penny and I are going after them, they took him by boat, somehow they followed us." He had another thought. "Tell the police we saw them, don't tell them how we saw them, they will only get confused and waste time." Jack was happy to see that Emma was calm now also.

"OK". She said, then "Be careful, this feels really dangerous."

"That's why we have to get to Gazza, tell the police to hurry." Jack said as he climbed down to the boat.

They motored out to mid stream and Jack said, still quite calmly, "Have you guys ever wondered how fast this thing is, cause we are all going to find out right now." He cranked the throttle on full and adjusted the trim of the motor for maximum straight line running. She jumped up on to the plane and powered off down river.

Emma watched them go and soon they had skipped around the bend and out of sight.

She told the river and the Rainbow Snake that made it, "The Keepers need you now."

Keepers
In the Forgotten Valley

Chapter Thirty Five
River Hawk

The police were not in, that happens in the Valley, "So please leave your details and we will return your call as soon as possible, Drink driving is a crime and -----   that was where Max Corndiff slammed down the phone.

He had listened to the story that Emma Kipley had told him about the Pearson farm and spying on people. About the guard dogs, the ugly big men who had wrecked his house and taken his son, that last part was all that he cared about for now. It sounded like the kids had upset some one with their games and nonsense but NO BODY was going to lay their hands on his son.
His next call was to his wife Maureen, she was almost home so he said, "No problem, see you when you get here."
Then he rang Alex Kipley.
Max explained things differently to the way Emma had told the story but at the end Alex agreed, they would find Gazza first, then deal with the kids. "Let me speak to Emma for a minute then we will sort out what we do," said Alex.
"Yeah sure," he waved Emma to take the hand piece.
"Hello Dad,"

"Hey baby, are you alright?"

"Dad I'm OK and the others are alright but we don't know about Gazza," now that she was talking to her Dad she could not control the tears and they ran down her cheeks as she spoke.

Alex could hear the emotion in her voice. "It's alright babe, we will work it out, just take it easy," he tried to be reassuring, "Did you tell Mr. Corndiff everything?"

Emma sniffled then replied, " Yes , but I think he thinks that we caused the trouble. Dad I'm scared, these men are bad, they shot down Gazza's plane and everything."

Alex did not think this conversation was helping Emma, "It's OK honey, Mum will be there soon, everything will be all right, put Mr. Corndiff back on and take it easy."

Emma just said, " Bye."

The men quickly settled on the first course of action. Since the police were not available, they would find out for themselves what was happening, Max would ring Greg Wilson, Alex would call John Walker, they were using telephones, Emma was not.

Kate had pulled her car to the side of the road when she had felt her daughters need to communicate.

At first it was difficult to understand what Emma was trying to tell her. Gradually she gathered that, Emma was at the Corndiff house, there was some trouble about Gazza, the rest of the kids were in danger and it was all Keepers business.

Kate sensed that Emma was under some sort of stress, she tried to tell the girl to relax, to rest, all she got in reply was,

"Hurry Mum."

Greg Wilson got the call on his mobile as he was driving down the winding road into the Valley from the Windsor side. From what

Max had to tell him he thought it best to drive straight to the Pearson place since he was on the same side of the river at the moment. Max and Alex had already decided to go by river and they were on the way as they spoke.

Greg said, "Are you sure that Penny is alright?"

Max replied, "It looks like my boy is the only one in real trouble at the moment but the rest are trying to join him, so let's just get there and sort it out."

They agreed to speak again from near the Pearson place. There was a spot just before the last bend in the river where the mobile signal was good, Greg would call from there and wait in his ute.

Greg called his wife Christine. She was always supporting Penny and her adventures with the gang but they agreed that this one did not sound good, she would head for the Corndiff house to find out what was going on.

Alex had been down at his boat when he got the call from Max, he had already checked it over since he had planed to take her out the next morning anyway. He made a quick trip back up to the house, unlocked the gun safe, took his shot gun and a box of cartridges, he did not like the feel of this.

When Alex finally got John Walker on the mobile he was on his way down river from Spencer where he and his crew had been installing peers for a jetty. John decided that the quickest way for him was to turn the work boat around and head up to Pearson's from the opposite direction. They agreed that whoever got to the bend with the mobile reception first, would wait to hear from the others. With luck this would just turn out to be some sort of kids dumb game gone wrong.

Keepers

John told his two crewmen that he needed to run half an hour up river and did not have time to drop them at the usual mooring, they shrugged their shoulders and went back to their card game.
He rang his home number, Cathy answered. When he had finished the story and told her that it seemed that Jamie was alright so far, she seemed distracted.
"I thought it would be longer before this happened,"
John was a little confused, "Before what happened?"
"I'm going to Maureen's," she answered and hung up.

Kate was a fair way from the Corndiff's and on the other side of the river but she was not far from the house that Pearl Kearns called home. She decided to head there first and was still trying to get Pearl to answer the phone as she entered the driveway and pulled up in front of the house.
Pearl slammed the front door and stepped as quickly as her walking stick would allow, over to the car. " About time," she said as she climbed into the passengers seat. "Drive, drive," she commanded, hammering the floor with her stick and reaching for the seat belt at the same time.
Kate put her foot down and drove.
"They were supposed to have time," Pearl groaned as they swerved back on to the road. "Time to learn the way."

Reg Kerry was driving his old truck down the road from his quarry as hard as he dared. All he had heard from Pearl was, "Reginald, get down here now, the kids are in trouble," he did not know exactly where 'Here' was. He had never been much good at mind talking with Pearl, occasionally the Ancients, once in a while dead people, sometimes even trees, but not Pearl. So, he thought he would head for the Kipleys and see what happened then.

River Hawk

Maureen Corndiff drove her fifteen tonne water tanker into the yard and shut it down in the usual spot. She knew from the way that Max had said, "No problem," that there would be a problem. Her husband and her son were the worst liars that she had ever known, especially when they had done something really dumb and were trying to make excuses.

Max walked over as she climbed down from the truck, he knew that she knew something was wrong. She was petite, attractive, very clever, and dangerous, when she got excited.

"Take it easy love, this could be a bit serious, Gazza is in trouble, young Emma is inside, you should hear the story from her. Oh yeah, the house is a bit of a mess so remember to breathe, OK?" By the time she had said, "What is going on Max?" they were at the back door and she could see Emma sitting at the kitchen table with a glass of milk and half a vegemite sandwich.

Max left Emma to tell the story to Gazza's mum while he went down to do a quick check on his half cabin. Batteries, fuel, ropes and stowage. He had been around boats long enough to know that when you are in a hurry on a boat, the fastest way is to take the time to check the basics before you cast off, you can't just pull up and call the NRMA if you break down on the water, you have to be prepared. Max checked the first aid kit as well, all that blood in his office had made him really nervous. He had agreed to wait for Alex to pick him up but if he didn't arrive soon he would go on his own.

On his way to the boat he stopped at his work shed and picked up two small aluminium tool cases. He left them on the jetty and jogged up to the house, Emma was just finishing the story.

"What do you think?"

"I think you had better find our son," she began, "Have you called the police?"

Max explained the absence of the police and told her that Alex Kipley would be there any minute and the other fathers were on the way as well.

"Alright you and the boys head up there but don't do anything stupid. Leave the police to me they will be on the way in about ten seconds if we need them, you can bet on it."

Max would not take the bet, Maureen Corndiff had been known as Maureen Crane for all her working life in the city. After law school she had worked her way up as a solicitor in the Criminal Prosecutors office. By the time she had had enough of city law she was the most senior prosecuting attorney in Sydney. She still had contacts all the way to the top in the N.S.W. police force. If he was a copper at Wisemans, he would be on his way in nine seconds or less, when she called.

Maureen was dialing the district commander as Max headed back to the jetty.

When he got there he could see the Kipley cruiser heading his way at full speed. It was almost ten metres long and with twin inboard V8 engines she had plenty of power. As she eased up to the jetty, Max climbed quickly on board and stowed his cases below deck while Alex steered back out into the main channel and powered up both engines.

The boat was called 'River Hawk' as she came up on to the plane the water under the hull was the wind beneath the wings of a hungry bird of prey.

This Hawk was flying to the Keepers.

Chapter Thirty Six
Think About It

Gazza lost a bit more skin when voice one dropped him into the boat, his shoulder landed heavily on the uncovered aluminium hull. He had decided that voice one with the boat, must be who Gunther had called Marty, when he was on the phone earlier.
So that was great, he was on first name terms with all the bad guys and they were still throwing him around like a floppy doll, he decided that Penny was not so rough after all.
"All right, nobody saw us, "Jimmy said as he looked back at the jetty while Marty powered the boat out to mid stream.
"Yeah, great so what now, all I was supposed to do was run you guys up and down the river and drop off supplies and now you've got me into kidnapping."
Jimmy cut him off, "What am I supposed to do? This grub and his mates have got pictures of us, they have been out at the house. We can't just leave him back there, shut up and let me think, I will work something out, just get us back to the cruiser and hurry up." He pulled the crumpled picture from his pocket, it showed Himself and Gunther arms waving, with the truck in the background.

He screwed it up and threw it over the side of the boat.

You should never throw rubbish into the river.

Jack was mind talking with the other two, "I tried to get Dad on the mobile just before we left but the battery is flat."
Penny, "I can't contact Emma either."
Jamie, "What channel have you got the two way on Jack?"
Jack replied that the radio was on channel 14, they all went quiet.
If their parents did not call before they caught up with the mob that had Gazza, they would be on their own against the bad guys.

All the women had now arrived at the Corndiff house, they each knew the story as Emma had told it and between them they had worked out where each of the men were, more or less. No one could find Reg but no one was bothered about that.
Kate had found Emma exhausted and had cleaned her up and put her to bed, Emma objected but G.P. told that she may be needed later and would have to be strong, so she agreed to take a nap.
Maureen had received a call from the local police assuring her of their interest and co-operation and asking for details.
Maureen thanked them and told them that at the moment the situation was being checked out by her husband and as soon as they were sure that this was not some misunderstanding, she would call them. The sergeant was very polite, he gave her his direct mobile number to avoid any further difficulty.
The women were undecided about what should be done, they were hoping for word from the kids or the Husbands, it would be dark soon.

Think About It

When Gunther had done as he was told and ridden the second trail bike up as close to the jetty as the bush would allow, he made his way along the track. Not far from the little beach he stumbled over the carry bag that he knew belonged to his boss, he took it with him as he walked the rest of the way to the jetty. He found no sign of the boss and no sign of Marty, the cruiser was still at anchor out in the channel but he seemed to be alone at Pearson's farm.

Thinking was not something that Gunther did a lot of, usually he didn't have to, there had always been someone to tell him what to do so that he could grumble and complain but not think about it much. This opportunity to be independent did not really suit him, he wanted his boss.

After waiting on the jetty for a few minutes, he looked carefully in the water around the jetty just in case Jimmy had fallen in. Then he decided that he must have misunderstood his instructions, Jimmy must be waiting somewhere else, maybe at the house. He could not understand why the carry bag was there so he did not try, he took it back to the bike with him and rode off to find the boss. For the next half hour he rode around the property, stopping here and there to call for his boss, "Hey Jimmy are you there?" he tried the house, tried the truck, the machinery shed in the middle of the paddock and that's where the second bike ran out of fuel.

It was going to be dark soon, Gunther did not like the bush anyway but in the dark he did not like it at all. He started to walk up to the house where the truck was parked, his shot gun was in the truck, if he couldn't find the boss at least he would have his gun.

———————

Penny was not one with the place, she was worried about Gazza and she could not relax. The mind talking in the boat had

205

become more and more difficult as they got closer to the Pearson place and still no word from anyone.

Pearl was not one with the place either, she was mind calling so loudly to the kids that it was giving Kate a headache.

She was also calling her brother but there was no reply from Reg either. Over the years it had been a bit like an old style post office with Reg, you just sort of send the message and hope he checks his mail from time to time.

The women were restless, their children were somewhere out on the river, at least one of them was kidnapped and they could find out nothing.

"Come on Jimmy, cut his hands free, we're almost at the jetty ,he's bleeding all over my boat," pleaded Marty.

"Shut up, don't use my name you fool, the only thing keeping him alive is that he doesn't know who we are," snarled Jimmy.

Gazza suddenly found that he had no saliva.

There did seem to be a lot of blood behind the kid, Jimmy pulled him roughly forward and looked at where the plastic binding had cut deeply into both wrists. "Hey kid, did you hear what I just said?"

Gazza nodded his head.

"If I cut you free and you touch that blind fold, then I cut your throat, understand?"

Gazza nodded vigorously this time and tried again to swallow.

Jimmy sliced the plastic clip with his hunting knife, Gazza winced at the extra pain as it shot through his arms but said nothing as he tried to workout what to do with his damaged wrists and then wondered if he was hearing things.

Think About It

Everyone in the boat felt a stab of pain when the tie was cut, Jack was the only one who understood what it meant, "OK Gazza we are coming," he thought.
"Is that you Jack," Gazza thought through the pain.
Jack said to the other two, "I've got him," pointing at his head. "Yes mate, we are not far behind you, are you alright?"
Gazza made sure he did not smile, but he found he was able to swallow again. "Yeah, I think I am, it's Marty and Jimmy, they've got me in their boat and we are close to the jetty," he thought, trying to stay rational.
Jack was trying to stay calm as well. "Alright Gazz, we are not far away either, the folks and the coppers know where you are, they're on the way so stay cool, we will get you out, don't worry."
Gazza took a deep breath, the pain in his wrists eased and he relaxed a little, and he lost contact.

_____

Pearl was ecstatic, "Oh, you beauty" she cried aloud, the rest of the women stared at her as she sat with her eyes closed thinking desperately.
Jack heard her call, "Is that you G.P.?"
"Of course it's me, I've been trying to reach you kids all day, all I got was danger and pain, it's been awful, you kids really need to practice communicating-----
Jack cut her off, "Sorry GP, but do you know where Dad is?"
Pearl got herself together, "Yes, yes of course, he left a message with your mother for Emma to send but the poor dear was just not up to it, she has had quite a day you know, what with you lot climbing things and -----
Jack was worried about the connection, "What was the message?"
"Message?"
"The message from Dad !"

"Yes of course, quite strange really, something like, 14 is not safe meet at 23, yes that was it, I'm sure that was it, now I don't where this 23 is, or 14 for that matter----
Jack learnt how to do a mind hang up.

He shook his head to clear it, then changed the radio channel to 23 and called, "River Hawk, River Hawk, are you receiving? over."
Penny rolled her eyes.

After about two minutes of rambling Pearl realized that Jack was not responding. She opened her eyes and looked back at all the interested faces watching her.
"All right ladies, I think it is time we all did our bit, Gareth is safe at the moment although in some discomfort. He has been abducted and is being taken to the old Pearson farm. The other children are nearby and will meet the men folk at 23 where ever that may be, I suggest we move ourselves closer to the action so that we can be of some use when needed."
Maureen cut in, "Pearl are you sure about this?"
Pearl looked offended, "I am most certainly sure of the situation, I am not sure how such new Keepers have found their way into this pickle but yes, I am sure they are in it."
"All right," said Maureen, "I am calling the police, then I am heading out there, whoever is coming with me had better get ready."

There was a rush of activity as she reached for the phone.

Chapter Thirty Seven

All for One

"River Hawk receiving, respond plus two, count three."

Jack switched to 25 counted three then said, "Dad they've got Gazza, we are almost there, where are you, over?"

Jack switched to 23 after three seconds he heard, "Understood. Max and I are fifteen, Bullfish is the same opposite, is Emma's story true, over? "

Jack switched to 25.

Penny wanted so much to hit someone.

"Yes the story is true, fifteen is too long, over." back to 23.

"Bullfish here", John Walkers voice boomed. "Jamie, stand by until we arrive, confirm, over."

Jack switched back as he handed the mike to Jamie. "We will look and call again in five, stay cool Dad, over and out."

Penny breathed a deep sigh of relief.

In the fading light, through binoculars, from the far side of the river, they could see Pearson's jetty. They could see the tinny tied to the stern of the cruiser and they could see some movement on board the tinny.

Keepers

For the tenth time Jimmy slammed his mobile shut, "Why is that fool not waiting on the hill where I can ring him."
Marty knew better than to answer, it wasn't that sort of question.
"I need my bag, otherwise I would leave the big useless dope behind."
They had tied up to the cruiser just a few minutes ago and Jimmy had been trying to call Gunther repeatedly, now he turned on Marty. "It's your fault that I dropped my bag."
Marty thought that he was about to get the four minute show but something made the boss stop and look across the river, then he stared up stream and down stream. When he spoke again he was very quiet, very clear, very precise and although Marty was not a man to be scared easily, it was lucky that Gazza was in the boat, the sound of Jimmy's voice scared him enough for man and boy.
"Take me over to the jetty, do it now and do it quietly," Jimmy almost whispered.
Marty responded just like a scared person would have. He undid the line to the cruiser, pushed off and started the motor, it only needed to run for a few seconds as he pointed the boat at the jetty and let it push through the shallow water until it nudged up against one of the pylons. He slipped the bow line over the pylon, moved to the stern, put another rope out on that end so that the boat was snugged up nice and close across the end of the jetty and looked at Jimmy hoping that he had 'done good.'
Jimmy said nothing as he moved across the boat toward the jetty, stopping as he passed the centre mounted control panel. He took the ignition key with its bright yellow float attached and stared at Marty as he put it in his pocket. "Wait here, you may have another way to start this thing but I have ten ways to track you down if you are not here when I come back, understood?"
Jimmy was still talking in that spooky quiet voice.

All for One

"Hey, yeah, Jimmy, mate, no need for that, I'll be here, of course I will," panted Marty as Jimmy climbed on to the jetty.

"Of course you will," mimicking as he turned and pointed at Gazza. "Don't talk to him. Don't let him move, speak, nothing, just both of you sit still till I get back, right?" he was very clear.

"Sure, cool, no worry's, we will be right here." assured Marty as Jimmy made his way along the jetty to the duck boards and set off toward the trail near the beach.

Marty and Gazza sat very quietly, listening to his footsteps grow fainter, man and boy had no intension of moving at all, at least while he was within earshot.

Jack only needed to watch for a few seconds, the river carried the message, if not the words, to him. He motored the boat slowly and quietly down stream until they were out of sight from the cruiser. He slowed the motor even more until the boat was just holding position against the incoming tide. "They are moving too fast, we can't wait for the olds, we have to get closer to Gazza."

Penny spoke first, "Jack these men are looking more and more dangerous, what can we do, we are only kids."

Jamie interrupted her, "Alright, Dad's brother, uncle Jack, likes to bet on the horses, he says the best way out when you've already bet too much is to have a little each way in the last race." He was not smiling and as the other two realized what he had in mind, neither were they. "Drop me just near the bend, I'll get close to Gazza and if anything happens before the Dads army lands, I'll be there."

Penny cut in, "Does your uncle win much at the races?"

"No, but he can afford to loose, we can't."

Jamie did not mention the rest of his uncles advice, the part about, 'Never bet if you can't afford to loose.'

Keepers

Jack was not happy but it made sense at the time, "Yeah, but you and Penny have to stay calm so that we can stay in touch, if you can't stay relaxed then you better get Gazza excited, that's the only way he seems to make it work."

Penny and Jamie sat facing each other for the couple of minutes that it took Jack to turn the boat and run back with the tide to a point that just hid them from the view of the cruiser. They practiced some deep breathing and relaxation that Penny had been taught at her yoga classes. Usually at yoga they left out the big scary men, the kidnapping , the blood, the guns and some other stuff, but they knew they had to make it work somehow.

As Jack swung the boat gently back around into the current, Jamie slipped quietly over the side. He joined with the river, the river had been preparing to settle, darkness was coming and it would rest from its journey to the sea but in this darkness there may be more to do, there were Keepers at work this night.

The majestic Hawkesbury river connects the mountains to the sea. She is a bridge of water for the spirits of the land and the ocean. Where the sea water travels back up the river on the incoming tide, it keeps company with the fresh water and they trade places with each other near a place that men call Wisemans Ferry.

Up stream from the ferry the water is more fresh and less salt, down stream is more salt, less fresh. The spirits of the ocean travel in the salt water, the spirits of the river travel in the fresh. They take the form of many types of creature, fish, sting rays, sea snakes, eels that live near the change of water and bull sharks that hunt in packs, they are vicious when they are hungry.

Now the river felt a spirit it had almost forgotten, as Jamie Walker swam quietly with the current to the aid of his friend, the Spirit of the 'Keepers' flowed with him and around him.

Keepers

Jamie had settled in to that steady smooth stroke, the one that had seen him do so well in the fifteen hundred. Jack pushed the throttle on just a little at a time until he decided they were out of hearing from Pearson's, then he wound her up and headed for the rendezvous with the fathers.

Alex had the River Hawk circling slowly in mid stream while Max spoke first to John Walker, he was nearby, then to Greg Wilson. He had just outlined what they thought was happening when Alex pointed up stream, then down stream, Jack was coming down, the 'Bull Fish' was coming up.
"Greg, we should have some answers in a few minutes, the kids are on the way," a pause, then, "Yes mate, she's OK I can see her in the boat," a pause, " I don't know, I'll call you in a minute Greg, I can only see two of them?"

Keepers
In the forgotten Valley

Chapter Thirty Eight
Moonshine

Maureen hung up the phone after reporting the kidnapping of her son. Cathy Walker squeezed her shoulders and said," It's OK, he'll be alright, the boys must be nearly there, they'll sort it out,"
Maureen shuddered as she took a deep breath. "I can't sit here and wait, I 'm taking the boat down there, who's coming?"
There had been some discussion while she was on the phone.
Kate said, "Christine is taking her seven seater to meet Greg on the road in case we need transport coming back, Cathy and Pearl are going with her, Emma and I are coming with you."
Maureen nodded, "Right let's do it, you girls take care," she said to the group heading for the front door. Kate was just returning from the bedroom with a bleary eyed Emma in tow when there was a commotion in the front yard with car horns and yelling. Maureen had been packing some things into a bag, she put it down and hurried past Kate, mumbling, "What else can happen?"
Reg can happen.
He had come speeding through the front gate as Christine was about to drive out in her land cruiser, she had just seen the headlights of the old quarry truck in time to stop and let him pass .

He narrowly avoided a collision but blew his horn anyway. The yelling part was Pearl out the window, "Watch out you silly old fool" Now parked alongside the water tanker Reg responded. "Me ! You want to yell at me, call yourself a Keeper, I've been driving around all over the place looking for you lot because you send a message that says "Get Here" Where's HERE,! you old bag?"
Maureen arrived on the scene just then.

To Christine she said, "Go Chris, just drive," to Reg she said, "Come on Reg, it looks like you are with us, settle down and we will fill you in on the way."
Reg was confused, "The way where? I'm already here aren't I ?"
Maureen shook her head as Reg followed her toward the jetty.

———————

The River Hawk and the Bull Fish were drifting side by side, Jack's tinny was tied to the stern cleat of his father's boat.
Jack and Penny had poured out the day's events and the men were getting some idea of what had gone on but the issue at the moment was the whereabouts of Jamie and Gazza. Jack explained about Gazza being blindfolded in the back of Marty's boat and Jamie being nearby incase he could do something.
Max Corndiff cracked up, "What on earth have you kids been up to? Who are these blokes? what are you doing with a spy plane?"
John Walker cut him off, "Look Max, we're going to have to get some of those answers later, for now lets just settle down and get our kids out of there."
Max took a breath, "Yes, you're right John but those answers better be good when they come."
John nodded, glaring at the kids, "Oh, Yeah, they better be better than good, that's for sure."

John sent his work boat back to Brooklyn with his two crewmen. She was too big to be stooging around in shallow water on the Macdonald, the men were quite happy to be leaving behind what sounded like a really loud family gathering.

Aboard the River Hawk, every one tried to focus on the situation at the moment.

Penny rang her father who was still up the road from the Pearson driveway, after he confirmed that she was all right, and that she would be involved in no more nonsense until he had spoken to her in person, he spoke to Max.

"Max I don't know what the kids have stumbled on but I drove up to the place earlier and the fence and the dogs would do ASIO proud, whoever put it there is serious about keeping people out, so let's get the kids out !"

Alex rang Kate and found out that the women folk were arriving soon by land and by water, he said, "OK," like what could he say. Pearl at the front gate, Reg on the water and all the women in between, if these blokes had any sense they would surrender peacefully when they found out.

He told Kate to use channel 25 on the radio when the phone signal dropped out, told her they should look for the River Hawk and anchor nearby, said, "Love you." and closed the phone.

Max was just finishing on his phone, as he hung up Alex said," All the wives and Pearl and Reg will be here in about fifteen minutes."

Max said, "Oh man, this will be noisy." he turned to Jack and Penny, "All right, you two know that you and the others cannot survive, no body may survive, if the mothers take over, the only chance , for all of us, is to sort this out in fifteen minutes. What was your plan?" Jack looked at Penny, she looked back, she did a little 'I don't know' type shrug that the fathers were not supposed to notice.

Jack jumped in, "Jamie will get a message from Penny, then he will create a distraction, release Gazza and the two of them will swim with the tide out to my boat holding position just out of sight of the cruiser."

The three men looked at each other, John Walker spoke first, "You watch too much TV Jack, if these blokes are dangerous I don't want my son playing games with them."
Max joined in, "He's right Jack, if anything goes wrong Gazza and Jamie could be hurt or worse."
As he spoke Jack had realised that the plan born in the last few seconds was really the only way to make sure that his two friends did not get hurt.
"Jamie is already in position, if we don't follow through and support him they could be in real trouble, we have to do it now, there's no time, then you can sort these blokes out."
The men sort of nodded to each other.
John said, "All right do it but I know who's going to get sorted out after," as he glared from Jack to Penny and back again.

———————

Jamie had floated past the cruiser and saw that the tinny was now moored at the jetty. He swam quietly in shore until the water was too shallow, then he drifted with the tide into the mangrove trees on the other side of the boat. The moon shone through the clouds as it rose, just long enough for Jamie to see what was happening. He could hear the man in the boat with Gazza.

"It's been too long, something is wrong, I can't stay here."
He was rambling about money and Jimmy, he seemed really nervous. Gazza seemed to be having trouble holding his head up, he had his hands across his chest, his shirt was soaked in blood

and his face looked white. The moon shone brightly again, this time almost like a search light on the man and on the jetty and he rambled again. "Yes that's it, I'll go find Jimmy, maybe he's lost or fell over or something, yeah I'll do that, yeah, hey kid." he had moved to the stern, he was shaking Gazza.

"Hey kid, are you kidding, wake up, Oh jeez," he was almost whaling as he looked closely at Gazza in the moonlight.

"Oh Jeez," I'm out of here but I'm gunna tie you up again, just loose, just in case Jimmy comes back or you're foolen me."

As he moved Gazza's arms to wrap the rope around them, he said, "Oh Jeez," one more time.

In the moonlight Marty could see that this kid was in trouble, he was pale and barely conscious and the blood from his cuts had made puddles on the floor of the boat.

"Oh bugger this," he stumbled across the boat and up on to the jetty, he stood looking across at the cruiser and then along the jetty. He could not make up his mind, finally, he looked down at Gazza slumped in his boat, he backed away, at first slowly. He stepped backwards as though too much noise might wake Gazza up, then he turned and ran, past the duck boards down on the mangrove mud, all the way to the gate at the end of the jetty he ran. There was no lock on the gate.

Just after he went through the gate, the moon went out like a light on a switch, it jumped behind the clouds and Marty charged on, into the dark valley night.

As soon as the moon went out, Jamie made his move. He half swam half crawled to the back of the boat, coming up beside the motor. Gazza was slumped against the side of the boat.

"Gazza, hey Gazz, can you hear me?"

No response.

Jamie climbed over the transom, he stood and looked along the jetty, there was nothing to see and the only sound was dogs barking in the distance.

He lent over Gazza. Now that he was close it looked was worse.

The ropes around his arms were just wrapped not tied but the blindfold was so tight that Jamie had trouble undoing the knot. When he finally got it undone and quickly removed it, Gazza let out a wail of pain. The blood surged into the area behind his eyes and into the eyes themselves. Jamie did not know what to do, his own blood was racing through his body.

When the blindfold came off, Pearl cried, "Oh my god," Emma half screamed and half fainted, Penny actually fell to the floor of the boat where she was, gripping her head with both hands.

Through the pain they each heard Gazza, strangely calm and clear, "It's OK, Jamie is with me, we will be out of here in a minute, all three bad guys are ashore at the moment."

In some part of Gazza's mind he was calm and controlled, his body was complaining loudly about the things his mind had done to it but he began to realise that the blind fold had been the biggest part of the problem, he was quickly feeling better.

Jamie sensed the connection through Gazza's pain, he had to use it, he took one of Gazza's hands from where it had been rubbing his head and held it.

"Just a sec Gazz, I have to do this, Penny are you there? Jack, anyone, can you hear me?"

Chapter Thirty Nine

Get out Now

Pearl quickly motioned for Emma to be quiet, this was no time for confusion. Emma held her mother's hand as the boat sped through the darkness and thought nothing, Pearl held her breath as she heard Jamie through Gazza call again.

"Penny I need you to connect Jack somehow." Jamie was close to panic, he was hoping Gazza would stay in pain until the message got through.

"Sorry Jamie, it was the pain, is he alright?" Penny finally replied. Jamie, Pearl and Emma all took a deep breath.

"Yes he is OK for now but I can't take him out in the river they've knocked him about a bit." Jamie explained.

"Hang on." thought Penny as she relayed to Jack, the fathers listened and waited. Jack was frustrated that he could not join in, he sat down in front of Penny on the floor of the boat, took her hands in his and squeezed.

"Jamie, Jamie can you hear me?" Jack thought as hard as he could.

"Yeah mate, look I have to hide him, they could come back any second, he's bleeding like a stuck pig, his eyes aren't working and he is dopey, like, half asleep."

"Can you get him into the mangroves on the far side of the jetty, if it's dark enough they won't see you, all the Dads are here, as soon as you two are clear we are coming in."

Jamie looked at Gazza, he waved a hand close in front of his eyes, no reaction, his friend was blind, maybe only temporary who knows but for now it limited their options.

He replied to Jack, "Right, that's the deal, give me ten minutes, no make it five, then, come on in. There will be enough water here for your boat but the big ones will have to stay in the channel, probably another hour."

Jack thought, "No problem, take it easy we are ready."

Jack and Penny stood up and sort of shook themselves. The fathers were in a circle around them, Max was first, "Well? what's this falling down stuff, is everyone all right? where is Gareth?"

Alex cut in, he thought he understood some of what had happened. "Settle down Max," then, "What's the story son?"

Jack addressed Max, "Gazza is OK, he is knocked about but Jamie is with him. He can't swim, he's got some cuts and his eyes aren't working, Jamie needs five minutes to move him into the mangroves then we can go in and pick them up."

Max had gone white and was sitting on the side of the boat, "These bastards are for it, I don't care what the kids did," his voice seemed to come from a dark place inside himself.

John Walker said, "Five minutes, we have got four left," he had checked his watch a soon as Jack said it, he was not leaving his boy in there a minute more than necessary.

Twelve years in the Army with the SAS had taught him the importance of many things but what he cared for most while he was fighting in the desert war was his family. When he finished that tour of duty he swore not to leave them again and let no body harm them, at a little over two metres and about 120kgs, he was the man. What ever needed to be done, is what would be done. Max spent one of their minutes wondering what sort of mongrel would do those things to a kid. He wanted his boy on board and if those blokes got in the way that would be their problem, he went below and opened one of the cases that he had brought with him.

He was about half way through a project for the federal Police. They had brought in some Taser guns from the USA, Taser guns are those things that look like a weird hand gun. They fire small needles with a fine wire attached, the needles go in through the skin of the target and the wires carry a high voltage electric charge. At the design voltage from the USA our Police were worried that it could be too dangerous so they asked him to have a look at maybe making the voltage adjustable, like a dimmer switch on a light fitting.
What he had in the case was the first modified test model, all he needed now was a test dummy.

Jamie told Gazza to sit forward. "Mate, I am going to bandage your wrists, I have to cut up your shirt, are you hearing me Gazz?" Gazza was feeling a little better but not really. "Yeah mate, whatever, I can't see, am I bleeding around my eyes, where are we, what's going on?"
Jamie cut the back of Gazza's shirt into strips with his hunting knife. He put the knife back in its scabbard on his belt and began to wrap the wounds. "It's OK Gazz, you're eyes and your head aren't bleeding, just your wrists, we are in that bloke's boat but I'm going to get you out, our gang is coming for us."

Keepers

Even as he started on the second bandage, the first one started to leak blood, he couldn't take Gazza into the river like this.

Jamie almost jumped when he heard Gazza's voice in his head. "It's fine Jamo, take me up the jetty into the compound." The voice was calm and clear, Gazza looked at him with eyes that were not seeing but something was.
Penny heard, so did Emma and Pearl, then they heard him again. "Don't worry about the dogs, we will be alright."
Penny relayed to Jack who was getting ready to cast off from the River Hawk, the fathers heard what she said, Alex was about to speak. Penny held up her hand, she looked toward shore and listened to Gazza again.
"Come on buddy we better go, I can feel them, they are on the way back, get me up there."

Penny relayed again, Jack said "What do we do now?"
John walker answered, "Enough ! I want to see these blokes," he lowered his solid frame into the tinny.
Max Corndiff said nothing but climbed down behind John, Alex followed, then turned to Penny. "Stay with the boat Penny, keep a check on the radio and look out for Max's boat, they should be here any minute, tell them to wait for us."
There was no discussion. He cast off the bow line and signaled for Jack to head for shore, Jack looked back at her as he steered the boat away, no need for mind talk, she looked worried.

———————

Jamie half pushed, half dragged Gazza up on to the jetty. "Sit still, just a sec Gazz." He said as he turned and made his way quickly to the stern of the boat. He reached down to where the hull met the transom and unscrewed the two drain bungs, water spurted into the boat through each hole. He was about to stand and leave when someone turned on a very bright torch, the beam was pointing directly at the wires running into the small bilge pump mounted in the back of the boat.

"Yeah, good thinking," he said as he grabbed the small wires and ripped them out of the connection. The water was already mixing with the blood on the metal hull, he turned to congratulate Gazza on thinking to disable the pump and ask him how he recovered and found the torch so quickly.

The tiny hole in the clouds opened steadily. The brilliant moonlight moved away from the wires, then away from the boat and spread from one end of the jetty to the other. Gazza was sitting exactly where Jamie had left him and there was no torch and no one else to be seen. He stepped off the rapidly sinking tinny up on to the jetty, helped Gazza to his feet and said," Come on mate, someone agrees with us heading inland."

They followed the moonlight up the jetty and into the compound where they knew there were two nasty Rottweilers. Jamie could see where they were going but did not know why. Gazza knew what they had to do but could not see.

They both knew that the Spirit of The Place was with them so they went without fear, almost.

Chapter Forty
Gazza & Co.

Gunther woke with a start. He must have dozed off while he was waiting in the truck, it was like a dream that woke him, he was in some bushes and he could hear Jimmy calling him, like on a telephone, that's when he woke up.

Uh oh , the mobile, maybe he should have gone up the hill and tried to ring Jimmy, maybe he should try now.

He grabbed his torch and jumped out of the truck, headed around the back of the house and up the hill. He did not like the bush in the dark but he did not like Jimmy when he was cranky either.

Jimmy had stumbled along in the dark from the jetty to the front of the house, on the way he had seen that his bag was not where he had dropped it. He saw no lights in the small house so he walked across the front and around to where the truck was parked, there was no sign of his bag or Gunther. Although if he had felt the seat he would have found it was still warm.

He looked for the torch that they always kept in the truck, it was not there either. The bag was important but he decided that leaving the area was more important, he headed back to the river.

As he stumbled back through the mangroves toward the jetty he was sure that for a few moments he could see lights, what was that fool Marty up to.

When he came to the jetty however, it was darker than ever. He climbed up from the duck boards, he could see almost nothing, "Marty," he called but not too loudly. He called again as he walked carefully toward the boat, by the time he reached the end of the jetty he knew that Marty should have responded.

He was squinting at where the boat should be and wondering how it could be so dark when suddenly the moon did the spotlight thing again. This time it lit up Marty's sunken tinny just as two large Bull sharks swam slowly over the sides into the boat, one of them turned toward the jetty and looked up at Jimmy. Sharks don't blink, this one stared at Jimmy for a long moment through the pinky brown water and then swam on.

Bull sharks do come into the river but they rarely bother people, no different to the ocean really. It would be nice to think the spirit in the sharks had brought them to help when they smelt the scent of Keepers blood in the water but it could also be that they were just hungry, the spirit is not always strong in sharks.

The bright light faded but it was replaced by a soft glow reflecting off the water between the jetty and the cruiser. The smooth shiny water was broken every few feet by the fin of a passing shark. Jimmy stood mesmerized at the end of the jetty trying to grasp what he was seeing, he could not accept it. His mind was saying stuff like, "There are sharks every where, they have eaten Marty and the kid, now they are waiting for me to swim for the cruiser, how do they know, where did they come from, how did they sink the boat?"

There is no way to know how long he would have stayed there if he had not been disturbed by the sound of an outboard motor nearby. He tried to see in the direction of the noise but it was pitch black again, he could not decide what to do, his gun was still in the boat. There was another back in the truck but it was too dark to get there, he turned away from the river just as a booming voice rang out.

––––––––––

Jack had automatically followed the directions of John Walker who was using hand signals from the bow of the boat to tell Jack what he wanted, Alex and Max kept out of the way. They both understood that John had experience in these things and Jack had plenty of practice at the controls of his boat. As they rounded the bend and the cruiser came into sight, John waved for minimum speed, the boat crept quietly forward. They could see no activity on board, a few seconds later the jetty came into view. The moonlight on the jetty was quite bright but their boat seemed to be under a cloud or something, it was dark where they were.

They saw a man looking down to where the front section of an aluminium hull was sticking up while the rear section was under water. They could see the top of an outboard motor just showing. The last they had heard the boys were in that boat. John felt his pulse quicken, he signaled for Jack to accelerate. As soon as the man started to look for the noise of their engine John called out in a voice that even Jack heard clearly over the noise of the engine. "You on the jetty, stay where you are, we are coming ashore, do not move, I repeat, do not move!"

Jack thought "Wow, that sounds official."
Jimmy thought, "Uh oh, that sounds official."
He spun back around looking into the darkness, still nothing to
see, but the motor sound was coming rapidly closer.
He had a quick flash of the future, courtrooms, charges,
kidnapping, maybe murder, the truck was his only chance.

The boat had made almost all the distance to the jetty by the time
the man turned to run.
John signaled for Jack to run down the right hand side of the jetty.
He did not signal to slow down, Jack followed orders. The boat
was running at full speed toward the side of the jetty, there would
be only a matter of metres before she ran out of water and hit the
heavy outer trunks of the mangrove trees.
John leant down to pick up the forward sand anchor, he coiled the
10mm chain leader and braced himself.
Max, Alex and Jack saw and understood, they braced themselves
for the collision.
The boat almost overtook the man, John signaled to cut power and
the same action he heaved the anchor up onto the jetty.

Jack yanked the throttle and gear lever back to neutral and kept it
going straight through to reverse, then full throttle reverse.
The engine screamed in protest as the boat nose dived, the front
of the keel slammed the shallow muddy water, the propeller threw
up a heavy spray of water, mud and minced mangrove suckers.
She still hit the first of the mangroves but only hard enough to
make a couple of small dents in the hull as she came to a halt hard
aground in the mud.
John's timing was perfect, he used the last momentum of the boat

Gazza & Co.

to propel himself forward as he sprang up and to the left. He landed at a run on the jetty about three metres in front of Jimmy who was face down on the walkway and moaning loudly.

The anchor was not really heavy but it was traveling fast, it hit the man just below the buttocks. Taken completely by surprise he was hurled forward, flat onto his face on the timber planks of the jetty. While the timber broke his nose and a tooth or two and cut his lip, the anchor rolled along his back taking some of his shirt and making holes in his skin, then it ran out of line pulled to the right and fell into the mud ahead of the boat.

Alex and Max were out of the boat by the time John had rolled Jimmy over and was saying, "Where are the boys?"
Jimmy had always found pain easier to deal with than threats and waiting, now through his pain he began to think, he spat out a tooth and growled, "Who the bloody hell are you lot? Coppers can't do this, I know the law."
Alex cut in, "You may know the law but you don't know us, we are not police, we want the boys now!"

Jimmy was no mug, "If you are not coppers then bugger off before I call them," He dragged himself to a sitting position as he spoke.

Max Corndiff was about two metres away, "Hey, tough guy,"
Jimmy looked up, he saw the gun in Max's hand, Jimmy was about to say, "No way!" but Max shot him.

———

When Jamie led Gazza into the compound where the dogs were, there was an eerie silence. Earlier the dogs had been barking and growling, now, there was not a sound to be heard.

Keepers

"Which way Gazz," Jamie whispered.

"Go toward the main gates up at the driveway."

They were about half way along the fence nearest the roadway when Gazza said, "Hang on here a minute."

Jamie could see that Gazza was thinking, but he knew that it was not working, Jamie could not hear what Gazza was thinking so the others wouldn't either. There were crashing and yelling sounds coming from the jetty, Gazza was fishing around in his pocket, at last he said aloud, "Yeah right, here mate, take this."

He handed Jamie a double cut security key. "Leave me here, go on ahead and unlock the two sets of gates, leave the inside one closed but open the other set."

Jamie was not happy, "I am not leaving you alone, what about those dogs and where did you get this key?"

Gazza cut him off, "Just relax, the key came from the truck when I was out there earlier and the dogs are not a problem as long as you don't do anything stupid."

Jamie did not agree, "Gazz, you are just a bit more insane than usual, if this is the gate key then let me take you up there and get you out of here, I've still got to contact the gang and tell them where we are and I can't do that if those monsters turn up and eat you while I'm gone."

Gazza was really calm, "Jamie I need you to relax, that's how this communication thing falls apart, you and Penny keep getting all excited then it doesn't work. For me it's the opposite but I am not going to get stepped on by an elephant just so I can have a chat with GP, so chill out mate."

Jamie thought he sounded so reasonable that he did begin to relax, then Gazza continued.

"As for the dogs, now remember we are calm and cool yeah?"

Gazza & Co.

Jamie was confused.
Gazza asked again "Yeah?"
Now Jamie was suspicious but he said an unconvincing, "ok"

"Well just keep breathing and all that, but the dogs have been standing behind you for about three minutes, I called them," Gazza added quickly, "Easy now, don't scare them they don't know you, well, actually they do, you are the only one that they saw the other day when they were tracking us so they might be a little familiar."

Jamie said, "You called them?" as he turned slowly.

In the moonlight about three paces away stood Hammer and Claw. The dogs saw his face as he turned, they looked at each other then back at him and each took a step forward.

Chapter Forty One
Who let the Dogs Out

When Marty followed the moonlight from the jetty into the compound, he had no plan in mind. He just wanted to get away from that kid who was dying in his boat. After the light faded as he went though the gate he stumbled on, trying to follow the path, it used to lead to the house before the fences were put up to keep the dogs in.

It was sort of like think evil, see evil, as soon as he remembered the dogs, he could hear them. He had only seen them once. They were big and looked mean, he never did like dogs anyway. They were coming from the other end of the compound, they knew he was there and he knew he was too far from the gate. He could hear the barking grow louder by the second. Pale pieces of moonlight showed that he was almost half way to every where, the bottom gate, the top gates, the fence on each side. The only thing that he was close to was a tired old paper bark tree about 20 metres down hill to his left. He started to run. This time the moonlight did not disappear, he was sure that without the light he would have had no chance.

With the light, he was still not sure. The sound of the dogs was gaining on him, Marty had enough sense not to look back. He put all his energy into his legs and thought only about the tree. From ten metres away he could see that he would only have one chance, there was a stump of a branch sticking out from the trunk a bit more than two metres off the ground. If he got that far he was sure he could grab it.

From five metres away he was sure that he could feel the dogs breathing on the back of his legs. The barking was roaring in his ears. Two metres from the tree he launched himself at the old branch, as he gripped the limb he felt a searing pain run down the back of his leg into his heel.

Marty swung up and on to the stubby branch, the dog had caught him by the calf muscle with a claw probably, it had dragged a deep tear down the leg and the side of his heel as it hooked his boot and pulled it off, his sock was torn and useless but he had made it, safe for now.

Claw and Hammer ran around the tree, even made a show of jumping at the tree but after a few minutes it got boring.

The human was not coming down, they could not get up, they took up a position opposite each other where they could both see the human. They sat, they waited.

Hammer had finished destroying Marty's boot, it would never be worn again, he was still chewing on it when he and Claw heard a new sound, more human footsteps.

They stood and circled the tree restless and undecided, without leaving the tree they followed the sound of the footsteps moving along the far side of the compound. Then there was a whole bunch of noises from down at the river, crashing sounds, men Yelling, strange human growling sounds. All the activity was unsettling to the dogs, they were becoming agitated.

Then there was something else, Claw heard it first, Hammer looked "Like What?" but at the same instant he heard it .

They were being called, no whistle, no barking, something older, something they only heard from their own kind, they could relax, they had a new leader and he wanted them.

They left the tree, forgot about the human there, and trotted off side by side to find their new boss.

––––––––––––

A few minutes after he had made the safety of the tree Marty had decided that maybe all his troubles were not over. The tree was not built for his shape, he was only just able to balance in the crook of the limb, he was sure that he would fall to the ground between the two dogs at any minute.

Now as he watched the dogs trot quietly off into the dark he was relieved, he did not know where they had gone or why but as soon as they were out of sight, he was down and running again. At least as well as he could with one bare and bleeding foot. The dogs had gone uphill, he went down, back toward the jetty and the river.

––––––––––––

Jamie stood tensed as the two Rottwilers considered him.

Gazza said "Sit, stay." They did, he leant back against the wire fence. "Lets go Jamo, there's stuff going on all over the place, unlock the gates, that will let the coppers in and there's two leashes hanging near the inside gate, bring them back would you."

Jamie looked at the dogs one more time, "All right," he said at last, "I'm going, but I'll be back in two minutes, you and your new buddies don't move an inch, right !"

Gazza knew he was being stared at, "Yes no problem, just go."
Jamie trotted off toward the gates, Gazza slid slowly down the
wire fence until he was sitting on the ground holding his head less
than two metres from the where Claw was thinking to Hammer,
"Did we get it right,? Is this one the boss ?"
They both heard the answer in Gazza's voice, "Yes I am the boss,
so sit still," then he lowered his hands and looked at both of them
with eyes that were still not seeing things from the outside.
Yep, this was the boss.

It was more like a minute and a half when Jamie came galloping
and puffing back down to where he had left Gazza and the dogs.
The three of them could tell it was him by the sound of his feet so
none of them moved. They just watched as he arrived all flustered
and worried, he did a sort of stock take on Gazza, hands, feet, no
new bleeding bits.
"OK, do you want me to put these on?" he said as he rattled the
heavy leashes.
The two dogs growled quietly.
"Probably not a real good idea just at the moment, I'll look after
them," Gazza held out his hand.
Jamie gave him the leashes.
Gazza continued, "You need to get back to the jetty, find our
people and tell them what's happening, I'll wait up near the gates
until the cavalry arrives."
He knew what Jamie was thinking as he looked at the two dogs
who would have ripped them apart just a few days ago.
"Things have changed," Gazza said.

Jamie put a hand on Gazza's shoulder and said, " Yes , things
have changed that's for sure, take it easy mate." then trotted off
toward the river.

235

The limping run that Marty was forced to use got him to the jetty gate more quickly than he expected. He leant on the gate post to catch his breath, what he saw toward the other end of the jetty took it all away again.

There were three men and a kid surrounding Jimmy who was half sitting half laying on the jetty, one of the men was pointing a hand gun at Jimmy. There was lots of talk among the group, Marty could hear a fair bit of what was being said.

"Do you really think it was a good idea to shoot him Max?" from one of them.

"I'll do more than that if he doesn't tell me where Gareth is !"

Then a shudder and a moan, and Jimmy saying, "I don't know where the kid is, he should be here if the sharks didn't get him. Another half scream from Jimmy, "That's all, turn it off, turn it off !"

Marty was not a quick thinker usually but something about what was happening to Jimmy gave him a shock as well. He thought that if he moved quickly, while they were all giving Jimmy a hard time, he could get to the duck boards and across to that little beach without being seen. He knew there was a old plywood dinghy in the reeds at the edge of the river, it should stay afloat long enough to get him out to the cruiser and away from this pack of lunatics and their bloody kids and Gunther's dogs and Jimmy and his guns. Bugger them all.

As Jimmy let out another yelp and the group all started talking at the same time, Marty took off. As quietly and as quickly as he could, he got to the point where the boards were laid on the mud, he lowered himself down on to them, nobody had seen him, he was safe now.

Keepers
In the Forgotten Valley

Chapter Forty Two
Call the Cops

The dogs each presented themselves to Gazza to have their leashes attached, then they stood patiently waiting.

Gazza wiped his eyes one more time, still no vision, just millions of tiny coloured lights flashing on and off, the pain had eased a little but it was really becoming a long day.

He thought about moving up to the gate to wait for the police and as he thought, Claw and Hammer started off at a very steady pace toward the gate. Gazza felt the leads take up and the three of them moved as one, along the fence line toward the gates.

Christine Wilson had driven as fast as she dared to get to the bend near Pearson's to meet her husband.

As well as Penny's parents, Cathy Walker and Pearl each had pieces of the puzzle to add. After few minutes they had put a lot of the story together and they knew that the police should be on the scene shortly.

Greg told his wife not to worry, he told her how he had spoken to

Penny while she was on the 'River Hawk' and he had instructed her to stay out of the whole thing until he spoke to her in person. So she would be alright, The women looked at him as though he had two heads. Christine just nodded and said, "Oh Yeah Greg, for sure, so she will just sit in a corner and wait for us?"

Pearl said quite seriously, "Yes of course, it will give her time to finish that quilt she has been crocheting,"

Greg looked back at them knowing he had said something but not knowing what.

"I'm going in," said Christine.

"I'm with you," joined Cathy.

Greg cut in, "Just a minute wonder girls, there is a double mesh steel gate up there, even if you did knock it down without killing yourselves you would be breaking in to someone's property, just hang on for the police, they won't be long."

As though on queue the sound of a siren grew in the darkness as Greg finished speaking. Very soon the flickering lights of an emergency vehicle began to bounce around between the trees. Greg left his ute and climbed in to the four wheel drive, Christine drove them all around the bend and pulled up at the side of the drive way to Pearson's, moments later they were talking with the local sergeant (Allan Grant) and the senior constable (Mick Kearns). Greg and Christine let Cathy Walker do the talking since, as far as they knew, Jamie was still on the property somewhere.

"So you are saying that at least one and possibly two, children have been forcibly abducted by up to three men who you believe are armed and on this property at the moment, is that correct?" asked the sergeant.

Cathy answered, "That is exactly correct, now please, lets get moving and get them out of there."

Call the Cops

"I understand your concern Mrs. Walker but we need to follow procedure here for a number of reasons, not the least of which is, that if what you say is correct, then we have to act in accordance with the law to ensure that any charges that are laid will not be undone by incorrect action on our part. Please just relax and follow us up to these gates you mentioned," said the sergeant as he climbed into the police four wheel drive.

The police car pulled to the side and stopped as it approached the now open gates. Christine drove straight through. The sergeant had been about to step out of his car, he hastily pulled his door closed and followed the civilians on to the property.

The searchlights on the Police wagon swung from side to side, then stopped as they picked out a figure making its way up toward the drive, actually it was three figures.

The head lights on the Christine's car were centered on another figure. On the opposite side of what seemed to be a compound, a large man in reflective green overalls was just opening more gates.

Gunther had tried Jimmy's number over and over, the message was the same each time 'out of service or switched off'. Where ever Jimmy had gone there was no phone signal. At first he thought he would wait a bit longer but, then he heard the dogs start barking. Then he saw lights down near the jetty and then there was yelling and more lights, he decided that it did not feel normal, it was way too active, Gunther decided to leave.

He did not use the headlights as he drove the truck down to the gates, he did not want to stir up those dogs, they had gone quiet a while ago and he preferred them that way. He sat in the truck looking for them when he got to the gate, they were nowhere to be seen. He took the dog whistle, unhooked the padlock and swung the gate open, he always left this one undone but made sure the other side was locked.

He was suddenly blinded by the glare of headlights and the flashing lights of a police car, he stood there rubbing his eyes in disbelief.

Some things came quickly for Gunther, not many but some, what came to him this time was something that Jimmy had been saying for years, "The way this deal is organized, there is no way we can be sprung on the spot, they would have to know exactly where to look, as long as we follow the plan that won't happen. So if you get bailed up by anyone, just be cool, be innocent because they can't prove that we are not."

He knew that there was no evidence of wrong doing lying around, everything was covered up, so he just turned around and walked back to the truck.

Allan had seen the boy with the two huge dogs walking up the paddock, Mick Kearns had seen the big bloke at the other gate, Christine had stopped the car in the middle of the compound, each of the occupants looking in a different direction.

As Gunther turned toward the truck, Allan stepped from his car and called, "Sir, this is the police, we would like to talk to you, please stay where you are."

Gunther ignored him, he reached the truck and climbed in. He put the truck in gear, revved the motor, let out the clutch, and it died.

The sugar in the diesel tank had found its way into the fuel injectors and that will stop any engine.

While Allan called to him again, Gunther tried to restart the engine, he did not know why but it was not going to start.

"Stay cool, you are innocent," he told himself as he stepped out of

the truck and walked toward the police. "Yes I am I'm Innocent, innocent, la, la, la."
Then he saw the dogs. He did not see where they had come from but they were charging straight at him from across the paddock. As he reached for the whistle in his pocket he noticed a group in the spotlight behind the dogs. A couple of women a bloke and, yeah, one of those kids and this one looked bloody and awful.

The whistle tasted of vegemite, that was strange, it didn't work, that was bad. Gunther nearly blew the top off his head but all he got was more vegemite.
Without realizing, he had started to walk backwards. The copper was yelling "Please stay where you are."
The dogs were still coming, he decided to go.
He had only one direction left, down the other side of the compound away from the coppers and the dogs, that's where he ran, "Innocent, yeah, tell the dogs. Stuff you Jimmy," !!!

Cathy, Christine and Greg had all leapt from the car as soon as they realized that it was Gareth with the two giant dogs. Pearl was not far behind, they left the police to deal with the man for the moment. They had covered most of the ground to Gazza and just before they reached him, he pulled the dogs to a halt and bent down.
With the leashes unhooked, Claw and Hammer waited, this would be fun. When the big bloke started to walk from the truck, their boss quietly said, "Go" they went.

Keepers
In the Forgotten Valley

Chapter Forty Three
Talking Mud

Penny heard the sound of the twin outboards before she saw the
Corndiff's cruiser, she had been deep breathing and mind talking
with Emma so she knew they were nearby.

Maureen skillfully eased the boat up alongside the River Hawk. As
the fenders touched, Penny leapt lightly from one boat to the other.
"Which way?" said Maureen.

Penny pointed, the bow of the cruiser climbed out of the water as
Maureen fed the power to the hungry twins.

Through Emma, the crew on the Corndiff cruiser were mostly up to
date as far as the point where the men left in Jacks boat. They
had heard nothing since. At the speed they were traveling there
was only moments to check with Penny for any fresh news, she
had none. Maureen knew more or less the layout of the beach
and the jetty, she planned to beach the boat and take it off later on
the rising tide.

Reg had offered to take over and drop them at the jetty.

Really she didn't care if the boat was aground or not, she wanted to get ashore and find her son in the quickest way possible, the plan was just in case Max asked the usual "What on earth did you think you were doing?" so that would be the answer, Or, it would have been the answer, plans change.

They rounded the bend in the river, in the moonlight they could see a crowd on the jetty, Maureen eased off the throttle.
Kate Kipley nudged her, on the other side of the jetty someone was moving in the shallows of the river.
Maureen checked to see if Penny was looking, "Is that one of them?"
"Yes it is, he is going to try for the cruiser," Penny replied.
"Hold on ladies, you too Reg" she fed power to the engines and flicked on the two powerful lights at the front of the boat.
The cruiser surged forward and everybody on the jetty turned to see what was happening, Marty turned to look as well. He was stuck in the light like a moth at a candle. All the men worked out what was happening in slightly different ways.
Max Corndiff knew that was his boat, he was sure Maureen was driving and she was coming in way too fast. Alex Kipley thought it sounded like Max's boat and it did look like the way Maureen would be driving if she was upset. John Walker noticed that the lights were pointing past the jetty and when he saw Marty in the center of the beams he had a bad feeling. Jimmy just did not care, this mob were insane and dangerous, he needed to find some nice professional police.
Jamie was a bit surprised at all the action on the jetty, he had arrived just before the cruiser appeared.
Marty on the other hand, had a really bad feeling.
He did not know whose boat it was but he had no doubt that it was coming for him. The harder he tried to get the little old dingy off

the mud and into the water the less it moved, it was like a slow motion comedy movie, but he was not laughing.

In only seconds the cruiser closed in on Marty and the dingy, Marty accepted his fate. He was going to be run down by a speeding boat while standing almost on dry land.

Max had time for a very quick thought, "What the hell does she think she is doing?" then he watched as the hull of his cruiser ploughed up the muddy river bank and sliced through the little plywood boat.

The man that had been at the front of the dingy disappeared behind the hull of the cruiser as an enormous spray of water and mud filled the air on each side of the vessel.

Maureen held the trim switch to raise the outboards as the water became too shallow for them to drive. As the propellers cleared the water the engines screamed, then she cut the throttle, that way the boat did not slow down until it was well up the bank.

She was over the side of the grounded vessel even before it had fully come to rest, she did not look back.

Jamie had only had time to call, "Gazza is safe," as he ran along the jetty before all that happened.

Now that Mrs.Corndiff was there as well, he told a little more about how Gazza was up near the driveway waiting for the police.

"Let's get up there," Max said, taking Maureen's hand, he didn't care about the boat either.

John said, "Ah, Max, what do you want to do with your electrical project here," pointing a thumb at Jimmy.

"OH yeah, let's take him with us, the police should have some questions for him."

Jimmy was recovering quickly but decided to say nothing at the moment. He sat still while Max pulled the Taser needles out of his neck and shoulder then climbed slowly to his feet.

He did not see what Max did with the Taser gun but he did see the wreckage spread around the cruiser at the beach. He assumed it was Marty who had been run down, since the kid was not eaten by sharks then Marty probably hadn't been either. There were lots of things that were not making sense about this deal but he had to clear his head, if the coppers were here, he needed to play clever, he thought he had a plan that would work.

The dogs were under orders 'not' to catch him. Gunther did not know that, he ran as hard as he could while he was thinking about what to do next.

Sergeant Grant watched the man run away with the two dogs close behind, he called to the group that had gathered nearby, "Young man, you had better call your dogs off before they do some harm,"

Gazza replied, "Sorry, they are not my dogs, I don't know who they belong to."

The sergeant was confused.

While Max and Maureen led the way up the hill, followed by Jimmy, followed by John, Jamie and Penny. Alex, Kate, Jack and Emma went to have a look around the grounded cruiser.

Now that things had settled down a bit Alex could hear some moaning coming from nearby, he hoped that it was not from under the boat.

Then they heard Reg speaking. "Well aren't you lucky, I thought she had you for sure," the Kipleys followed the sound and found Reg talking to a giant lump of mud that was stuck about two metres up in some heavy mangroves eight metres from the starboard side of the cruiser.
The mud was just moaning, not really making much sense but it did not sound like happy mud.

The policemen were at a loss. There were people coming from everywhere. The original group from the driveway had taken the kid who had the dogs but did not own them, and put him in the back of their four wheel drive. Two of the women were working on his wounds with their first aid kit. Then another mob had come up from the river with a bloke who looked pretty battered and they were claiming that he was a bad guy, they had three kids with them. One of them had a fresh bandage on his right arm and two of them said they were the parents of the boy with the dogs. There were supposed to be two other bad guys, one being chased by the dogs and one unaccounted for.
What these bad guys had done before they allegedly kidnapped the first kid was not known, the only things known for sure were that they had a truck, a fence and some gates.

Allan needed to get some control over the situation before it turned into a circus. The injured bad guy had sat himself on the ground with his back up against the police wagon, Allan thought that was a strange place for a bad guy to get comfortable. Even stranger when he heard him say to Mick, "Man, am I glad to see you guys." Every one else was gathered around the kid in the car and everyone of them talking at the same time.

Chapter Forty Four
Who is Who

"Folks, please, ladies, gentlemen, can you settle down." He tried to calm the group, "Please can we just quiet down for a minute, I need some answers so we can sort this situation out."
Slowly the group began to respond, as soon as he had their attention he began, "Folks it seems there are some issues here but we need to follow procedure, even if it seems like a waste of time at the moment. I can assure you we will sort this out as quickly as possible so please just co operate with Senior constable Kearns while he records some details."
The group seemed to be listening so he continued.
"First off, does anyone need an ambulance or medical attention?"
Maureen Corndiff answered, "Our son has been beaten and blinded by this man," pointing at Jimmy. "We will get Gareth to a doctor you just make sure that he gets what he deserves."
Jimmy piped up, "I never touched the kid, look what this mob have done to me, they attacked me on the wharf, then they killed the other bloke with their boat and I don't know what they have done with my offsider!"

Allan moved closer to Jimmy, he had already decided this was going to be a long night, "Who do you say got killed?"
Jimmy answered quickly, "The bloke that owns this place, Martin Pearson, they ran him down on the beach just before they dragged me up here."
Maureen looked a bit worried.

Gazza said "Wow, who ran over Marty?"
Max and Maureen were looking at each other, every one else was looking at them.

From the darkness on the river side of the compound, Reg could be heard saying, "Don't worry, no one has killed nobody yet."
A few seconds later he came into the circle of light around the vehicles walking slowly behind a mud covered limping, very sore looking, Marty.
They were followed by the Kipley family who rushed ahead and mixed in with the rest of the group and every body started talking all at once again. Marty staggered up to where Jimmy was and sat down slowly and painfully beside him, "They've broken my ribs," he moaned as he tried to get comfortable, "I'm sure they have."
Allan and Mick looked at each other, the increasing size of the group, and at their note pads.
Mick said, "How many more are there out there in the bushes? I moved to the country for a quiet life, this place is busier than Oxford street at 'Mardi Gras'."
Allan answered, "I don't know if there are more out there and I certainly don't know about 'Mardi Gras' but you better get some names and details down while I go and find that bloke that the dogs were chasing. Oh yeah, keep your eye on that pair until we get sorted," he said pointing at the two leaning on the police car.

Who is Who

When Allan made his way through the group to Gazza, he was impressed with how much better he looked with a lot of the blood wiped off and cleaned up.

"Excuse me he said to everyone, Look young man-----"

"His name is Gareth" Maureen put in.

"Call me Gazza," said Gazza."

"Argh" said Maureen.

Allan hesitated, then he said, "Look ,young fella, what can you tell me about those dogs and the man they were chasing?"

Gazza replied, "They won't hurt him, they've got him bailed up at a kennel down on the other side of the compound."

Allan was still confused, "Well, I want him back up here, how are you going to get him back?"

"No problem, you can go and get him."

Allan seemed unconvinced, "And why should they not eat both of us if I go down there?"

Gazza would have laughed at most other times, "It'll be ok, take Emma with you."

Allan looked around the circle of women and said "Emma?"

He looked at Kate when she spoke, "Gareth are you sure?"

"Really no problem Mrs. Kipley, she is the only one that won't make them nervous just now, she'll be fine."

Emma bounced off the tail gate where she had been sitting.

Kate looked at Jack.

He shrugged "ok",

She looked at Alex.

Alex looked at Allan, " Well it does seem that we don't want to make them nervous," but he made sure that Allan saw him looking at the Policeman's pistol on his hip as he said it.

Gazza was suddenly very serious, "Really Mr. Kipley, he might need that for the bloke but he won't need it for the dogs, just let Emm handle them, they know she is coming."

Alex looked at Gazza in surprise, his eyes now had a gauze bandage and padding over them.

The sergeant looked at Emma in surprise and said, "You're Emma? !"

Emma said, "Yep, I sure am", as she marched off through the parting crowd. "Are you coming?"

Allan looked at Alex one more time.

Alex shrugged and said, "Guess you better stay close to her."

They looked a bit funny as the big burly sergeant did his best not to step on the smallest Keeper while she marched off on more serious business for the valley.

"Don't worry," she said as they sort of got into a rhythm, "Just stay behind me and you'll be safe."

Gunther was not really much of a runner and he did not really expect to outrun the dogs, even if he had somewhere particular to run to, which he didn't. So he thought it was odd that he had not been jumped on and chewed up after a very short distance.

Finally he chanced a look over his shoulder into the darkness. There were no dogs behind him. He started to slow down, there was a low growl from his left, he veered to his right, there was a growl from there as well. The dogs steered him down the hill and directly to the kennel that he had erected for one of them.

He stood in front of it breathing heavily for a moment. There was a bark and a growl from each side, Gunther was not psychic but he dropped down on all fours and crawled inside, there was only just enough room for his large frame. He was facing the back wall and could not turn around but all of him did not fit in.

Only once did he try to back out, the barking and growling made him feel rather vulnerable so he crawled back in and wondered how all this had happened.

———————————

He was still wondering much later when he heard a mans voice saying, "Hello are you in there."

Gunther answered, "Of course I am in here, my arse is out there, were else could I be?"

Allan responded, "I am a police officer and I would like you to come out please."

Gunther was unimpressed, "Well officer, as soon as you shoot those bloody dogs, I will be happy to come out."

The night was getting weirder for Allan. This big bloke was hiding in a dog kennel with his bum stuck out, so that a pair of giant Rottweilers would not get him. The giant Rottweilers, which no body seemed to own, were now sitting on their haunches one each side of a little girl with boofed up red hair.

They reminded Allan of those Sphinx statues guarding the Princess in Egypt, except this princess was standing hands on hips, tapping her foot, as if to say "I know who should be getting shot and it's not these sweet little puppies."

"Sir," he began, "I am sure that the dogs are under control at the moment, if you come out of the kennel you will be all right, although it would be best if you don't make any sudden movements."

Gunther backed out of the kennel. He was not looking very confident and was definitely not making any sudden movements as he pushed himself to his feet using a length of aluminium that he had found in the kennel, it had been chewed and twisted but for Gunther any weapon was better than nothing.

Keepers

He turned to face the policeman, at the same time raising the aluminium like a club.

Allan stepped back hand on the butt of his pistol. Claw began to growl dangerously, that was his toy, he found it, this bloke better leave it alone.

Emma stood very still and realized that these puppies were not always cute.

Allan was thinking that he should not really be surprised, this joker had come out of the kennel with what looked like part of a toy airplane and now he wanted to play 'Conan" with it, how dumb can you be?

Allan heard himself say, "Please put the wing down sir," he hoped no body else could hear, "You are upsetting the dogs, it would really be best to drop the wing, do it now."

Hammer was starting to act up, he didn't care about Claw's toy, that was dumb anyway, no, he just did not like this bloke, never did.

Chapter Forty Five

That's my Dog

So, back at the cars Allan now had one more 'bad guy' sitting with the other two. He had the 'Macdonald Valley P&C.' and all of their offspring milling around telling stories about everything from mountain climbing and river spirits to high speed chases and talking trees.

Oh yes, he also had two large, un-owned black monsters sitting quietly, one each side of the inside gate to the compound.

The police manual covered all of this, crowd control, investigation, animal welfare and family counseling. It was just a bit unusual to have it all at the one place at the one time, especially in the middle of the bush in the middle of the night.

"Hey folks", he began again clapping his hands for attention. "Does anyone know of any other people or animals or anything interesting that is on this property at the moment?"

Mick and Allan watched as all the family group counted each other and nodded and murmured, like, "Yeah we are all here, yeah we're right."

The three blokes just looked at each other and said nothing.
Mick continued, "All right then, just to confirm, we are expecting no one else at this party, no one else is missing, eaten or killed."
No body responded. "Good, what I would like to do is move every one over toward the house where we can get some lights and maybe sort this story out as quickly as possible."
No body argued. Looking at the family group he said, " If you folks would like to drive and walk over that way," he pointed along the driveway, "There is enough room to get your vehicle past that truck, we will follow you over."
The Kipley's, the Corndiffs, the Walkers, the Wilsons and Pearl and Reg, all moved around the car like a windmill and within a couple of minutes had loaded it with non walkers and elderly. The leftovers paraded each side of the four wheel drive like a military escort, they set off toward the house. The dogs followed about ten metres behind. Allan was impressed
The three men refused to get in to the police wagon.
Allan assured them that it was just for a ride to the house but none accepted the offer. Mick drove the car and Allan just sort of wandered ahead of the men who waited until he was out of ear shot before they started talking to each other.
It seemed to be mostly the first bloke, Jimmy they called him, doing the talking, the other two were just nodding and limping along beside him.
They had just walked past the truck and the big fella could be heard saying, "I don't know, it just stopped and would not start, no it's not out of fuel, it just stopped."
A pair of headlights lit up the scene as a vehicle entered the compound. The three turned, when the vehicle stopped in front of the truck the headlights went off and only the parking lights stayed on, a man stepped from the utility and spoke to the men.
"Sorry I'm late", He said as he approached them, then "Bloody hell

what happened to you two," when he was close enough to see the condition of Jimmy and Marty.
Jimmy was doing a really weird sort of cutting action with his hands low down. Gunther was nodding his head toward the truck like he had a bad twitch of some sort and Marty just did not care, he turned and continued limping toward the house.

The man tried again, "What's wrong, where are the dogs?"
Allan stepped out from behind the truck and said. "Good evening," The man saw the uniform in the poor light and responded in surprise," Ah, yeah, hello."
Then while Jimmy rolled his eyes to the heavens, the man said. "I'm just here to pick up my dogs, then I'll be gone."
"Oh" said Mick, "That's fine , so they are your dogs are they?"
The man answered "Yes that's right," he pulled a dog whistle from his shirt and blew into it.

The dogs stood for a moment looking at Gazza then started off at a trot. As they got closer to the truck they separated one going each side, they slowed down to a careful walk.

The man with the whistle stood nervously fidgeting at the back of his ute. Mick had joined Allan at the truck by now and Jimmy stood with Gunther about half way between the truck and the ute. Nobody actually saw the dogs until the man looked around and started in surprise. "Oh, there you are," he said when he saw Hammer on the left and Claw on the right of the gate way. "Come on, in you get."
Neither of the dogs moved. The man blew one blast on the whistle again, Hammer barked but stood still, Claw growled softly.
The man reached in and took some rope leashes from the back of his ute, he walked toward Claw.

The dog tensed and growled, louder this time. The man turned the other way. Hammer had stepped forward, he was snarling and showing his fangs.

Mick and Allan both had their hands on their gun butts.

"What have you done to my dogs?"

Jimmy snarled back louder than Claw, "Just take the bloody things and go."

The man was not happy, "Yeah right, what about my money?"

Mick noticed a change in Jimmy, up until now he had been behaving like he was the innocent party who had been attacked by three generations of 'The Village People' but something about this dog man was making him nervous, it seemed as though he did not have control and he did not like it.

Mick said, "We would like to have a word before you go."

The man looked from Mick to Jimmy and back to Mick. "Sorry, I, ah, I'm too busy, no I'll have to go."

He stepped toward Claw with the leash in his hand, Claw leapt, he clamped his jaws around the extended hand.

———————

Back at the house Gazza said out loud, "Wo, hey take it easy."

GP. was near enough to hear.

She said quietly, "What are you up to Gareth?"

Gazza realized his mistake, "Who me, nothing, I'm just, ah, hallucinating, that's it, yeah I am imagining things."

Pearl looked around to make sure no one was listening.

"Communicating with animals is a great gift but don't abuse the power, that's not the Way."

"Yeah, you're right, it's alright now."

———————

At the same time, Claw released his grip on the man and Hammer took a small nip at his left leg, the man yelped and sort of stumbled backwards to his ute, he got in and started the engine.

"What about your dogs?" Allan asked.

"Bugger the dog's, they're ruined, keep them or shoot them I don't care."

Mick joined in, "What about your money."

By now the ute had turned around, through the open window he yelled, "Stuff the lot of you," as he sped off down the driveway.

"Got the number?"

"Yep," Mick made a note.

Allan addressed Jimmy and Gunther, "Gentlemen, if you would be so kind," he gestured toward the house, "Let's get on with this before the next event on the program, whatever that might be."

The men moved off in the direction of the house, one of the dogs took up position on each side of the gate sitting quietly, they were calm and controlled again. Mick had the impression that nobody would be coming or going without permission, he just was not sure who was giving permission?

The general noise had settled down when they reached the house. The clan had sorted the place pretty quickly. There was a shed type lean to along one side of the house, it had a few bare light bulbs hanging from the roof, they had dug up a couple of old tables, some chairs, crates and buckets to sit on and the kids were all tucking into a feed of cold chicken and bread rolls that the adults must have brought with them.

Mick had another impression, this mob worked well together and they looked after each other.

Chapter Forty Six
Who Done It

One of the women waved the policemen to a crate at the head of the makeshift table, she ignored the other two who made their way across the shed and settled on the dirt floor alongside Marty who had washed himself down and found some of his uncle's clothes in a box in the corner. He was looking less miserable but was still sore and a bit nervous, Jimmy signaled to stay calm by pushing both palms down at the floor. It was only a small sign and if Allan had not been watching he would not have seen it.

On the table in front of the policemen were two lots of a policeman's favourite items. There were two plastic cups full of hot coffee, poured from one of the large thermoses further down the table, and there was a neat stack of pages from a note book, each one of the pages had the names and addresses of each of the family groups.

This was real progress. Mick and Allan were both impressed this time, at least half of the life of a policeman is taken up with taking notes of exactly that sort of thing. Between that and the coffee the police had just about decided for sure who were the goodies and who were the baddies.

However, procedure is procedure. Allan went through the pages and called out names until he had a pretty good idea of who was who and how they were related.

Mick took his notebook and started to quiz the bad guys, the ones with no list and no coffee.

He started with Marty. "Sir is your name Martin Pearson?"

Marty looked a little nervous, "Yes"

"And are you the owner of this property?"

"Yes, more or less,"

Mick stopped taking notes, "Could you explain, 'More or less?"

Marty shot a quick glance at Jimmy, then he said, "Well the place is in the name of my Dads brother but he died a while ago and the Aunt is crook so Dad said when she is gone we will get it."

Mick took a few more notes, "I see."

He turned to Jimmy, then he had a thought, back to Marty, "Do you know these two gentlemen?" pointing at the other two.

Marty looked up with his eyes the way kids do when they are remembering spelling, or when they want to get the story right to tell mum, yeah ,it was the cat that broke her favourite vase.

"Yes, these men are contractors, I hired that one," indicating Jimmy, "to do some work and he brought Gunther with him."

Mick nodded as he wrote, "I see and do you know a man with a white utility who turned up just now to pick up, as he said, his dogs and his money?"

That was not on Marty's spelling list, " Ah, ah,"

Jimmy cut in, "Mr. Pearson does not know that man, security was part of our contract, we hired the dogs."

Mick nodded again, "I see, and may I know your name sir,"

Jimmy had been waiting for this, he replied in his most pleasant voice, "Certainly officer, my name is Smith, James Smith, people call me Jimmy."

Allan kept writing, " H'mm I see, so Mr. Smith what sort of contractor are you?"

Jack , Emma , Penny and Gazza had been elected to tell the family story since there were pieces that each one did not know about this days events. Their parents had already told them to be honest with the police but not to bother with the powers of the Keepers just to avoid confusion.

Between them they outlined the last few weeks, the truck, the drums, the TV Show that had the same drums being taken out of the ocean near Sydney harbour, and on until today with all the drama, ending with Gazza's abduction and the rescue mission by the families.

Allan had started to write the whole story down but quickly realized that he would be better off just with key points for now.

"So after your trespassing and snooping, you are alleging that at least two of these men abducted and assaulted young Mr. Corndiff here, is that correct?"

Jack jumped in, "Yes but what about the dumping, what about the toxic stuff?"

Allan looked up from his notes, "Do you have any evidence about dumping? do you know where the site is? do you know what it is? do you even know that it happened?"

Emma tried, "We know they did it, they've got tractors and diggers and everything down in the back paddock."

Allan was trying to be reasonable, "Lots of people have that gear, this is a farm, that doesn't mean they are burying toxic waste."

Gazza had a go, "Then why did they shoot my plane down If they weren't hiding something?"

Allan said, "Look, just relax all of you, your plane could have Crashed, there could be some other explanation for the noise."
The parents were all lined up on the other side of the table, they had been listening and kicking each other whenever one of them was about to butt in.
Now Allan turned to them. "Thank you for your silence, I am sure that you all support your children but let me say this, at the moment it will be best if no more is said about the activities of the children today." He held up a hand to silence at least three of them, "Let me finish, I will pursue the matter of the injuries to Gareth but frankly,-- You had all better hope that these men don't choose to lay charges against almost all of you for most of the things that you have already admitted doing to them."

That was exactly what Jimmy was in the process of doing.

Mick had also stopped taking detailed notes by the time Jimmy got to the part about being tortured with a Taser gun, he was not sure how to proceed. He tried to sum up, "So you want to lay charges against all of these kids for trespassing, malicious damage, and theft, then you want to charge most of the parents with, assault and all of them with trespassing."
As he finished Marty joined in, "Me too, whatever you call running over someone with a boat, don't leave that out."
Mick sighed and made one more note.

Allan and Mick met back at the table.
Mick started, "These blokes reckon that the 'Partridge Family' here," nodding at the mob, "are a cross between the mafia and the 'men in black', did anyone say that they ran 'Marty' down with a motor cruiser?"
Allan answered as he looked through Mick's notes, "Yes as a

matter of fact, one of the mothers did that, which one of the blokes got hit by the anchor?"

Mick was amazed, he took his note book back and made another entry then continued, "So it was an anchor, he wasn't sure, it was that one," pointing at Jimmy.

"What about the Taser gun?"

Allan stared at him blankly, " The what??"

Mick explained, "Yeah that's right, the same bloke reckons that, that one there," pointing at Max, "Shot him with a Taser gun then wound the power up and down to torture him, he showed me two nasty looking wounds, one on his neck one on his chest, I don't know what did it but they look bad."

Allan leant on the table with his head in his hands and moaned, "I think I will go back to Oxford street with you, when is 'Mardi Gras' on?"

Mick slapped Allan on the back, "Well what do we do now boss? If we lock them all up do we get a bulk bonus?"

Allan pulled himself together and replied, "Very funny, no senior, tonight we will take some photographs of the scene, make sure that we have everybody's details and hand the whole mess over to district command in the morning."

"Rodger that, this mob have all confirmed their I.D.s I'll check on our mates over here then grab the camera."

Chapter Forty Seven

Wasn't Me

Allan went back to where the families had gathered in the corner.

He just made a general announcement since it seemed like almost every one was some how involved in everything." Ah, folks, we will need you to show us where some of these things happened so that we can get some photographs of the scene or scenes." He looked at the size of the crowd and imagined trying to get them all to and from the river and listen to each of their stories again.

He shivered, "Maybe you could just decide among yourselves to pick, say, three at the most, to come down to the jetty, to begin with anyway. Oh and Mr. Corndiff, could I have a word with you?" Max left the group as they elected their representatives to go with the police. Back at the table Allan said, "Mr. Corndiff, do you by chance know anything about a thing called a Taser gun?" Max answered, "I certainly do, I have done some research on them for the government."

Allan spoke slowly, "Hmm, I see, so you know they are illegal for civilian use,"

Max nodded.

"Now you need to think carefully before you answer this next question, Did you --------------

There was a loud crash behind them as part of the table collapsed and fell against the iron walls of the shed, in the middle of the debris was Gazza moaning and holding his head moaning, "Oh, my eyes, my eyes."

Max rushed over to him and Allan wondered how Gazza had gotten so far from the mothers club that had been caring for him.

As the hubbub from that event settled down Mick returned with the camera and said, "Well, are we right to go?"

Allan hesitated, looked at the group who were not paying him any attention as they cared for their own. Then he looked at the three men who, despite their injuries seemed to be twitchy and nervous. He decided that he could ask the question later. "Lets go, those who are staying please don't wander off , we will be back as soon as possible, then we will all leave together, yes?"

There was a general murmur of agreement and three of the family stepped forward, Max was not among them.

"Oh just before we go," said Mick, "Mr. Smith do you have some ID. With you, drivers licence, business card, that sort of thing?"

Jimmy replied, "No I don't, I lost my wallet and all that stuff when this lot assaulted me on the wharf."

Mick was not surprised, he turned to Gunther, "And you sir, I'm sorry, I didn't get your name earlier."

Gunther was caught by surprise. "Who me, I'm Gunther, "He blurted out."

Wasn't Me

Mick was patient, " I'm sure you are, and your sir name?"
Gunther's eyes darted from place to place, he looked at Jimmy
who had his eyes shut in frustration, he could not remember what
they had agreed, he took a chance, "Smith, I am Gunther Smith,"
Jimmy did not hit him because that would look suspicious, he just
sort of smiled weakly.
Mick said, "Oh I see, any relation," looking at Jimmy.
"Yes I've got relations in Germany and Denmark and,---
Allan cut him off, "No , you and Mr. Smith here," pointing at Jimmy.
Jimmy tried to salvage the show, "No officer, no relation,
Gunther is from the European Smiths, I'm a local boy."
Mick responded, "I see," and to Gunther he said, "And by any
chance Mr. Smith, do you have any ID, on you ?" Gunther looked
blankly, then went to reach for his wallet, winced and stumbled as
though he had been kicked by someone in the dark, then groaned,
"Oh, no, sorry I left it at home this morning, I can drop in at the
station tomorrow if you like."

Mick replied, "I see, yes that will be fine Mr. Smith, we'll do it
tomorrow, that will be nice," he walked away making more notes.

Marty stayed behind because of his injured foot, leg, ribs, back and
head, the other two joined the expedition to the river.

Alex, Jack and Jamie represented the families. At the jetty they
stood around for a few minutes while Mick took some general
pictures. The tide was still rising and Jacks boat was beginning to
float off the mud beside the jetty, he secured it with a line while
Jimmy went on about how he was hit, battered and shot all over
again.
Allan and Mick were pretty impressed with how far up the bank
Maureen had managed to get the cruiser considering how far back

265

the water would have been when she did it, the groove through the mud was mostly covered by the tide now but the wreckage of the little dinghy was still strewn around.

Marty's boat was sinking deeper as the water rose around it.

Allan asked Jimmy what he knew about the sunken boat. Jimmy explained how he had found it like that when he came looking for Marty, just before he had been assaulted.

"So," said Allan, "You had not been out in the boat earlier, with Marty, ah, Mr. Pearson?"

Jimmy lied quickly and smoothly, "No sir, definitely not."

Mick came back from examining the boat with his torch, "Mr. Smith, do you own a gun?"

The two Mr. Smiths looked at each other for a moment, then they both said, "No."

Mick made a note, "M,mm, I see," he said "Oh and I should have asked earlier, who owns the truck that you were in when we first met this evening?"

Jimmy answered quickly, "That was on the property when we first came here, so we don't know who owns it, probably Marty."

Mick made a note , "I see, so since it has no number plates, I assume it is not driven on the road."

Jimmy again, Gunther was sweating, "No of course not, only around the property."

Gunther nodded.

Mick made a note, then directly to Gunther he said, "Then Mr. Smith, where were you planning to drive to if the truck had not broken down tonight?"

Jimmy had seen that one coming, he had been staring at the boards on the jetty and found what he was looking for at just the right time. "Hey look, there,!" he started loudly as Gunther continued to sweat. "That there is my blood, did you get a picture of that?" he demanded, pointing to some vague stains on two of the boards, then he launched straight in to a repeat of his story one more time.

Mick made another note.

———————

Penny and Gazza were able to move away from the group when the police took the others to the jetty.

"What did they say about your eyes?"

Gazza was distracted, "Your Mum and GP. think that they were sort of squashed by the blind fold and the blood was cut off, they should be ok soon. They are taking me to the hospital at Gosford after this." he continued, "Do you know how much trouble we have got the folks into?"

Penny was quick to reply, "That's what I really wanted to talk about, my Dad, your Dad and your Mum are all in real trouble, what are we going to do?"

"The problem is there is no evidence of anything, I was listening to the cops before they went down to the jetty, it's our word against those blokes and we can't talk about the spirits or we'll all end up in the loony bin,"

Penny was despondent, "They look like they aren't worried about the police looking around at all, you don't think we were wrong all along do you?"

Gazza was positive, "No way, these blokes are up to no good that's for sure but if they don't mind the cops poking around they must have some sort of plan, I don't know what it is but we better figure it out before we all end up orphans."

The Wilsons drove back up to the house just then, Christine had taken Greg back to get his ute as soon as the police were out of sight, Greg, Reg and the rest of the folks had been talking also.

They had all decided the same thing, if they could not prove that these blokes were breaking the law, then the whole family would be seen as the bad guys.

The kids had been looking for evidence of a dump site, everyone guessed that the men must have dug a hole, put the drums in it then covered them with dirt.

Reg was sure that he would be able to find out where the hole had been by driving back and forth across any suspicious areas and looking to see if the tyres went deeper in one place than another. Reg knew a lot about excavations, he had been digging holes since he was a baby. He knew how difficult it was to put the soil back at the same density after you had dug it up, that's why builders are always so careful when they excavate to prepare for a building, if one part is hard and another is soft, then the whole thing could fall down.

Greg agreed with the theory and mentioned that he had a metal detector in the back of his ute, he worked with a construction company and lately they had been surveying a site in the city that was to be redeveloped. They needed to be sure that they did not disturb any artifacts from the early days of the settlement of Sydney. Part of the method was to use the detector to show any old iron in the ground before it was dug up, it would work the same here. If Reg found a soft spot with the vehicle then Greg could check it with the metal detector, if the steel drums were in the ground they would find them.

There was only one part of the property that did not have trees all over it so that had to be the place. It was quiet a large paddock and Greg had to agree that the idea of using the plane had been a good one as long as there was actually something to find. He knew the kids believed it and he knew how much trouble everyone was in if they could not prove it.

The only problem was that the Wilson's four wheel drive was not very heavy and it had wide tyres on it, that made it a very good off road vehicle because it would travel over soft ground without sinking, that was exactly what Reg did not need.

On the other hand, the police vehicle was nice and heavy and it had skinny road tires on it, for some reason they always do that on government vehicles. That should be good enough to find loose packed soil, the keys were in it, Max was watching as Reg compared the two vehicles, he could see what Reg had in mind.

He approached Reg "You are surely not going to add a stolen police car to our list of crimes, are you?"

Reg looked across to where the women and the kids were now watching also, loud enough for all to hear he said, "If we don't find some evidence against these blokes it will be us in jail and them out and about."

For a few moments they were all quiet, then Maureen said, "You better go if you are going, we won't be able to delay them for long when they get back," the rest of the women sort of nodded then started to plan a distraction.

Max walked to the passengers side as he spoke to Reg "Well, you heard the lady, lets go, you might need another pair of eyes."

Greg followed in his ute, he would use his headlights to see if the tires of the police wagon made any deep marks, then he could test the area with the metal detector. The bottom paddock was not very far away by car, it was a large paddock which sloped down toward the river. Just about in the middle there was a big new machinery shed, it had a concrete slab laid at the front of it. They stopped to have a quick look. There was nothing to see but Greg thought a couple things were odd as they drove away. There was a type of steel frame on the ground all the way around the slab, he had not seen that style of frame in a building before, it looked more like it should be in a railway yard. The other thing was, with such a nice big shed it seemed strange that so many machines were left outside, there were several types of digging machines, another old truck and even a fairly new dirt bike laying around the place. He noticed the bike partly because there was a carry bag still on the handle bars like someone just stepped off and left it there. Anyway, all that did not matter, they were here to find some soft ground, Reg had already started to drive in a pattern across the paddock. Greg set himself up far enough behind so that he could clearly see the tire marks.

They were looking for a big hole so they drove across the paddock with about ten metres between each run, that way they could cover a large area quickly. They did not think that it would take long to find the truth.

Keepers
In the Forgotten Valley

Chapter Forty Eight

Bet it Was

Allan led the group as they returned from the jetty. He knew that the kids had gone way too far with this detective game that they were playing. They did seem like good kids and a couple of them had certainly picked up some injuries along the way but there was just nothing to prove that these blokes were breaking the law, at least not as much as the family had.

The kids and some of the parents had already admitted to all sorts of illegal things, he did not want to charge them because they were being honest and thought they were doing the right thing by each other. Also he really did not like these blokes, they were lying, he knew that. They were up to something, he was sure of that. It would not be too hard to find some charges against them, like there was a shotgun in the truck and another in the sunken boat and he expected finger prints to prove who had been using them. But shotguns in the country were not as bad as, say, handguns in the city. Then, there might be a serious reason that two of them were lying about their names but then again maybe not.

Even the story about the kidnapping could not be proved. The kids said one thing, the men said another. If the boat had not been sunk they might have found young Corndiffs blood there but now it was washed away by the river. There was supposed to be damage at the Corndiffs house but that would need a finger print technician to come up from Sydney and that was not going to happen tonight. All in all things looked worse for the family than the 'bad guys' at the moment.

Pearl and Emma loomed suddenly out of the darkness ahead of him. He got quite a start but did not let on.
"There you are," said Pearl, "We have been looking for you lot."
Alex came forward," Pearl, what's wrong?"
Pearl seemed to be flustered, short of breath, she stood trying to breathe deeply, "No," she said, in between breaths, "nothing wrong really, Gareth had another bit of a turn so they are all keeping an eye on him but Maureen remembered something that she thought the officers should see before the tide gets too high, it's on the cruiser," she stopped to do more breathing, she seemed somehow older than usual.
Jack asked, "What are you doing here Emm?"
Emma sounded a bit younger than usual , "Mummy did not want Great Aunt Pearl to be on her own while she went to find you."
The group was all bunched up now so everyone could hear.
Jimmy said, "That's all well and good but I have had enough," he turned to Allan, "We have been more than co-operative considering what this mob have put us through, now I have had enough, I am going home and I will be pressing charges against all of these maniacs in the morning."
Allan did not like Jimmy or his attitude but he was just about right and that was annoying also. "Well Mr. Smith and Mr. Smith, there is the matter of a shot gun in the truck and another in

that boat at the jetty, then there is the truck registration and the fact that there is no other vehicle here so how did you arrive, it wasn't by boat, you said you had not been in it."

Gunther had a brain wave, Jimmy saw it happening but before he could say be quiet, Gunther blurted out,
"Bikes, we came on the dirt bikes."
That was it. He just stood there with a grin on his face as though he had won ' Stump the Stars' or something.
Jimmy knew it would make things worse if he hit Gunther but it seemed like such a good idea.
Mick replied, "I see," he made a note, " And where are the dirt bikes now?"
Gunther began to think that maybe he had not won first prize after all. "They are out of petrol," he answered "One is back there in the bush, the other one is down at the machine shed."
Mick made a note.
Allan said, "It seems, Mr. Smiths, that you may be able to help us with our enquiries for a little longer after all, Yes?"
Neither of them answered, Allan turned to Pearl and Emma, "So ladies, what is this important thing back at the river?"
Emma answered, "Mrs. Corndiff said not to tell you if the bad men were listening."
Jimmy began to splutter.
Allan said, "We should not call them bad men, sweety, at least not at the moment."
Emma replied sounding more like herself, "And we should also not call me sweety anytime please."
Allan mumbled, "sorry," then, "Ah, senior take these two back to the house, the rest of us will duck back down, check out the cruiser,-----

Pearl cut in, "Sergeant, the reason we can't tell you is that they will find a way to explain it but if they are there and you all see it at the same time then they won't have time to make up a story."
Allan looked a bit dubious but he could not see what could be gained for the family if this story was not true. "All right, he said , after a few seconds, "Off we go, all together, ladies if you please," he gestured for them to take the lead.

With the oldest and the youngest of the family leading the way, it soon became obvious that it would be a slower trip than it was before. Jimmy continued to grumble and tried to trip Gunther without the police noticing. He thought that he might make him fall and hit his head so that he would be unconscious and not able to say any more stupid things.

Jack and Jamie had both received the message from GP. and were now busy trying to think of something to show the police when they got back to the river. Alex got no message but there was something about the way that Pearl and Emma were acting that made him think the night was not over yet.

––––––––––

On the third run about half way across, Reg felt the police car sink lower on the right hand side, he drove another ten metres and the ground became hard again, he moved further across to the right and reversed, this time both wheels marked deeply. After another couple of runs the tire marks showed a soft area about ten metres wide and fifteen long.
Greg stopped his ute on one side of the marks, from the back he took out a thing sort of like a giant weed cutter or wipper-snipper, except it just had a disc on the end that did not spin. It worked a

bit like underground radar.

He turned it on and started to walk slowly across the area, he made several passes in one direction, then tried crossing at right angles.

When the detector finds metal it beeps, the closer to the metal, the more it beeps.

The machine made no sound, none at all.

Reg was annoyed, "They all knew that it was not uncommon for farmers to dig a hole to bury tree stumps and that sort of thing, that must be what they had found but at least the theory about the weight of the police car was right.

"All right," said Max, "We better get on with it, we haven't got long."

Reg and Max started the pattern again, there was no short cut. Almost the whole paddock had been worked with one machine or another so it was all bare dirt, with no other way to tell if a hole had been dug or just the surface cut off.

It did not take all that long anyway, Reg was driving a bit faster now but by the time that they had been across the entire paddock they had found no other soft spots. The three of them stopped to look back from the far end of the paddock, they all agreed that if there had been another spot they would have found it.

Reg got out of the police car, "You better take this thing back Max. I'll be along shortly."

Max and Greg were depressed also but Reg was right this time, they had better return the car and hope they got back before the police.

Chapter Forty Nine
Litter Bugs Me

The way that GP. and Emma were taking turns to stumble or stop to rest or wonder which way to go made Jack believe that Reg would have long enough to do the survey. The problem was coming up with something to show the police so that they would not think it had all been a plan to delay them.

They reached the point on the jetty where the duck boards led across to the small beach and the grounded cruiser.
Pearl said, "Well off you go, I'm not going down there I would never get back up."
Jamie made his way to the front and climbed down, then he helped Emma get her footing, Jack followed and the three of them moved ahead far enough to talk quietly.
"Well?" he whispered to Jack, then looked at Emma .
Jack shrugged, "I've still got nothing."
Emma was picking her way along the boards,
"Me too," she said over her shoulder.
Pearl had wandered out to the end of the jetty, the kids looked

back and saw her staring into the never ending waters where the Serpent Spirit lived. They had reached the cruiser which was starting to be surrounded by the flowing tide, the men caught up to the kids as they stood in the shadow of the moon near the starboard side of the boat.

Allan watched as the three looked at each other and shifted nervously on their feet, he was getting a feeling that he did not like. "Well, what are we here to see?"

Some people can whistle very loudly by putting two fingers in their mouth, at that moment the kids discovered that this was another talent of Great Aunt Pearl.

The piecing whistle made them all turn toward the Jetty, now they could hear Pearl yelling, she was waving her hands in a circle and yelling , "Go around, go around," then, "When will you kids learn how to listen?"

Mick said, "What does she mean, listen, I can hear her, can't you hear her?"

The kids all nodded, Jack said, "She must mean the boat, go around to the other side of the boat."

The moon was brighter on the other side without the boat making shadows, it was shining on the water and on a piece of paper floating there.

Allan saw it first, floating near the waters edge and coming in with the tide was an A4 sheet of paper with a coloured picture printed on it. He quickly took his note book out of its plastic cover and used the cover to carefully lift the soaking paper. The others crowded around except for Jimmy and Gunther, they had no interest in rubbish in the river.

Jamie was first to recognize the angle of the shot and the two that

were featured in it, Allan could not quite see the faces and was
trying to focus on the other details when Jamie said, "That's one of
the shots that Gazza took , he was going home to print them."

The two men moaning in the background heard what was said and
suddenly became very interested. Jimmy pushed through to the
front and began to say, "What shot? what are you,"----then he got
a clear view of the picture that Mick was holding, "That can't be I,
we, ah ---" he stopped himself but too late.
Mick said, "Please go on Mr. Smith, you what?"
Jimmy was flustered, he knew that could not be the same picture.
That was miles away, that meant there must be more somewhere.
That woman knew it was there, what did that mean?
Jimmy tried to recover the situation again, "Oh, I was saying we
took that picture before, of ourselves but I didn't like it so I threw it
away," then he was quiet. As he thought about what he had said,
he began to understand what it meant to think like Gunther, he
wished he could hit himself this time.

Mick made another note, "H,mm, I See."

Emma commented, "Don't you know, you should never throw
rubbish into the river?"

Right at that moment Allan was not sure exactly what the picture
meant but from Jimmy's reaction he was sure it was important.
That should be a good thing for the family. He folded the note
book case over the picture and said, "We can sort the picture out
back at the house, now what did you bring us to see young lady,"
looking at a surprised Emma.

From the jetty came a wailing sound, " Ohmyills--, maills,"

They all turned to see Pearl sort of lying on the jetty leaning on one elbow and holding her chest with the other, she looked quiet dramatic.

Jack took off first, then Emma and Jamie realized that they should attend to their great Aunt who was in obvious distress.

Allan and the others had no choice but to follow the kids. By the time they climbed up on to the jetty the kids had got her on to her feet and were walking her carefully back towards the gate.

"Her pills," Emma said "It's her pills they are up at the car, we have to take her back."

The three kids supported a now feeble Pearl as she took small steps along the jetty.

Mick looked at Allan, Allan shrugged as if to say, "I don't know," and turned to the other two who were arguing in whispers about something and said, "Well gentlemen, it looks like we are off again," motioning for them to follow the old lady and the kids.

A few minutes later Allan looked at Mick again when it became obvious that the old lady without her pills and the little girl who did what mummy says, were going uphill at about twice the speed that they could manage just a while ago when they were coming down. In fact it was the two men following them who were tripping and stumbling as they tried to keep up. It did not help that Jimmy was pushing Gunther in the back every time he got close enough and Gunther kept mumbling that it was not all his fault and what about Marty.

Allan wondered how long it would take to get a transfer back to a nice predictable city station.

Both policemen noticed headlights moving around up near the house as they came over the hill toward the gates, they kept walking each with his own thoughts.

Litter Bugs Me

As they passed through the inside gates they were both impressed with how much more relaxed the dogs had been since their 'owner' had left. Claw and Hammer watched them come and go but they had been ordered to rest so they just stayed at rest, life was much more comfortable for them now.

They were just about at the house when Marty came toward them out of the shadows in a sideways scurry with a limp, like a hunch back without the hump.
"Sergeant, they took your car and the others went away, then came back and one of them is driving my tractor, I can hear it down in the paddock."
At the last part Gunther looked quickly at Jimmy.
Mick said, "Alright Mr. Pearson, just settle down, we need to get some pills for this lady, then we can listen to your story."
They had continued to walk while talking and now found the other women had quickly seated Pearl and were giving her something from what looked remarkably like an Aspirin bottle, Allan followed his gaze and said, "Hmm."

Allan also noticed that there was an extra vehicle in the yard and that his wagon was facing in the opposite direction to the way he had left it. They could hear the sound of a heavy diesel engine working somewhere nearby. Mick looked around the gathering mentally ticking off faces, then to no one in particular he said,"
Where is Mr. Kerry,?"
Some one said "Reg?"
"Yes, Reg."
The group started to look at each other to see if any of them looked like Reg.
"All right, every one into a vehicle, no argument this time, I want to know where every one is, lets go," he clapped his hands.

for emphasis.

Jimmy and his mates were given no choice this time. They looked nervous as they were bundled into the police wagon, Allan noticed, so did Mick. The headlights of the three vehicles lit up an interesting scene as they drove past the machinery shed, in about the centre of the paddock toward the bottom end, a hill was growing, it had not been there earlier. The hill was made up of dirt, old logs and even older stumps.

As the convoy came to a halt, the top of the hill started to roll over and move toward them, then with the roar of a heavy engine a large bulldozer topped the crest, its own tired old working lights glowing like the eyes of some beast from the past, on the monsters back sat Reg squinting into the glare from the brighter eyes of a new age of mechanical beasts.

Mick walked in front of the vehicles and motioned for Reg to cut the engine. For a moment it seemed that he had not seen the signal, then, the motor slowed to an idle and starved to a stop as diesels do when you cut the fuel supply.

Reg sat in the glare knowing they could all see him, he turned his palms up and shrugged his shoulders, the hopes of the family sunk. Jimmy and his mates were suddenly on top of the world, Jimmy nudged Marty with an elbow.

"What on earth,! Sergeant, enough is enough, I want these people charged, they have torn up my property they have broken a dozen laws,---

He would surely have gone on with his impression of an outraged citizen but Allan did not want to hear it. He had seen how scared they were when they did not know where the tractor was working and he saw their obvious relief when they found it was not in the right place, or the wrong place, depending on your view.

He spoke brusquely to Marty, "Yes, understood Mr. Pearson, don't worry I intend to make sure that everybody gets what they deserve for their efforts today."

If the three of them were not so busy being relieved they might have heard some menace in the sergeant's voice.

Reg had rejoined the group now, "Sorry kids, it's just a stump dump, no drums no nothing," He looked at Greg, "Yeah, I know, you knew, I was just hoping your gadget was wrong, anyway, now we know for sure."

Mick directed everyone back to the house, Penny was giving Gazza a commentary on the way, "We are coming up to the shed, there's one of the dirt bikes, the shed doesn't look like it has had much use, there's a carry bag on the handle bars of the bike, I suppose they will be coming back for it. Now we are------

Gazza suddenly came to life. "Did you say a carry bag, sort of a dark blue bag, like an overnight bag??"

"Yeah that's what it looks like."

To Christine, "Mrs. Wilson, please stop the car, please."

Christine stopped.

To Penny, "Quick go and get it, make sure the police see you, then take it to them, tell them to look inside the newspaper in the bag."

Penny jumped out of the car and trotted to the bike. Mick had stopped the police car almost opposite the bike, he and Allan saw the girl take the bag from the bike and carry it to them, she held the bag out to Allan's open window. "Gazza says you should look inside the newspaper in here."

Allan said out loud, "Who owns this bag?" Jimmy was in a panic but he said nothing.

Allan tried again, "What about the bike, Mr. Smiths is this one of the bikes you spoke of earlier?" Jimmy looked 'death' at Gunther, they said nothing.

Penny said, "We saw them on that bike earlier today."

Mick put the bag on the floor of the car. "OK, please tell your driver to go directly to the house with no more stops."
Penny returned, gave the message and reported the conversation.
Pearl said, "What is in that bag Gareth?"
Gazza told them about the map he had found hidden inside an old newspaper, the markings on the map included Pearson's and he believed it was a chart of the places where the men had dumped either before or would dump later.

Maureen Corndiff said, "That's fine son but there is no evidence to show that they are dumping here, so the police can't do much no matter how suspicious these men look."

Chapter Fifty

Last Chance

Back at the house the kids quickly got in to a huddle in the far corner of the shed. Jack started off, "That's it, I know the police will let these blokes go and whatever they have done they will keep doing. The only possibility is the plane, if there was nothing to see they would not have shot it down."

Penny cut in, "We all agree but we can't find it in time, if it's in the river we may never find it."

Jamie began, "What if,---

He didn't get to finish.

Emma said quietly but clearly, "It's not in the river, oh my goodness I don't believe it."

They looked as one.

Jack said, "What Emm, what don't you believe?"

Emma had tears in her eyes, "I saw it, right at the start I saw it and I never thought, I just did not realise ----

Jack went to speak, Penny held up her hand to stop him, she spoke instead, "It's alright Emm, what did you see, it's OK, just breathe deep and talk slowly."

Keepers

Emma shuddered and through her tears she said, "The dogs, the dogs have got the plane, or some of it, when we went to get that big bloke out of the kennel, one of them had been chewing on one of the wings. I saw it and it just did not sink in, I don't believe it--- she started to bubble again.

This time Jack did speak, "Hey Emm, chill out, It's all good, we can work it out, come on, get it together, you're my big little sister." The others joined in with words of encouragement, all except Gazza, he had his eyes shut under the bandages.

The messages were mixed, he and the dogs would need more practice at this, planes, wings, aluminium, crash, flying, none of it meant any thing to the dogs but all those weird questions did get them restless and a bit nervy.

Allan had the parents gathered at the table, he was explaining how there would be further investigation of the charges against everybody over the next few days. He also said that they would all be expected to report to the station in the morning to make formal statements.

Then he told them that he would have to tell the other men the same thing, even though he was not sure that he would ever see them again.

Mick was explaining the situation to the three who were now in high spirits and full of agreement at everything the officer suggested.

At the station in the morning, "Yes sir."

Formal statements, "Yes sir."

Complete ID, "Certainly sir,"

In the end Mick could not handle the smirking faces of the two Smiths, he had a thought.

"So gentlemen you are free to go, although it does seem that you have a transport problem, can we offer you a lift??

Jimmy stopped smirking immediately, "Oh no, thank you, we will be fine."

Mick liked that better, they were nervous again, he continued, "Oh good, where will you go then?

Jimmy was getting it together, "Marty said he would take us down stream in his cruiser, it's parked just out there in the river."

Mick said, "I see but how will you get to the cruiser? Mr. Pearson's tinny is submerged."

Jimmy tensed as Gunther joined in feeling comfortable. "Marty and I will drag it over to the beach and bail it out, those little buggers have taken the drain plugs out that's why it sank..

Mick liked talking to Gunther, "I see, and where do you need to go tonight?"

Gunther started just a word in front of Jimmy, "He will drop us at Brook-----

"Brooky's, a mate of mine at St Albans," he spoke over Gunther, "That's where we will go tonight."

Gunther just nodded and said, "Yeah, that's it."

Allan looked over at Mick, Mick shrugged and nodded. Allan said "Well then, we will see you all in the morning, drive safely."

The three got to their feet and started off toward the river, Jimmy hesitated at the police car where his bag was, then changed his mind and followed the other pair.

Allan called after them, "Oh of course you realise that this is a crime scene and will be under police lock until all the charges are settled."

Jimmy did not even slow down, he called over his shoulder, "Yeah fine, what ever you think best sergeant,"

Allan turned to Mick "This feels really wrong, there is something here but we need a search team, we need more people on the ground but for all that we need some evidence and those three are just going to disappear while we get sorted".

Mick said, "Yeah."

Allan addressed the group, "Well folks, I need you all to leave the site so that we can lock up until those gentlemen come in to press charges against you in the morning."

All the faces looking back at him were grim, except the kids. They were all in a huddle in the far corner.

He continued, "Once this site is locked down it will be an offence for anyone to be here without a police presence, is that clear?"

From the back came, "Sergeant, we know where the plane is."

Allan looked blank for a moment.

Jack continued, "With the camera, from this arvo.!"

Allan nodded, "Young man, if you find that plane on this property it will most likely only add to the evidence against you, I don't think you need that."

There was a murmur among the adults.

He continued, "If you can make reasonable charges, or better if your parents do, Tomorrow, I will try to have the place searched but really you have already done a good job of that, it's best if you just let it go for now."

Penny spoke, " Sergeant, we know we have made a mess of this and we have gotten our folks into trouble but these men are doing real harm, you know that, you can feel that. Let us have one more chance while they can still be stopped, please."

Allan and Mick had a short conversation, then Mick addressed the group again.

"Young lady, I am sorry but we can not condone any further activity on your part at this time. Therefore the constable and I need to inspect the property boundaries to make sure it is secure. If you find anything as you are leaving I would expect you to report to us in the morning."

He looked at Mick and continued, "The constable thinks it will take about fifteen minutes to do our checking, then we will lock the gates, understood?"

The kids huddled quickly. Emma jumped up and said "Aunt Pearl might have another attack and not be able to be moved for a while."

Allan looked at Pearl, who was suddenly fanning herself vigorously and said, "That would be serious, how long does an attack last?" Jack whispered in her ear.

"Sometimes an hour."

He shook his head, "I would have to call an ambulance after half an hour."

The kids looked at each other, Jack nodded.

Emma said, "Alright, she will be well in half an hour," Penny whispered to her and she added,

"Oh yes, thank you sergeant."

Allan turned away to hide a smile, "Right then, we are off to inspect, please leave the property in an orderly manner."

Before the police were out of sight Jack was working out the plan. "Gazza are you up for this?" he began.

Gazza replied, "I'm not sure Jack, my eyes are starting to work, I can see some light through the bandages but I can hardly move and one of my legs has stiffened up."

Penny put in, "That will be the blood you have lost and the bruising, I think you should stay here."

Jamie said, "You might be right but who's going to work the dogs?"

Gazza came back, "If I could be sure of talking to you lot, it would be alright but I can only reach the dogs, so, I think there is only one other dog handler here."

Keepers

Jack did not know who he meant but he did know that they were short of time, "Right Gazz, who are we talking about,"
"Now stay cool and give this a chance," then he called his mother.

Maureen Corndiff listened while her son explained. The dogs were the only way to find the plane in time and she was the only other one experienced with working dogs. He would tell the dogs to do as she said and how everything would be all right and when he was finished she said, "No way son, not me."

The other parents were listening, none of them were keen to become dog handlers either.
Gazza's mother explained a little. "Gareth, I was never much good with the dogs. Your grandfather said that I did not relate. Why do you think we never had a dog at our house, I don't like them and they don't like me."
Gazza persisted, "Look mum, these dogs are well trained, they just weren't happy before but now they are. You must remember what you learnt, Grandma always says you had good technique and I know you're not scared, you're not scared of anything."
Maureen answered slowly, her eyes swelling with tears of pride, "Son , it looks like we each have some things to learn about the other. Alright, I will lead the dogs but if they kill me, I am never going to speak to you again."

Gazza lifted the cord from around his neck and gave his mother the dog whistle that her father had given him. "Don't use it unless you have to, it annoys them some times."
Maureen knew the history of the whistle. She took it, held it for a moment, kissed her son on the forehead, looked around and said, " Who else is on this expedition?"

Max moved over to join his wife, "I may not be 'Crocodile Dundee' but I think I'll tag along just in case."

The rest of the kids formed up, Jack made sure that they had three torches between them, Jamie had a length of rope that he had found in the shed, Penny was feeling a little twitchy, they did not know what they would find so preparation was difficult.

"Let's go," called Jack and continued talking as they headed for the gates, "So we pick up the dogs, take them to the kennel where Emma saw the wing, show them what we want and they take us to where they found it."

Max, replied, "Yeah, Sure, they will probably want to help us rebuild the plane as well, no problem, are all your plans so easy?"

The four kids looked at each other in the moonlight, man that was spooky, now they knew where it came from.

At the gate, Claw and Hammer stood and waited while Maureen fitted the leashes. As soon as she said, 'Kennel', they were off. They knew where they were going.

Chapter Fifty One

Perfect Penny

Mick drove back down to the paddock and stopped the car near the machine shed, he turned off the engine and said, " Sarge, you know we should just put that mob off the property and let the investigators sort out this plane thing."

Allan climbed out of the car and gazed up at the sky, it seemed to be jammed full of brilliant stars. "You will probably think I am mad, being a city boy as you are, but look up there, you don't have to be a nature freak to appreciate what you see. There is a story about the family that you met here tonight, I'll tell it to you some time. I didn't pay much attention to it before but for now let's just say that all they want is to keep the valley alive. If these blokes are dumping toxins here, it could be the end of the Valley and everything in the district, so yes I am bending the rules and yes I hope they find something soon."

Mick shook his head, "Wow I was going to call you a 'Greenie', but it's more than that, isn't it? That's what I was seeing in that family, they're not here to wave a flag and save the whole world, they want to save this piece of the world. I have to be honest, to me it's

just trees, bushes and lizards but I like the idea that there is more to it, maybe if I am here long enough you can show it to me."
Allan was still gazing at the sky full of glitter, "If you are here long enough, I won't have to show you, some people see it all, some see it in pieces but in time everyone with a soul feels the spirit of the valley."

Allan wandered over to the iron building, "This shed should be part of the puzzle but I don't know where it fits."
Mick shone his torch through the small gap between the sliding doors," Yeah it seems odd that it has a sheet steel floor for one thing and as well as that it looks like it has never been used."
They walked idly around the outside of the shed. Allan ran the beam of his torch along the roof line, "There's another odd one, the rain water tank is not connected to the guttering," he held the light on the gap between the shed and the tank.
Mick said, "Maybe they forgot, or the pipe fell off or something."
Allan shook his head, "Down here, rain water is a way of life, you don't forget to hook your tank up and it's too new to fall apart, he checked his watch, "I hope those kids find something useful."

The piece of wing from the plane, was still on the ground where Gunther had dropped it. Claw went directly to it and sat down, "That wasn't a tough job and it was done now," he thought.
The group stood around looking at each other, Hammer sat down beside Claw. Jack picked up the wing section, Claw did not mind, it wasn't much fun anyway. Max held out his hand and Jack gave him the chewed and bent aluminium. Maybe Maureen was more surprised than Max by what happened next, but he just had a feeling, he squatted in front of claw and put the piece on the ground between them. Then he waited.

For a full minute nothing happened. Maureen stood holding the leashes. Max and the kids stayed where they were. Claw and Hammer sat quietly.

In the second minute Claw began to whine and grow restless. He growled at Max only a metre away.

As the third minute ticked by, Claw slowly got to his feet, he stood, face to face with Gazza's father then, he barked, loudly just once. Hammer sprang to his feet and together they turned and trotted back toward the river but on the other side of the compound.

Maureen and the rest were running to keep up with the dogs, it wasn't long before they were most of the way back to the river. At a stand of tall old 'Blue Gums' the dogs stopped. There were five trees growing close together, Claw sat at the base of the one that was second closest to the river, then he lay down with his chin on his paws and closed his eyes.

"Well," said Jack, "This must be it."

They spread out and searched the ground with their torches. Not far from Claw Emma found another fragment, then Jamie saw a larger piece, they were starting to think that the dogs had destroyed the whole thing. Max borrowed the torch from Emma, he positioned himself in about the middle between the biggest pieces, then he pointed the beam straight up.

Almost immediately, the light found a long narrow white reflection high up in the branches of the tree. The Australian Eucalypts number about eight hundred species, the gum they were looking at was a good example of one type. It had grown straight and tall and the nearest branch was about sixteen metres from the ground, the fork in the branches that was holding the fuselage of the plane was more like twenty five.

Keepers

It looked like the plane had dived into the tree on a pretty steep
angle, the nose and bent propeller were poking through the fork.
The other wing had folded up and was jamming the rest of the
plane in the vee of the stout branches, the body of the plane
looked to be pretty much intact so maybe the camera had survived
but how to get it down.
Jack had a thought. "Hey Jamo, duck down to my boat will you?
grab Penny's bow and quiver and that short boat rod of mine as
well, you know, the one with the heavy rig."
Jamie did not ask questions, he just nodded and went.
Jack moved close to Penny who was staring up at the plane.
"What do you reckon?"
"Well," she said "That depends on what you want me to do."
"If you can put an arrow with a line on it through each end of the
plane, we might be able to pull it loose and lower it to the ground. I
don't want to just knock it down, if the camera is in one piece it
might still be working."

Penny moved from place to place looking for the best angle, she
had only just decided which place to try from when Jamie re-
appeared in their midst. No one heard him coming and it gave
Maureen a start. "You should wear a cow bell," she breathed,
holding her chest.
Penny checked her quiver, "I've got three target and three hunting,
that does not give us much room for error."
Jack cut the fishing rig from the line and said, "It'll be fine, just
take your time, and hurry up." they all had a nervous laugh.
Jamie tied the line on to the first arrow, they had decided to use
the target arrows to practice. Target arrows have a pointed steel
cylinder at the end, they have no barb so that they can
be pulled from the target and reused, that would be alright to get
the range right, then they would need the classic triangular arrow

294

head shape to hook into the body of the plane after it had gone through, so that they could pull it down.

The first smooth tipped arrow pulled well under the target. The weight of the line was more than Penny had thought, the arrow lodged somewhere high up in the tree and although they will pull out of target material it would not release from the tree.

With a last pull on the heavy fishing line, the flights stripped off the arrow and the line cascaded down in a knotted jumble. They lost some time untangling the mess but on the next one Jack cut a grove in the shaft just forward of the flights so that the line would hold on the shaft, instead of the flimsy flights.

Penny's adjustment was perfect, the second arrow hit the center of the engine cowling, pierced the outer skin and fell back out.

Another tangle of fishing line but this time a bit quicker recovery. Max spoke with Penny, "That is excellent shooting Penny, but when you go for the real shot you will need to hit further back so that you don't hit the engine, otherwise the arrow will break on the metal like the last one did."

Penny was in full target mode, "No problem Mr. C. how far back do you reckon?"

Max looked up for a while, then he said, "I think you will have to use all the room there is, try to get as close to the tree trunk as you possibly can."

Max was definitely impressed when the first of the hunting arrows passed within a whisker of the trunk, went through the top and bottom skin of the plane and fell back to lock itself in perfect position. Emma squealed and started her own Mexican wave, the rest of them clapped and laughed.

They moved to the other side of the tree while Jamie took the rod, ran to a bush about thirty metres away, tied the line off, cut it and rejoined the group as Penny was setting up for the next shot.

"Any tips on this end Mr. C.?" she asked

Max had been calculating and remembering the structure of the plane. "This end looks easy because there is so much of it but there is a bulkhead about two thirds of the way to the tail, I think we need to be forward of that."

Penny looked blankly at him and said, "Yeah?"

Max looked back and said, "What !!"

Maureen said sternly, "Maxwell !!"

Max said, "OH, I see," he pointed up and said, "Just where the first letter of the name is, put it through there."

Penny said, "Not a problem, I hope."

Emma said, " Struth, they're twins."

The boys just nodded agreement.

Penny put the arrow through almost exactly where she was told, it was a beautiful shot, unfortunately it went through the plane and kept going until it lodged in a branch about ten metres higher, the audience was quiet.

"Oh stuff it," said Max, "the skin is very light back there to save weight, there is not enough to slow the arrow down."

The kids could see him talking to himself, working through ideas.

Jamie mumbled under his breath, "Man this is spooky, he's come back to haunt us and he's not even gone yet."

Jack nodded, "Tell me about it."

Max came back to earth, "Right, one arrow left, one chance, no pressure, eh Penn."

Penny was in a time warp, "Gareth I told you, don't call me Penn you moron----! !" even as she said it she realised, she put her hand to her mouth.

Maureen was first to react, "Well said Penny, right reaction, wrong Moron."

Jack and Jamie laughed first, then Emma, then Maureen and Max and finally Penny.

Max said, "That is really spooky," he shook himself, "Now, the position is fine we just need to change the angle, can you , say, use the same hole on the bottom but have the arrow going more to the back as it goes through? You need to hit that bulkhead that I wanted you to miss before, or get close maybe."
Penny moved back about three paces, hunched her shoulders, then relaxed and took a deep breath, "No problem, here we go."

The last arrow went through the underside of the plane at an approximate speed of ten metres per second. The hunting tip hit the internal structure of the bulkhead exactly as planned, the arrow slowed dramatically as it went through the heavier material but not enough. There was just sufficient force left for the whole arrow to come out through the top of the plane, it did not jam on anything else. It was just hanging on the outside of the plane. It was still another perfect shot, now it was a question of whether or not the ragged metal in the body of the plane would cut the line before the job was done.
Max congratulated Penny once more on her truly amazing marksmanship and explained the risk of the metal rubbing on the line instead of the shaft of the arrow. After one last look up he said "There is only one way to find out."
Jack said, "Watch your heads, let's do it."
Jamie went back to the bush, he picked up a piece of fallen timber on the way, tied it on as a handle, took some tension on the line and called out, "Ready."
Every one moved back until they were a safe distance from the tree then Jack started to put some strain on the tail section of the plane.
The tail swung down slowly as Jack kept constant pressure on the line. It came down to horizontal, then its own weight started to work for them, the metal groaned as it freed itself from

the grip of the tree and with arrows stuck all over its bark, the tree was happy to be rid of it, all part of working with new Keepers.

The rest of the plan was perfect. Jamie just walked slowly forward letting the line run over the limb far above, as gravity took the damaged plane on its last controlled descent

Once it was settled safely on the ground the group ran forward. Jamie and Max rolled it over so that they could see the cargo hold where Gazza had installed his first aircraft camera.

Chapter Fifty Two

Connections

The group stood together in disappointment. The cargo bay was empty.

Animals loose hair over time, snakes shed their skin to grow, flowers drop petals and trees drop leaves, seeds and wood. As a tree grows some of the branches die off. This dead wood can stay in the tree for years, it can be shaken out by wind but mostly it just drops. No warning. It falls to the ground and decomposes to enrich the soil to feed the tree, it is another cycle of life.
Hardly anybody gets hurt by falling wood, it's like lightening, usually no body gets struck by that either.
But people don't camp under the drip line of trees in Australia. You only need to look at the amount of fallen wood to know why. You are pretty safe near the trunk usually, the group was standing about midway. Both of the dogs were at rest near the base of the tree, Maureen had sat them further out, when she was not looking, they moved.
As Max stood holding the shell of the crashed plane, both dogs

tensed, hey sat up, then they stood, staring at the group.
Max was in the centre, Emma on his left, Maureen on his right, the rest gathered on each side, nobody was watching the dogs.

Hammer barked. Nobody noticed.

Back at the house Pearl felt edgy, she glanced at Gazza. He was lying in the back of the Wilson's car, moving his head from side to side in his hands as though he was trying to focus on something. She felt the same, something was wrong but she could not tell what. Gazza suddenly rolled over, pulled the loose bandage from his eyes and yelled, "NOoooo,"

The policemen heard him, the group at the tree might have heard him too if the dogs had not, at that instant, both barked and launched themselves violently into the centre of the gathering. No one had time to react. Hammer took Emma's left forearm with the back of his mouth where there are no teeth, he clamped down, and turned his body. Emma was swung like a rag doll around the rotating dog as his body collided with Maureen and Jamie knocking them sprawling backwards on the ground. As he spun he let go of her arm, she flew about two metres before hitting the ground and rolling two more.
Claw went directly at Max, the dog weighed about fifty kilos, he hit Max head first in the chest. The impact sent Max back three metres, the leftovers of the plane went up and away to the right where it landed heavily on the tail end.
Jack and Penny shared the same 'slow mo' view of how it all

happened.
The heavy branch had fallen vertically with the pointy end first, it hit Claw behind the shoulder just as he hit Max in the chest
Max lay winded where he landed, Maureen was quickly to her feet and went to help him, Jamie was already standing. He had instinctively rolled with the blow, Emma was dusting herself off and preparing to bite the dog.
Hammer was standing beside Claw, the branch had gone straight in through his tough hide like a spear and probably hit something vital inside. Most of It had broken off on impact leaving about ten centimeters protruding from his back.

He lay on his side, his breathing was shallow. The group gathered around him as they realised what had happened. Maureen and Emma sat beside him, they watched his eyes as he looked from one to the next then the next, you would swear that he was counting to make sure they were all there.

 Then he died..

All lives will end and the ones who suffer most are those that are left behind. It is a natural process even when the cause is unusual, Hammer sat beside Claw and waited for his next orders.

People talk about 'being in shock' or 'suffering from shock,'
physical shock is a massive interruption to the normal processes of the body. Mental or psychological shock is a massive change in the way you see the world or what you see in it, everyone is affected in a different way by what happens to them.

Maureen, Max, Penny, Emma, Jamie and Jack were all in shock.

To be so close to sudden death is way outside the normal boundaries for most people.

For some it was what could have happened to themselves, for others it was how quickly the world can change from brilliant to buggered. And for some it was the amazing bond and awareness that can develop so quickly between people, animals and the rest of the place.

Emma was shaking and crying.

Maureen was holding her as she helped her to her feet and said, "I am taking her back to the house."

Max had sat down beside Hammer and had his hand on the dogs shoulder, "Yes love, take it easy, we'll be along in a minute."

Jack, Jamie and Penny were sitting opposite Max and Hammer. The tears in their eyes were not out of love for Claw, they had not known him well and he seemed mostly spooky anyway. It was about the stuff that takes pages and pages to write, then, when you read it, it's still not what you wanted to say, not everything can be put into words.

There is nothing wrong with laughing when you are happy and nothing wrong about crying when you feel that deep in your soul a connection to another spirit has been broken and will never be replaced.

With a final pat on Hammers head Max climbed to his feet, " Well kids," he began, "Claw did the best he could and I am grateful, I am extremely grateful, so now we have to do our best to finish this thing, only I don't know what that is, without the camera I am afraid we might be out of the game."

The other three got slowly to their feet, dusting their clothes and wiping their eyes.

Jamie had his hands deep in his pockets, he wandered over to where the wrecked plane had landed, said "Man this sucks," and swung one of his best soccer kicks at the end of the badly bruised shell. His boot sunk into the light alloy and the tail end snapped of at the bulkhead that Max had spoken about. The tail section spun away to the right, the larger section spun to the left, the camera shot out of the larger section and landed on the dirt in front of Hammers nose, he did not move.

In fact no body moved. They looked at each other, it was a bit more of that shock thing, like, "Is this for real?"

Eventually Penny bent down and picked it up, she pressed the power button, then auto, then review.

Like she was talking in her sleep she said, "It's working."

Jack took it from her, checked the screen, it was showing an image. He did not register what the image was, "Yes it is," he said. There was none of the excitement from earlier when they were searching, Jack turned the camera off and put it in his pocket.

Jamie removed the heavy leather collar with 'Claw' scribed in silver and together they walked slowly back to the house.

The mood in the shed was very somber indeed when they got back. The police had arrived just ahead of them and were hearing the last of the story from Maureen.

Allan looked up as they shuffled in. "Sorry about the dog," he said to no one in particular, then continued, "I don't know how these things work, but it seems that the dog saved at least one life and that should be cause for celebration after he has been put to rest, and don't forget this fella here," he bent and roughed up the back of Hammers head, "He did the same job, he just had a bit more luck from the sound of it."

There was some mumbled agreement from the group.

"Now I am sorry to say it but without further evidence, I really do have to ask you all to leave."

Keepers
In the Forgotten Valley

Chapter Fifty Three
Picture This

Jack moved forward and handed the camera to Mick without a word, then went back and sat with Emma and his parents.
Allan was elated, "Well, well," he said," what do we have here?"
Mick lent over his shoulder while Allan scrolled through the memory of the camera. It started at one of two hundred and five, according to the screen, after going in order for a few and seeing mostly trees and bush, he started to skip numbers.
The first bit of interest was number 135, it showed the machine shed and the area in front of it. Allan looked for a minute thinking there was something different about the shed, when he and Mick began to show some interest, the group started to wander over. Soon most of them were gathered around trying to see the images on the small screen.

At 172 the shed was in the picture again from the opposite direction. Reg and Jack saw it at the same time.
Reg said, "Those sneaky buggers, come on Jack,"
Allan had still not seen what 'it' was, "Wait on where are you two

going?"

Reg kept walking toward the paddock, over his shoulder he said, "Go back one frame at a time and you will see, then go and stop those mongrels from leaving."

Alex followed Jack.

Allan scrolled back one shot at a time, then he went forward again at 169 he stopped. "Well I'll be !"

He jumped up, almost sending Pearl flying.

"Sorry," he mumbled, "Senior, get down to the jetty, see what those blokes are up to and if you can, stop them from leaving. I'll be with you in a minute, I just want to make sure the Kipleys don't ruin any evidence."

Allan could hear the sound of another tractor as he drove down to the shed, as his headlights lit the area he could see Reg at the doors of the shed waving to Jack who was reversing toward him on one of the machines he had seen earlier.

"Take it easy Reg," he began, "If this is what it looks like I don't want to contaminate the scene."

Reg was calm, he replied, "No chance of that. Just enough to prove the point, that's all."

The group was pretty much divided, half of them walked down to the shed, the other half headed for the river.

Mick arrived at the jetty just in time to see the three men struggling to paddle Marty's tinny out to the cruiser. They had bailed most of the water out of it then discovered that the engine would not start after being submerged. Jimmy insisted that they push off using the oars from the old dinghy as paddles, they were about half way when Mick called out.

"Hello, gentlemen, we have a couple more questions if you would come back in."

Jimmy called back, "Sorry officer, it will have to wait till we come to the station tomorrow."

Mick tried again, "I am afraid that I must insist, please return to the jetty now."

The boat had just reached the cruiser, Jimmy clambered aboard and while the other two did the same, he answered, "Look mate, you are out of luck and we are out of here, bye bye." His tone was sarcastic and confident.

Allan arrived with Reg and Jack as Marty was dragging up the anchor, the twin outboards were already idling.

Mick had his hand on the butt of his pistol, "Have we got grounds to fire at them?"

"We may have but I don't want to risk an excessive force issue ruining the case."

Jack butted in, "I don't think you will have to shoot, they won't be going far."

Normally Allan would have asked questions but he had the feeling that he would get the answers soon enough.

Marty pulled the motors into gear, Jimmy and Gunther saluted the crowd on the jetty while laughing like school boys.

Allan and Mick looked at each other as the boat steered out into mid stream, the stern went down and the bow rose up as the powerful motors pushed it ahead. Then both of the engines suddenly screamed at full revs but the boat settled back into the water. Marty quickly shut the motors down and the arguments started.

Mick and Allan both looked at Jack as the cruiser drifted with the current while the men on board yelled at each other.

Emma was not far from Jack, "I wondered what that was

supposed to do, did you know that would happen?"
Jack explained to the police men, "When we were out there earlier
I didn't know what these blokes were up to, so to be on the safe
side I ran one of my 20mm mooring lines around the bottom of
their motors."
Allan laughed and said, "You cunning little bugger, well done."
Mick looked blankly at them both.
Allan winked at Jack, nodded at Mick and said, "City boy," then he
explained. "Out board motors are fitted with a thing called a sheer
pin, it's supposed to stop major damage to the engine if you run
aground or hit a log, that sort of thing. What the young bloke did
was wrap a heavy rope around the motors so that when they took
off it was picked up by the propellers, tightened up and snapped
the sheer pins. Now the propellers are on the bottom of the river
and our friends out there are going nowhere."

Mick laughed with the rest of them, "I'll put a call in to the water
police but what if they decide to swim for it?"
Pearl was near enough to hear that part, "Officer, you or I or the
children might swim tonight but that lot would be silly to try," she
was gazing at the river as the cruiser drifted in the moonlight.
The only ripples on the water were where the fins of the bull sharks
broke the surface as they slowly circled the boat. Maybe the spirit
was with them after all.

John Walker found some tools in the shed. He and his son walked
with the whole group up to the tree where Claw still lay, they all
took part in the digging and for some, it was the first time that they
actually felt the power of The Place.
This was not the legend, that didn't matter, tonight they had
worked together for each other. Some of what they had seen and

done could be explained in lots of ways but some of the events were beyond normal explanation.

The parents had seen their kids put their lives on the line because they were sure that the valley was at risk. The kids had seen their parents put themselves at risk to back their children.

Claw had found a connection to something that he had only heard about from older dogs. He met the end of this life while he was feeling that connection and now his spirit is one with The Place

The police would have had trouble explaining some of the nights events but now that there was evidence. Well some things did not need to be mentioned after all. One of the Smiths did have a couple of nasty mosquito bites but they would fade in time.

Some left by boat, all of which were floating on the high tide by now. Some went home by car. They had all agreed to assemble at the Kipley's for a family conference in a few days time. The members of QuintX gave each other the thumbs up as they separated. Their job was done for now.

Hammer traveled with the Corndiff family, as he would for the rest of his life. It was his first trip on a boat but he was not concerned, he knew he was at home where ever this family was. Maureen did not let him drive the boat but she thought that he probably could if he had to, Max was sure he could. How could her father have been so wrong, of course she liked dogs, she had just not met the right ones before.

Chapter Fifty Four
Told you so

It was in fact a lot more than a few days before all of the group got together again.

Jack and Gazza were taken to separate hospitals. Jack was treated and released after the doctors expressed amazement at the recovery rate of the burn on his forearm. When they asked what treatment had been used he had to say that he did not know but he would ask his sister and tell them later.

Gazza was admitted for observation and treatment for severe bruising to his eyes and blood loss. Then he was given shots to guard against infection in his wounded wrists one of which required several stitches. He was released three days later but was ordered to rest for a week while he finished a course of antibiotics.

Penny and Emma both went to bed that night and slept for about sixteen hours each, they both had dreams and were both happy when they finally woke.

Jamie talked with his Mum and Dad for most of the night. They talked about all sorts of things, it was like they were seeing each other differently after their adventure together. When he finally slept he went through until the following afternoon.

Each of the families heard more details of the adventure as time went on. The parents mostly, were uneasy about the number of risks that the kids had taken. They decided that another parents meeting was in order before the kids became mobile again and this time Reg and Pearl had better be there.

The two Smiths and Marty spent all night on the cruiser. They had dropped anchor again after realizing that they had no chance of escape. Right up until the water police arrived the sharks continued their vigil around the boat. When Jimmy looked for them as he climbed aboard the Police boat, there were none to be seen, not one.
The men were first charged with firearms offences, then kidnapping and assault, obstructing a police investigation and some motoring offences. That was enough to have them held in custody while the real offences were confirmed.

Allan and Mick were on hand the following day to unlock for the officers from the Environmental Protection Agency. Allan showed them the surveillance pictures and helped them hook the tractor to the cable across the shed. When the tractor moved forward the shed followed, rolling on the tracks that had been included when the concrete base was laid. The shed moved about ten metres to uncover a hole in the ground that was almost as long and as wide as the shed itself and about three metres deep. By connecting to the cable at either end of the shed it could be moved to open or close the hole at any time. The EPA People had to admit that it was a very clever and simple way to avoid discovery and would not have been found by their normal methods.

In the hole, stacked two and three high were the drums that Jack had seen and other types as well. Two hundred litre chemical disposal drums, specially built drums which would resist corrosion for many years in the right circumstances.
These were not in the right circumstances.

The ground in which they were buried was low and close to the water table. That meant that they would be damp a lot of the time. This would encourage the break down of the metal containers and then the contents would flow with the ground water directly into the river. Once in the river any contamination would spread to all forms of life from that point, on both banks, in the river and out into the ocean. Some of the toxins in the drums were easy to identify. They still had labels and names of the factories they had come from. Some of the others had code numbers designed to be difficult to understand so that people would not know what sorts of poisons are traveling on our roads, even on the way to legal dump sites.
The legal dumps are supposed to be safe and controlled. Tell that to the land made useless forever by the dumping of chemicals and poisons which mean that land can never ever be used or worked with for any purpose. New comers to this country still see some of it as dry and useless desert. They think that it does not matter what they do to it so they destroy it bit by bit, they call this, part of the price of progress but they are not the ones who pay.

Over the next couple of weeks the EPA tracked the drums to an industrial waste disposal company. It turned out that Jimmy had an arrangement with a couple of the workers at that company. They would collect the waste from different companies, those companies would pay the high cost of disposal according to the law. Jimmie's mates would then change the records and split that money with Jimmy who used Gunther and some others to hide the drums in different parts of the country. Parts like Pearson's place where normally no one would notice what was happening.

People like Marty were happy to take money without concern for the future. They would say, "It's my place I can do what I like with it," luckily the law says. "Not when it affects the rest of us, thanks very much."

The EPA used the map that Gazza had found to track down nine other sites, some of them were ten years old. All of them were in places where the chemicals would have wiped out whole communities of people or of nature, mostly both, once the containers became rusted and broke down.

Even Allan and Mick were amazed to learn how permanent these poisons can be. Because they are so concentrated they can stay active for ever. Although some industrial chemists would say that is an exaggeration, really it might only be a thousand years or so, for some of the better ones.(Derrrr!)

The same as a plastic shopping bag or those plastic six pack can holders do not look dangerous when they go down the storm water drain or wash off the beach and out to the sea.
It might be years later when it finally gets caught on the nose of a dolphin or a turtle or in the stomach of a whale.
Which ever it is, the animal will grow weaker and weaker because it can not eat, then painfully and slowly it will die.

Told you So

It will not die because it came to be in tune with the place like Claw. It will die because mankind does not know how to measure the cost of what it calls Progress.

The story made headlines in the papers and all the news programs. The parents managed to convince Allan and Mick to take credit for the discovery as a result of their exceptional policing skills.
They knew what sort of circus could be started if the media thought there was a team of super kids roaming the valley looking for wrong doers. The kids were happy about that. They were embarrassed enough with Reg turning up at every bodies house raving on to the parents about how this would be the greatest bunch of Keepers that the valley had ever known. It did not take long before he started to add that he thought his training and mentoring probably had a lot to do with how clever they all were.

The new school term started the next week. Gazza missed the first two weeks, Jack missed one. Emma was way to wound up for the first three days so she stayed home as well. When she did go she was under strict orders to tell no body about what they had gotten up to over the break.
Jamie and Penny started on the Monday but it was pretty boring without the other two on the long ride to school. They went over the details together more than once and although Penny especially would not say so, it was just not the same without that goose Gazza and his dumb comments.

When Jack came back things improved quiet a bit and the following week when the 'dumb goose' joined them. Things were back to normal only better.

They talked through their adventure repeatedly and each time there was a different hero. Jack with his preparation and boat handling, Jamie swimming the river to rescue Gazz, Gazza got the pain management and dog whispering award and what about Penny, so cool under pressure for not just one but three of the best bow shots that the world has ever seen, or not seen. But as they say in boxing, the hardest hitter pound for pound would be Emma, mind talking, first aid, boat driving, the girl was unstoppable. Then they started on the parents.

They listed the super powers of each of their parents. They actually agreed out loud that the most super thing was they way they just turned up and joined in. As Gazza said, "They were just so cool, once they knew we were in trouble they just became like an army, those blokes never stood a chance."

After they had settled down a bit the other parent topic came up. How would they be the next time they all got together? There was sure to be a pretty heavy reaction now that everyone was back in one piece and things were normal.

The kids sort of knew they deserved some grief but none of them could imagine what form it would take this time.

Keepers
In the Forgotten Valley

Chapter Fifty Five

It's for the Best

They found out the answer the following weekend. It was Sunday at the Kipleys and all the usual mob were expected at the BBQ. As each part of the group arrived the gang got the impression that they had missed something, the parents were sort of smug, like we know something you don't know. Childish, but some grownups are like that.

The kids got together in a corner and pieced together their bits of information. After ten minutes they had to admit that it looked like the parents had held a meeting among themselves some time in the last two weeks and QuintX had missed the signs and therefore did not know what was coming.

This was not good, apart from not being prepared. It meant that the parents had outsmarted them, now they needed a plan of their own and it had to be quick.

Keepers

The kids were good but no one is that good. Within minutes of the last arrival Reg had ordered all of them to the stone house.
The kids knew they were out of time so they marched off to their fate ready for the worst, they thought.

Reg settled them down and waited for the murmuring of the kids and the giggles of the parents to stop. "We are here this time because of the events of a few weeks ago, when our magnificent Keepers took on the forces of evil ---
"REGINALD." called GP in a voice that would have stopped an avalanche.
"Yes, well, as I was saying," he continued, then in a cheeky voice quickly, "One more time, well done kids," and before GP could shoot him, "This is my last duty as guardian of the valley legend, I have already handed the book over to the new guardian and now I am happy to pass the rest of the duties to Kate Kipley, who has already shown how well she can work with the Keepers and even do that mind talking thing, please step up Kate."

Every body was clapping and cheering. Emma was jumping up and down, Jack was looking very happy and Kate was so red in the face that she could have worked as a stop light.
Slowly the cheering and clapping wore down, by the time that Kate's blushing was under control the noise was too.
"Thank you," she began, "Guardian of the legend is mostly a book keeping job so I do not expect too much trouble there. Now that all the parents are convinced that our Keepers are some how connected to the power of our valley we have decided to be involved and help where we can."

Every body was still listening, Kate continued, "Because our Keepers are our children we have made some decisions that we

316

think will be the best for them and for the valley."

The kids were getting restless, parents decisions for the good of things usually meant trouble for them.

Kate looked directly at the kids and went on, "The five of you have done an extraordinary job and saved the valley from certain destruction at some time in the future. The skill and bravery you have shown has made all of your parents very proud."

There was a murmur of agreement from the rest of the parents and some nervous smiles from the kids.

"The risks you have taken and the danger that you put yourselves in however, has made the same parents very nervous." More murmurs of agreement.

No smiles this time, whatever was coming was almost here.

Kate was a little nervous, "I will ask Pearl to explain a couple of things before I continue."

She gestured to GP who stood and cleared her throat. "Yes, right,"

The kids each had exactly the same thought and it was not magic. "What could possibly make GP Nervous? and if it made her nervous, how could they hope to survive it??"

Pearl found her voice, "You will remember when we all met here last time, there was talk of some training for the boys by other male Keepers."

The kids nodded, still suspicious.

Pearl continued, "Well I am happy to say that after weeks of negotiation and discussion with relatives, parents and school principals an arrangement has been made."

Like a flashing sign yelling Danger, Danger, they heard the words School principals. The rest of the 'arrangement' did not matter. It

involved more than one Principal, they only attended one school, this was not going the way they thought it would.
The girls had not been mentioned but Penny felt a sense of dread, Emma was feeling many signals but mostly confused.

Pearl could see their faces, she hurried on to finish her part , "The parents have managed to convince your school at Galston and the high school at Maroubra to undertake a student exchange program for one term as an experiment in cultural exchange."
Reg looked shocked, he called out loudly, "What are you saying woman, you can't mean that you are sending the boys out of the Valley!!"
Pearl tried to quiet him but this time he did not listen.
"Why was I not told about this? What are you people trying to do?- John Walker spoke to Reg in a quiet and controlled voice " Reg settle down, listen to the rest, this is why we didn't tell you what was happening, it will be for the best."

Pearl continued even more quickly, "You will each change places with the kids of Keepers on the South side of Sydney for one school term. Then you will be able to learn some of The Way and still not miss any school."
Reg was quietly fuming.
Pearl finished but her voice lacked conviction, "This is for your benefit and for your safety, this last adventure was just too dangerous. It happened before any of us expected and it may not be the last, you must learn more about being Keepers before there are more serious injuries or worse."
Jack called out with an edge to his voice, "We have time to learn the way, you told us that, the legend always said that. We don't have to leave the valley, I am not going anywhere."
Jamie voiced his agreement, "All of you said we did terrific on the

Pearson job. We can be more careful if there is another one, I am with Jack, I am staying put."

Gazza was nodding his head furiously as his mates spoke, now he put his bit in, "Yeah," he almost yelled, "We saved the valley you all said so, even if we did nearly get killed a bit."

Penny glared at him as he finished, Gazza looked back like, "What??"

She jumped in quickly, "Why are the boys being sent? Why not me? I'm a Keeper, I was in danger, there should be no difference. It's not fair, leave them here in the Valley, this is where we belong." she stopped as the tears in her eyes made her even more cranky.

Emma was already crying when she said in a voice much softer than the others, "I don't want Jack and the boys to go away, it's my fault because I had those feelings," She sobbed, "I won't have them any more, honest never, just don't send them away, please."

Jack was ready to go again, "What about the Ancients? Aren't they supposed to help us? Where were they when we were in trouble? Where are they now? they are just dreams, I agree with Emma. Leave us here and we will stop having dreams. We will stop being Keepers, leave us in the valley."

The rest of the kids voiced their agreement even though each of them had a sudden strange feeling when Jack said, "Stop being Keepers," he felt it too.

Alex was on his feet, "Wait on, settle down, all of you, relax, it's alright, breathe everybody, chill." He looked at Reg who was still looking defiant, "Reg we did not need that, what we do need is your experience and common sense."

Turning to the kids he said, "All right you lot, you have all had your say. Now think about the 'Pearson job' as you called it Jamie, who was there as soon as they knew you were in trouble?" he did not wait for an answer and his voice softened as he continued, "We were, that's who, every one of us was there to back you up, We took chances too remember, big chances, with the law, just because we trusted you kids and wanted you safe."

The gang started to feel a bit less angry and a little less determined.

Alex finished off, "We know none of you want to leave the valley even for a short while, and that's all it is, just one term but if it helps you to understand how to be safer Keepers then it should be a good idea. So just relax, listen to the rest of the deal, then we can discuss it, yeah ?

There was a sort of murmur from the kids and Alex sat down.

Maureen Corndiff stood and began to speak immediately, "The three of you will still go to school together over at Maroubra. You will just live at different houses, fairly close to each other actually. The families you will be with are sending their kids here to live with us and attend your school while you are away. It will be like a hostage situation. If they don't send you back all in one piece we will roast their kids on the barby."

Trying for a laugh did not work. Even the other parents were too tense to join in. She continued, anxious to be done, "The men in two of the families are official Keepers, that is they are descendants of the Kerry's the third is not a relative but when you get to know him you will find no difference. They will be able to answer all your questions and help you understand how to stay safe."

One last look at the kids showed that she was not making too many friends, "We will visit while you are there, there are some great beaches and of course you will come home for some weekends as well." Her speech sort of dried up and she sat down.

Kate took the floor once more, "Well, that's just about all of it. We can answer any questions any time you like, just one more thing.

It's for the Best

We expect the five of you might want some time, so why don't you go to your headquarters for tonight. You are all excused from school tomorrow so come back about lunch time, alright?"

Jack was quieter now, "How come we are off school Mum?"
"Well son, on Tuesday we are taking you all over to meet the families at Maroubra," her voice tailed of uncertainly.
Jamie said, "Mrs. Kipley, you said meet them, when do we move there?"
Jamie's mother answered, "We are going to do the swap on Tuesday as well son. It was the only way that we could get all the timing right, sorry to spring all this on you so suddenly but it has been incredibly difficult to work it all out."

The kids sat in shock. The parents had been so busy with their plans that they had not really thought about how hard their children would take this. Now as they realized the significance of the plans they had put in place, there were doubts. This was all about their children. Like all parents, they wanted their kids to be happy and safe but their kids were Keepers so things were different. That must be part of 'The Way.'

Keepers
In the Forgotten Valley

Chapter 58
Real Magic

As though they were in a trance the five of them picked up their gear, said their goodbyes and headed up toward their headquarters, leaving behind some very nervous parents.

They even went the long way since there seemed to be no hurry.
It was not as if they had plans to make, or anything like that.
They were more than half way before anyone even spoke.
It was Gazza, "Hey Jack, remember when we read that Harry Potter book, like way back when we were young."
"Yeah, I remember," Jack was not interested.
"So if we were 'Wizards' instead of 'Keepers' we could do stuff like him and his mates did, couldn't we?"
"What on earth are you talking about?" growled Jamie.
Penny chimed in, "Do you want to dance around with a magic wand putting pigs tails on kids and mumbling magic spells?"
Gazza was a bit disappointed but he persisted, at least the walking pace had picked up a little, "No, although that Ben on the

school bus would look good with one."

He was so dumb that a couple of them almost laughed. That was bad, he was encouraged, "And we could have flying broomsticks instead of all this walking."
"And the food Gazz, remember the magic food, as much as you want." Emma whispered loudly like a witch casting a spell.

'Oh yeah, that's right, hey how come Harry was always skinny. Come to that everyone was except that dumb kid, what's his name?"
Jack finally had to give up being sour, it was too hard when Gazza got going," That was Neville you Neville."
The others almost giggled.
"And when you get older you can be a Troll," added Jamie.
Yes laughed Emma, "You can be Gareth Neville the Mountain Troll."
"Not me", Gazza shot back "I want to be the next 'Dumbackdoor' !!"

That was it. They all cracked up, even Penny," I have no doubt about that Gazz, it would be the perfect job for you."
Jack was still laughing as they crossed the stream near the cave, "It might be just as well that we don't have that sort of magic here, you get in to enough trouble in our own world." He said to Gazza who was now looking much happier, like the rest of them.

They had not been to the cave for a while, by the time they had tidied up. Chased a pair of sleeping brush tailed possums out from under the sleeping bags, got the fire going and filled their water bottles at the stream, it was almost dark.
After a hot meal of canned food they sat outside the cave.

Watching the stars and the planets in a sky so clear that they felt that they could have been suspended among them not dreaming so far below.

The anger was gone now.

"I guess I did make a mess of the Pearson thing," said Jack slowly. Jamie stared at the sky, "You don't get all the credit, I nearly got us all caught twice."
Gazza added drowsily, "You two are my heroes, have a go at the strife I got into."

A little later as they moved into the cave for the night. Jack took one more look at the brilliant sky and said to no one in particular. "We have got plenty of our own magic here, I guess it would be dumb if we didn't learn the best way to use it."

Some how the next morning was even brighter and fresher than usual. Over breakfast the boys started to give the girls instructions about how to look after the place while they were away.

Gazza was saying," Don't go bringing any of those city blokes up here while we are not about. There's no telling what they will get up to."

Penny was offended, "Oh yeah Gareth, like we would, this is QuintX headquarters, no one else comes here."
Then she had a thought, "Hey what happens if another job comes up while you guys are loafing around the city, do you think we can mind talk that far?"

Keepers

Jamie said " You know some of my ancestors were aborigines,"
"Yes" said Emma, waiting to hear some history.
"Well," he went seriously, "I don't know about back then but these days they can still talk over enormous distances, no trouble at all,"
The girls were both interested, the boys realized that they had heard this one before and took cover.
"Yes, from here to South Sydney would be the same method, you might have to practice but if you just lift your hand up to the side of your face you will be able to hear us perfectly, as long as there is a phone in it.

He just had time to duck as the missiles flew fast and furious over his head, when the dust settled and the laughing stopped it was time to pack up.

It was time to head back and learn more about how to be better 'Keepers in the forgotten Valley.' and remember,
                              'Its all good'

                    The end of a beginning